THE COLLECTIVE

KENAN HILLARD

ISBN:0692360735
ISBN-13:9780692360736

This book is for my father and mother:

CHARLES
For instilling persistence, determination and a no-quit attitude

&

RACHEL
For blessing me with my creative spirit and enduring will

CONTENTS

ACKNOWLEDGEMENTS

CHAPTER 1   XONOX

CHAPTER 2   THE MOUNTIE

CHAPTER 3   ABEL

CHAPTER 4   BOURDAIN

CHAPTER 5   WARDEN

CHAPTER 6   THE TOURNAMENT

CHAPTER 7   GRAZEN WOODS

CHAPTER 8   KEERA

CHAPTER 9   TOMMIE GUN

CHAPTER 10   UPPER HOUSES

CHAPTER 11   THE FIRST OF FIRSTS

CHAPTER 12   RISE OF HOUSE IOSSEC

CHAPTER 13   RALSTON

CHAPTER 14   THE RETURN

CHAPTER 15   WAR ROOM

CHAPTER 16   THE WATER FACILITY]

CHAPTER 17   ADVANCED
             TECHNOLOGY
CHAPTER 18
             DISTOR
CHAPTER 19
             INNER CIRCLE

             EPILOGUE

ACKNOWLEDGMENTS

Thanks to everyone who helped THE COLLECTIVE become a reality. A few short years ago it was just a thought, something I wanted to share and hoped that readers would enjoy.

CHAPTER 1
XONOX

"Father, may I have a word?" The words hung in the room. Victor Xonox turned surprised to see his daughter, Pheona and trusted aide Dante. She had grown so much since her mother's passing. She was dressed in a silk evening dress, her arms and neck adorned with her mother's jewelry, long dark hair fell over her shoulders. Xonox marveled at the striking resemblance to his wife. Dante was dressed sharply in a custom suit from Xonox's personal tailor. A purveyor of information, Dante was a valuable asset and often had vital information to share. He waited silently for Xonox to conclude his conversation.

"Pheona, what brings you to my study? Shouldn't you be preparing for the soiree?" Xonox asked trying to get a sense of her abrupt appearance.

"Is it true? You've found the House member who tried to end Hilson's life?" Pheona shot back.

Xonox stared at Dante, the only person who could have enlightened his daughter on the situation. He was not angry, but now he understood why his daughter had come to him. She regularly inquired about the Xonox Empire. She desired to take his position one day and Xonox loved the idea. Circumstances out of his control had robbed him of his only legitimate son. There was only one problem. For all of Pheona's aspirations for the finest of life, she was too soft. Too caring and giving. Too much like her late mother. If only he had a son, Xonox thought. He looked at his aide as he addressed Pheona. "I presume Dante has imparted the details to you."

"Sir, she was quite persistent and I know how you like to keep Miss Xonox abreast of developing situations." Dante struggled to give Xonox clarification.

"True. But I distinctly remember telling you to conceal this bit of information until the deed was done." Xonox peered at Dante out the corner of his eye. Though he was valuable, Dante had to be reminded occasionally that he could be replaced as easily as Xonox changed his suits. Dante was seldom on the receiving end of one of Xonox's stares. He witnessed and heard stories of their devastation. One too many and the recipient could end up missing or worse. An incompetent chef had seasoned Xonox's dinner incorrectly too often for his liking. Reprimanded with a stare twice in one week, by the third time he was relieved of his station. His quarters were invaded in the middle of the night and he was dragged from his bed, with his wife screaming in the background. Stripped to his under garments he was dragged through the street by twelve of Xonox's guards for all to behold. Finally he was driven to the edge of the city and thrown out, to be shot on sight upon return. He lasted three days before trying to enter the city.

Pheona sought to take her father's thoughts of displeasure away from Dante. "Father, it's not Dante's fault. I can be quite persuasive. I am your daughter."

"True." Xonox agreed with her. "And that is the only reason I won't throw Dante into my tiger pit."

Dante visibly shook at the thought. "Thank you, sir."

"I jest Dante. You are family after all." Xonox said half-heartedly.

"As I am honored to be, but I have news on the House member we spoke about. Should I speak freely?" Dante spoke quickly attempting to work his way back into his master's good graces.

"Yes." Xonox replied. "We both know she will get the information from you later. Let us sit."

Xonox made his way to the desk and chair backed against the clear glass. The city was his backdrop. Pheona and Dante set on the U-shaped couch in front of him with their feet settled on the black bear rug. A server appeared from the side room placing cups, plates, tea and sandwiches for the group. She waited as Xonox sipped the tea. It was to his liking as he waved her off. He made a mental note. She had worked with him for over a year and after the first month her tea was always the perfect temperature. Perhaps this attention to detail could be useful in other arenas.

"What information do you have Dante?" Xonox asked sipping his tea.

"The suspected conspirator has left the Water Facility with a caravan and all the water he could carry." Dante informed Xonox. "Supposedly he told Distor the water was for the city."

"How many and what is his destination?" Xonox held his cup as he waited for Dante's response.

Dante did not hesitate. "He's traveling in a luxury vehicle with his aide, four hummers armed with four men a piece, four men on motorcycles and one cargo truck with supplies and eight men inside. It appears he's headed for asylum with the Croman Family under the House of Janus two-hundred miles west."

"As I suspected." Xonox placed his cup down. "I've had my suspicion of Croman for many years."

"What is your course of action? Should we try to intercept? It will be hard to catch him now." Dante was unsure how to proceed, but he knew what the final results would be.

"My course of action is always the same and unwavering." Xonox paused for effect. "Death to anyone that plots against the family. Gerrius Crispus will be dealt with in good time."

Pheona was startled by the name. "Gerrius! Father...No!"

"Pheona. What have I taught you?" Xonox sat up in his chair as he recited his father's favorite quote. "Power belies lenience."

The young lady Xonox persisted. "But Crispus's son, Juda. We have been friends for years. This would ruin him. What about him?"

"Actually he is on the ballroom floor as one of our guests, very unaware of his father's deception." Xonox replied undaunted.

"Father, please." Pheona begged.

"I have no intention of harming the young man." He sighed as he responded forcing a fake smile. "He is here for your gathering."

"If his father dies the blood will be on your hands." She was incredulous.

Xonox looked at her sternly. "No child. My hands will be unsoiled."

"I'll never forgive you." Pheona snapped back. "It's like mother all over again."

Before the first of the House of Vancrew could gaze in Dante's direction, the aide was excusing himself from the room. No one mentioned Xonox's wife or the tragic circumstances of her death. Xonox pounded the desk as Dante retreated. "Your mother knew the risks. I told her to take a private jet. She insisted on flying with the other philanthropists. Who knew terrorists would attack?"

"You, obviously." His daughter said cynically.

He raised one of his eyebrows, staring at his daughter. "What are you implying?"

"What everyone else whispers." She spoke frantically. "You downed that plane. You killed my mother and your son, my brother. I guess a required sacrifice for the ascension of the Xonox Family."

"Is that what you think?" Xonox asked taken aback by Pheona's bluntness. "You believe these lies over your father?"

"Not at first. Not when I was younger." Pheona wiped the tears from her eyes. "But I've seen how you operate. Cold and heartless. You care about nothing and no one in your quest for absolute power."

Pheona's vicious words nipped at Xonox's heart. She came by her venomous tone naturally. The tears streaming down her face were her mother's trademark. He walked from behind his desk and wrapped his arms around his daughter. Compassion was uncommon in Xonox. Holding Pheona he tried to express his feelings. "I loved your mother and brother. She was lovely and stubborn like you. Your brother was young, but already being reared as my successor. All I have left is you. Of all I've gained in this world, you are what I prize the most."

"Then prove it. Let Crispus live." Pheona said softly.

Xonox was unmoved. "In time you will see why these decisions are made."

She pushed her father away as the tears dried up. "You're wrong. I'll never be like you."

Pheona headed to the exit and Xonox watched her leave. She was smart and she was right. Xonox had given up a great deal to secure his position. He was not remorseful. There was no success without sacrifice.

"Sir." Dante broke his thoughts. "Just to inform you, your party has begun on Level Forty-nine."

"Thank you Dante." Xonox sat back in his seat.

"What do you want to do about Crispus, sir?" Dante asked, patiently awaiting Xonox's directive.

"It's already taken care of." The ruler adjusted his coat and grabbed the tea cup.

His aide was dumbfounded. "May I ask how? I just gave you the information."

Xonox let the question linger in the air for a few seconds before he answered. "I spoke with Distor two days ago. I told him if any caravan comes to the Water Facility to inform me. He was able to stall Crispus while I notified someone to take care of the matter permanently. He should be meeting them on the road as we speak."

"Who's meeting them?" Dante asked still puzzled.

Xonox spoke through his teeth with a wicked smile. "The Mountie."

CHAPTER 2
THE MOUNTIE

"Driver, pick up the pace!" Gerrius Crispus shifted forward as he shouted.

"Sir, this is as fast as we can go." The driver responded without turning around.

The caravan was on schedule despite the delay at the Water Facility. Crispus was pleased with how smoothly everything was going. He was prepared to fight his way out of the city. His attempt on Hilson's life had failed. Had he succeeded he would have gained influence and moved to the third position in the House of Vancrew, placing him within striking distance of Xonox. When the Collective was imagined it was for the elite to have complete control over the commoners. Somehow Xonox had positioned himself to have complete dominion over one of the upper houses, The House of Vancrew. Crispus and his peers were more akin to his staff than his equals. Xonox's unprecedented reign had thrust him into a 'God amongst men' status in the region. The mention of his name brought dread to the rich and poor alike. Crispus believed he had to be stopped to bring the power scale back into balance. Now he sought sanctuary in the House of Janus. If Vancrew was the third, Janus was often considered the second House among the eight. Once under Croman's protection he could send for his family. Xonox could not deny him then or he would risk waging a civil war with Croman. But if he failed to reach Croman, he shuddered to think of his family's fate. His son Juda had befriended Pheona, Xonox's daughter, but his wife, mother and innocent daughter may not be so lucky.

"The water cargo truck is slowing us down. Should we speed ahead?" The driver noted.

Crispus broke from his thoughts. "No. How far do we have?" He had no intention of leaving the precious cargo unescorted.

Crispus's aide answered, leaving the driver to focus on the road. "We are halfway to the the House of Janus. We should start seeing the towers in a few hours. Your family will be joining us soon. Relax Crispus, we are home free."

"Just seemed too easy." The former fourth of the House of Vancrew's voice was shaking as he spoke. "And nothing ever is with Xonox." The words scarcely left his mouth before the driver called his attention to something in the road.

"There's someone in the median up ahead."

Leaning past the driver, Crispus could see a figure in the distance. "Run him over if you have to. I want to keep time."

Four hummers rode in front of Crispus's car, two on each side. The motorcycles ran in pairs along the sides of the vehicle. Behind was the slow cargo truck carrying the treasures; water and gasoline supplies. Speeding towards the lone wanderer, the lead Hummer driver switched on the microphone and broadcasted over the truck's speakers. "Exit the street. You are in the path of Gerrius Crispus of the House of Vancrew."

The man in their path tilted his head up. That was exactly what he wanted to hear. Stopping in the middle of the paved highway he brushed back his long trench coat to show his full body armor. Blue-tinted goggles shielded his eyes. Rolling up his sleeves he unveiled the metal bracelets on his forearms. Around his waist running up beneath his biceps were slim metal boxes with an unknown purpose. He tapped a button on his left wrist and lifted his arms up so the metal boxes were unobstructed. "Target Acquired" the computer chirped into the chip implanted behind his ear. The convoy was bearing down on him full speed, but they were slightly out of range. At eighty-five feet away from the drifter the computer spoke again "Launching". Two cylindrical shaped metal disks whizzed from the boxes. They magnetically attached to the front of the Hummers.

The Hummer driver exclaimed. "What the..." His last words as the front of both Hummers exploded simultaneously, flipping the vehicles as they crashed upside down onto the pavement. The rear Hummers screeched to a halt forming a 'V' barricade in front of Crispus's car. Men filed out of the jeep with M-16 rifles in hands. The first man's head exploded as he exited the wagon. His body dropped limply to the ground. The guard behind him dove for cover, but never came up. The bullet cracked his sunglasses as it passed through his head. Precise, lethal rounds were coming from the two-gun wielding assailant through the fire and debris; they couldn't get a lock on his position. Three more of Crispus's guards hit the ground, one still staring at the hole in his stomach in disbelieve. A guard yelled. "Take cover behind the Hummer!"

The onslaught continued. One brave defender advanced, discharging rounds past the cover and into the stretch of conrete. The bullets bounced off his armor. His goggles had switched from blue to infrared in order to detect his opponents' movements behind the vehicles. His accuracy was unparalleled as he downed his enemies one at a time. Zooming in on the next target, positioned behind the front of the vehicle, he cocked the pistol. Shooting through the flames, the armored bullet was unaffected by the heat. It cut through the light-plated escort vehicle, under the guard's elbow, through his heart, lodging into Crispus's car bumper beyond. Crispus pleaded for the driver to back up, but they were boxed in by the cargo truck inches from their bumper. As the bullets ricocheted off the attacker, the two remaining guards took cover behind the Hummer to reload. Crispus watched in horror as the glass shattered on the trucks and the two men fell in unison. Crimson fluid soaked over the granules in the ground. Two motorcyclists took off to intercept the threat attempting to slow his advance. The remaining guards dismounted moving swiftly to pull their leader to safety. Opening the doors, the guards pulled out a stiffened scared Crispus. His aide broke free making a mad dash up the highway back to the House of Vancrew. The motorcyclist closed in on the armored antagonist. Pulling out Uzis they aimed to hit him in an uncovered area. They wanted to test the durability of his protection. Before they could prove their theory, the mysterious man squeezed off two shots from his handgun. The bikes skidded past him leaving the two owners face up on the pavement. The guard driving the cargo truck was flabbergasted. He never saw someone move so quickly. At first he thought there was no way one man could take out twelve armed guards, even with the jump on the first eight. He was wrong. In a matter of minutes only two guards were left as they tried to drag Crispus back to the truck. The driver peered into the holding area of the truck where six armed men had not moved.

"Someone get out there. We're losing everybody!" The water truck driver screamed to the small army sitting behind him holding their weapons looking visibly shocked at the carnage. His navigator was sitting still next to him. The main driver thought he was paralyzed by the bloody display. He was wrong. His partner's dismay was over the man causing the storm of mayhem. His voice was low as he spoke.

"Everyone...stay put if you want to live. I've seen this man before. He's a member of the Redstone Mercenary Guild. He goes by 'The Mountie' and he's the most dangerous killer on this planet."

"The Mountie...heh...heh." The main driver chuckled nervously.

The navigator did not look at the driver as The Mountie approached, but he offered a stern warning. "Trust me. You don't want to laugh at this man." The driver sat back in his seat. The co-driver was not easily rattled. To hear the quivering of his voice was unsettling.

Crispus stared at the truck waiting for the men to come out. His survival instincts overrode his fear. "Someone do something! Why am I paying you?" Crispus sat on the ground with his back to the truck. As the words left his mouth, the guard facing away from Crispus head lurched back as the bullet pierced his skull. His most loyal protector shielded him and fired wildly, before succumbing to the bullet hole through the stitched 'C' on his chest. She dropped face first to the pavement. Crispus was uncontrollable. "Help me! Somebody, please!"

The Mountie walked near Crispus, but his gaze was focused on the two men in the front of the truck. The main driver had his hands on the wheel, while the co-driver had his hands in the air. The Mountie knew there were more guards in the truck. Though Xonox would prefer his resources returned, he contemplated blowing up the transport.

"A gift from me to you, Xonox." The Mountie said inaudibly.

Crispus used the distraction to grovel at the killer's feet for his life. "Please...wait...please."

Mountie extended his hands to quiet Crispus. It always amused him how these people of prestige and riches could be reduced to whimpering idiots begging for their lives in a few seconds. They perceived themselves as being untouchable until they were touched. He looked in the distance and he could see Crispus's aide running in a straight line down the road. Falling to one knee, he pulled out a foot long shaft, screwed it to another shaft, attached a pre-assembled handle and trigger, flipped up the arm and placed the final piece, a scope. In the crouched position, he lifted the rifle up to his shoulder and fired one shot. The aide slowed to a walk as if he was out of breath, clutched his chest and dropped into the street. Who could pass up that kind of target practice? The Mountie thought. Two-hundred yards out with one shot. He rose to his feet to better admire his work; surveying the bodies, burning flames and twisted metal around him. Breaking down the rifle he placed it back into the compartments and moved closer to Crispus. He hated this part of the job. Crispus was an old, dumpy man without a shred of muscle or an appetite for any physical scuffles. Most targets would be offered a fair fight with the weapon of their choice. That is what he loved; the combat, the strategy, one man versus an army, one man versus a worthy opponent. There were few to be found. Every now and again he would run up against a rogue mercenary or gang leader who could make him break a sweat. The outcome was never in doubt. They would be given the chance to go down fighting. But eventually they would go down. Sure, he had a thirst for blood, war and all that came with it. Yet it was the search for the ultimate challenge that propelled him. Now it was time to dispatch of this little prince. Unfulfilled, he stood motionless for a long time. His surroundings were frozen and quiet. The wind swirled and lifted the dark-crusted dust. Fires crackled behind him. No one moved in the truck. Crispus cowered before him. He breathed deep, sucking in all the chaos he caused and the quietness that came with it. A serenity that was about to be broken. With the Luger in hand he moved closer to Crispus. The barrel of the gun stopped two inches from the bridge of Crispus's nose. He could smell the man's despair. Sweat dripped down Crispus's face. His hands were up in a pleading manner, but he knew there would be no escape.

"Xonox says hi." The Mountie said through a harsh voice that sounded as if he had swallowed nails.

"He would have done the same thing in my position." Crispus whined.

"Maybe..." There was no shred of sympathy in his demeanor.

Crispus knew it was the end. He could not reason with this man, this killer. All he understood was violence. He mustered his courage to say his last words.

"That pompous prick, I'm glad I attempted to stop him. Someone should have. See you in..."

The Mountie squeezed the trigger to send him to the place they would all have their final rest. Unfortunately, Crispus was next in line. Maybe he could hold a spot for him and Xonox. The mercenary turned towards the cargo drivers who had not moved or breathed. Good thing, any excuse would usually do. Luckily they caught him on a good day. He was feeling generous. Besides, Xonox would be pleased to get the truck back. Perhaps he could borrow the prototype laser sword his technicians were working on for the next mission. Locking eyes with the driver, The Mountie placed his hand in the air, extended his index finger and motioned in a circle. The universal sign for turn it around. The men exhaled and quickly began backing up the transport. They would return to the Water Facility. Leaving with their lives outweighed the punishment awaiting them. The Mountie watched as the truck pulled away. Heading in the opposite direction, he tapped his wrist band. The computer linked to a familiar number.

"Xonox. It's done."

"I never had a doubt."

"Thank you sir." The Mountie said in a soft growl.

"And the other matter?"

"Heading there now." He rasped.

CHAPTER 3
ABEL

"Is everything alright?" Abel asked quietly, with a bit of concern.

His father shouted back. "Yes, but quickly son, the water." Abel could discern from his father's tone that everything was not okay. His father's voice trembled and they never accessed the well early in the morning. Abel stepped out into the cool morning air with the water bucket in his hand. He approached the side of the house, where the well was hidden under an old boat hull with some bushes hanging over it. Removing the hull, Abel took a quick look around before lowering the bucket into the darkness.

Few in the Gravope community knew about the well, but many suspected. Loun, Abel's father, shared and traded out of this limited resource sparingly. In these times, it was similar to having oil in your backyard. If the House of Vancrew found out; they would confiscate as much water as possible, close the illegal well and discipline the perpetrators who concealed it. That was the right that power brought. Many were against the Water Protocol laws, but few dared to rise against the Collective eight Houses.

As Abel turned to head back to the house, he was startled by a face peering over the gate. It was Forsum, his playmate since childhood. Abel froze in stride and a few drops of water hit the ground. Forsum looked with a knowing glance. "I always suspected." He whispered and vanished before Abel could respond.

Loun bellowed from the house. "Abel! What are you

doing?"

Still in a panic, Abel entered the house. Loun took the water out of his hand staring at Abel. "What took you so long?" Abel was silent, and then he began to stammer out his words. "I need to tell you something..."

His father placed a finger to his lip to silence him. He had no time for one of Abel's explanations. "Later, your mother has fallen ill."

Loun headed back to the room leaving Abel to speculate what trouble may come from the exposed well. There were only a few bargaining chips used to procure water; scrap metals or coins, fresh meat, people sold into servitude or the sale of information. The last one was where Abel's worry laid. Though Forsum was a childhood friend, he never shared knowledge of the well with him. But questions often arose as Abel's family always seemed to have water. Abel sat down on the floor trying to calm down. Surely Forsum would not sell out his family and bring wrath to the village for a few drops of water. Maybe he should find Forsum before a problem occurred, he thought.

Before he could act, his father called him from the bedroom. "Abel, come in here."

All thoughts faded as he walked into the room. His mother's sweaty body was on the bed. An old faded sponge was held to her forehead to cool the fever. Hovering over her at the head of the bed, his father spoke slowly. "I won't be able to hunt with you today. Grise will take you out. Shoot something nice for your mother..." Loun turned from Abel to his wife, the emotion welling in his face. Abel felt the tears coming from his eyes as he answered. "I will."

With a look of determination, Abel bent over to kiss his mother's cheek. She had been sick for weeks, but it was getting worse. The only hope was to bag a wild deer and trade for medical supplies at the Water Management Facility. Guns and ammo were easy to come by. A gallon of water would buy you enough weapons for a small army. But few wanted to part with the limited medical supplies that they possessed. In this world if you didn't die by dehydration, sickness would slowly rot your body. Medicine was second to water in scarcity.

Grise was a hardened man with scales for skin. Like Abel's

father, he was a former Army Ranger. The two served together before the government collapsed and the military became defunct. His training mixed with his Cherokee blood made him a formidable survivalist. As the pair walked towards home, Abel's eyes were filled with hope. The hunt was a success. Abel had bagged a small buck. He and Grise carried the animal to his home. About an eighth of a mile out Grise signed off. "Give my regards to your mother and father."

Abel grasped Grise's hand. "I will. Thanks."

A firm exchange and Abel was left to carry the buck on his own. How happy his father would be, he thought. It was no easy feat to bring down the animal. Last time out Abel had shot a huge hole through a boar destroying most of the meat. This time he had snuck up on the deer without a sound and shot it cold before it could react. Obviously all those years of hunting had finally paid off. His father had taught him well. He beamed at the thought of his mother getting the help she needed. Suddenly, he was startled by loud sounds in the distance. He could make out a large engine and men shouting in the direction of his home. Instantly the smile on his face was replaced by a look of terror. He dropped the buck and started to run.

Loun was outside the home with his hand raised in protest as the Captain of the Xonox Water Management Facility read him the articles of the Collective Water Distribution Protocol. The remaining guards watched with guns lowered but ready for action. The community was aghast, some were angered at the intrusion, but none came to Loun's defense.

"Per article 6, section 2 of the Collective Water Distribution Protocol, any consumable water must be reported to the Collective for appropriate division and metering for public consumption." The Captain held the small electronic palm device in his hands, reading the words as they scrolled on the screen. "The penalty of non-report is death as authorized by the Collective and the corresponding house."

The head of the Water Management Facility, for the House of Vancrew, was a man named Distor. His lack of patience or empathy for the rank and file was an attribute that the community was painfully aware throughout his tenure. A potent mix of cruelty and intelligence guided him in his rise to his position of status.

Stepping out of the helicopter, he surveyed the dismal town. His pets lived better than these people, yet they refused to die. Rarely were any of them of use, lest for entertainment. Now he had learned there was access to an illegal water source, which would undoubtedly cut into the House of Vancrew water supply. This could upset the power generation for the Xonox family. Every drop of water was precious in his bid to become a member of the House. His goal was the unlimited access gained by inclusion into the Collective. Once a member, mere thoughts frequently became reality. He would make an example of these peasants and halt any future insolence. As he strode towards his Captain, with two guards in step, he could hear the reading of the Distribution Protocol. To his left were two Hummer trucks with nine guards standing in a half circle. The sunglasses on their faces shielded their eyes, but Distor was sure they were unblinking. These men were the lucky few, pulled from the depths of poverty and given a station in life. They were not among the elite, but lived a life of comfort none would forfeit. The small army was more for show. The townspeople would not defy him or water would be the least of their concerns. Distor interrupted his Captain as he continued to read Loun's crimes. "Thank you Captain. I think this man fully understands his crime. What is your defense?"

The Water Facility leader spoke calmly as he glared intently at the criminal sizing him up. Loun's age and clothes seemed to shield an inner power. Taut arms and legs told Distor that this man had served the old country, killed for it and was not to be taken lightly. His aggressive stance was tempered by a void in his eyes that he could not place. It was haunting.

"Sir, my wife is dying. She has been ill for a while." Loun fumbled over his words looking from the armed men back to his home. "I only hoped to get her stronger again before I reported the well. We need medical supplies..."

Distor raised his hand to silence Loun's pleas. "You test my intelligence with your lies. You have stolen from the Xonox Family and therefore the House of Vancrew. Do you have anything that I can consider in a trade for your life?"

Reaching to his waist, Distor unholstered the small pistol at his side. The gun shone as he removed it, catching the glint of the sun. It looked fresh off the manufacturing line for good reason;

Distor rarely used the weapon. When he did, people died. Normally he would let his guard beat and dispose of the culprit, but the charge was too grievous. This situation called for a public execution, fired by a single bullet, the way only he could administer. The atmosphere was deathly silent. The whirring of the helicopter propellers cut thru Loun's plea for leniency. Suddenly running out of the woods, half out of breath, Abel appeared. The scene was disturbing to behold; thirteen soldiers, two armed vehicles and a dark helicopter swirling the dust in front of his home, his father surrounded and begging for mercy. Abel could see the two straddled 'XX's' which was the crest of the Xonox Family. All the guards, equipment and vehicles bore the mark. He heard stories about Xonox and his so-called kindness. Some teenagers from the village had broken into a Water Mediation area for a bath and a few sips, but were discovered. They were supposed to be killed, but Xonox showed kindness. He employed them as slaves in his House until the debt was paid. But all the townspeople knew the payment would be too steep for the unlucky pair to gain freedom. Concern was etched across his face as he imagined the penalty for his family. Repayment did not seem to be an option. Half the guards spun around to face Abel, locking their weapons on him. They were rarely approached by civilians and itched to show their resolve. "State your name!" The closest guard shouted with his weapon aimed at Abels' chest.

Abel froze and started unsteadily. "I am Abel, Loun's son." He pointed toward his
Father. The guard was still menacing, but did not respond. Abel lowered his hands and began walking towards his father. The Guards barked in unison adjusting their guns. "Stay there!"

Frozen, Abel looked at his father and knew this encounter would not end well. Loun could see the fear in his son's eyes. His father spoke slowly and with a calm that belied the situation. "Abel, did you bag something on the hunt? If so, maybe we can appease the Xonox Family with a trade for our insignificant use of water."

Quickly scanning from Loun to Distor, Abel seemed assured of the situation. He had forgotten the hunt and the buck he left behind. Maybe there was a way out of this, he thought. They were going to use it for medical supplies, but now they could trade for the consumption of water. His demeanor began to brighten. "Yes...about a few yards back. I'll go grab it now."

Before Abel could dash off, Distor motioned for him to stay still. The situation was getting out of hand and he was not going to let the monkeys run the zoo. It was time to restore order. "Boy, there is no need! Your father has knowingly taken from the Power Generation of the Xonox Family and this act will not go unpunished!" Distor stalked towards his victim. "The crime has been committed and by the power of the House of Vancrew I will meter out the sentence."

Distor could have accepted the animal as penitence, but the situation was far removed from negotiations. Besides, once his pistol was drawn it had to be used. Showing mercy would be deemed as weak and nothing would stop his ascension. Abel felt the words fall from his mouth in a frenzy. "No! My mother...please...show compassion!"

Abel tried to determine what went wrong. In his mind a deal was imminent, but now his father was facing death. Stepping forward to assist his father, he felt the butt of the guard's rifle strike him in the head. The world went black. As he collapsed to the ground he could hear the shot and Distor's words trail off in the distance. "There's....your....compassion."

CHAPTER 4
BOURDAIN

The town of Bourdain was ten miles south of Gravope and more secluded. Whereas Gravope laid outside the city walls and the towering Vancrew Houses could be seen in the distance, Bourdain was more remote. The people there were akin to late eigthteen hundreds North American settlers possessing better fields and wildlife than Gravope, but in constant search of water. Residents often traveled to the Water Facility to trade. In these small communities the inhabitants banded together. It was essential to survive against marauders and gangs on the outer limits. Unless you were a member of a House or ready for war, it was dangerous to travel deep into the barren areas. Gangs were becoming an increasing problem. Taking what they needed, while trading and sometimes wasting the rest. Gangs were another thorn grown out of this harsh world. One person in particular was always on the lookout for suspicious people in Bourdain, Isnor Profik. Isnor ran the local trading store. As expected, his water rations were low, but he kept a steady supply of items that made him a popular man. In a pinch he would get water from the man named Warden, but that came at a steep price. Isnor worked with four other gruff men, who hunted, traded and guarded against bandits. Peering out of his shop-home he was shocked to see a single Xonox truck pull up. He rarely saw one truck alone. Was there trouble, he tought? Had someone broken the Water Protocol? The guards never came to help or inspire, but to oppress and instill fear. His thoughts were getting away from him as he prepared for the worse. The guards stepped from the vehicle and he could hear them arguing as they pulled a young man from the rear.

"We should have disposed of him as Distor commanded, Franke. How are we going to   explain this? What if he finds out? We'll be dismissed from the Facility. I don't know about you." The guard paused surveying the surroundings. "But I'm not going to live like these   people!"

His panicked tone was returned by a stoic look of the lead guard. "The father knew better, he knew the consequences. The boy...I have a son and I'm not going to kill this young man. Is that clear!"

"Yeah, yeah Franke, cool out. Just drop him near the curb so we can get out of   here."

Franke carefully laid Abel on the ground with a backpack under his head. His gentleness spoke more of his conviction as a father than the ruthless acts he had committed as a soldier. Franke stood up slowly, clearly thinking of his sons and the decisions they will face in this new world. Almost instantly the moment was lost as he shifted back into his hardened demeanor. Softness led to death and he had a family to get home to. He jumped into the vehicle and directed his attention to the remaining guards. "Alright you stupid maggots, lets push out! Any word of this and you'll all be spending quality time with your maker."

The truck sped off and disappeared out of Isnor's view. He had just witnessed a miracle, a guard with a heart. Who was this young man that pulled the emotions from the ruffian guard? He had never seen such a thing. These men killed without thinking and on command. Many of the guards enjoyed their work. It was a small price to pay for the luxuries afforded within the city walls. Isnor's curiosity was piqued as he replayed the scene in his head.

As Abel came to his senses he felt the sharp throbbing of his head from the gun butt. There was a bandage on his bruise, but he had no idea who dressed it. His parents! Their image shot through his mind and he stood up quickly, too quickly as he stumbled around the room. As his eyes focused, he realized that he was not home. Where was he and what had beome of his father and mother? The last thing he remembered was the desperate look in his father's eyes. Was his mother even alive? Suddenly he heard footsteps approaching him. Bracing himself, he thought how he would never get caught off guard again.

Isnor stepped from the back of the store and he could see

the angst on the young man's face. He knew Abel was still injured, but he had a determined look in his eyes. Isnor empathized, being knocked out and dropped in a new city would rattle anyone.

"Calm down, I'm the one who brought you inside." Isnor gestured around the shop as he tried to clarify the situation. "Lying on the curb is no place to be when you're new in town. Welcome to Profik Trades, you can call me Isnor. Seems that you've hit a rough patch my friend, where do you call home?"

The man did not seem to be a threat, but Abel was still suspicious of his hospitality. He was short and stout with white hair that barely made it to the top of his head. His shirt hid his weight well, but did not cover his large forearms. Shopkeeper indeed. Abel stood to his feet, still holding his head. He was in the foyer and could see the town from the window. There were no familiar landmarks. Trinkets for trade, weapons and more exotic items were neatly placed around the shop shelves. Abel was standing near a table and Isnor was behind the counter, with a machine gun resting below his hands. It wasn't pointed toward Abel as Isnor ran a cloth over it. It appeared that he was cleaning the firearm, but Abel knew better. You don't clean a gun with your finger on the trigger. He respected his host's caution.

Abel took a second to mentally recount what had transpired. The last he remembered was a gun shot before he blacked out. Did his father survive? His mother? How long had he been out? Glancing over the counter, he could tell that the shopkeeper was getting anxious. Slowly he began to speak. "Last thing I remember....I was being knocked out before Xonox's guards shot my father. I have to get home. My mother was very ill. She may still be alive."

Isnor's eyes perked up and he stopped cleaning the gun. "Xonox you say? That's strange, because it was Xonox's guards that dropped you in the street with your backpack."

Now Abel was shocked. His eyes conveyed to Isnor that he was more a victim than a threat. Abel wondered aloud. "They shoot my father...leave my mother to die, but I live. If only I wasn't caught off guard!"

Reality was setting in and the fury rose in him. His anger grew so quickly it startled Isnor. Looking to lighten the situation, Isnor motioned toward the table. "Come, sit. I have some bread and gelatin. We'll settle the debt later."

Still clenching his fist, Abel sat down. Who had informed Distor about the well? Was it his friend Forsum? Did he realize what he had done to his family? What would happen when he was able to get back home? Forsum would be dealt with quickly, then he would set his sights on Xonox. Life had been sort of a game until that point. Hunting, trading and scraping for water. There were times when it seemed his family would not make it, but they always pulled together. Xonox and his horrors were always stories that never affected anyone close to him. In his mind, those people were careless and brought the wrath of Xonox upon them. But now he could see clearly. The House of Vancrew was evil, the whole Collective was a sham. Now he had nothing but a fire that burned in him. His father had taught him, trained him to handle himself, but when the time came for action, he froze. Quietly he vowed to never freeze again.

Isnor reappeared holding two plates with bread and gelatin in a cup as he promised. "So where is your home?"

"Gravope." Abel responded looking at the red gelatin and moldy bread.

"Ah, I've been there before." The merchant said as he sat at the table. "I traded with Aaron, he was good and fair. Do you know him?

Abel slid his fingers around the cup. "Yes. My father traded with him often."

"He always kept a good stock of water." Isnor stated while dipping his bread into the gelatin. "Well, next time I head to Gravope I'll carry you with me. We'll figure out something for you to do to earn your way."

Abel slurped the gelatin and broke off a piece of bread. "No. Thank you. But I need to leave right away. I have to find out what happened. I appreciate your help, but I have no way to repay you."

Isnor was a trader by heart, but even he was soured on this deal. Normally he would demand debts were paid immediately, with a hunt, information or some form of currency. But the young man had been through enough and he did not want to pile on. "Don't worry." The trader said. "I'm sure you'll find something to trade in your backpack."

The bag rested in the corner. It was dusted and worn, but still sturdy. Abel often carried it when he hunted, but he was surprised at the way it bulged. Cautiously, he reached down and slid the backpack to his feet, as if it would explode if it were picked up too quickly. Who knows what the guards left for him. Unzipping the bag he gazed in, slowly sat back in his chair and looked at Isnor. Smiling, Isnor took another bite of bread. Inside was everything Abel needed for the distressing situation he had been thrust in. Bottles of Xonox water overflowed the bag and a 9mm pistol sat stiffly in the inside pocket. Isnor saw a debt being settled, Abel saw the first step in exacting revenge on the man that had taken his family.

****

Abel awoke with a start, discombobulated by his surroundings, neck stiff from sleeping in the chair. His rest was broken by prodding children who giggled at his dazed look. The children were in good health, if not a little dirty, and their eyes sparkled as they poked at the newcomer. It was obvious he was not from town. Abel playfully jumped at the children, they laughed and scampered into the street. Isnor was at the counter trading with an older woman. As she made her way out of the makeshift store, Abel could see the bottle of Xonox water in her hand. Even as he slumbered, his debt was paid. Isnor nodded towards Abel. "Sleep well?"

Abel grabbed the back of his sore neck. "I've slept better." Before he could inquire about the water, a woman screamed outside the store. "Help! Someone please!"

The woman who left the store was in danger, Abel quickly deduced. He swirled towards the window were he saw a woman in the distance. She was young, her clothes were dusty but even from where Abel sat he could see her subdued beauty. It was not the woman from the store. Three bandits were surrounding her on motorcycles, they seemed more concerned with the package in her hand. From their posturing, Abel knew trouble was imminent. In one smooth motion he stood up, grabbed his vest and headed to the door. He turned back to Isnor. "Watch my back. I may need you."

"Sorry lad I can't get involved with these affairs." Isnor stepped back with his hands in the air waving Abel off. "They come every so often to pillage. It's best to give them what they want so they'll be on their way. I'm too old for these constant scuffles."

Looking at Isnor, Abel knew he had been shaken down before by these ruffians. "Alright old man, watch my bag." Wiping the front of his vest, Abel smiled as he strode toward the door. He really hoped these bikers gave him trouble.

The gang members were focused on the young woman and her bag. Two were hovering around, while the leader had his hand on her shoulder harassing her. "Hey sweetie, stop struggling and hand the bag over. Nobody is going to help you, unless they want my boy Merck to rip their heads off."

The gang leader pointed towards the brawny man who gave a wide smile, with few teeth to show. If teeth equated to smarts, the man had little of both. Holding Uzis at their sides, the two goons were covered in a thick layer of brown dust, except for the clear rings left by their goggles. It was clear from their easy manners and general disregard for their surroundings that this was not their first time in Bourdain.

The leader kept fixated on his prey even as Abel approached. He was confident that his two henchmen would take care of any small problems. Only Warden and his people dare challenge the gang. Warden was a powerful man encamped on the edge of town. People pledged themselves to him for his protection. He traded freely with the Water Facility and kept an ample supply of water, which he kept as a reward for his monthly tournaments. The gang thought they could overrun the Warden taking control of his water supply. Many brothers were lost in that battle, weakening the gang and subsequently growing Warden's popularity. A mistake the gang would not make again. They always traveled with automatic weapons, steering clear of Warden's domain. If this young man challenged him, he would be easily dispatched. The town people had to be kept in place.

The two men tensed as Abel got closer, they were seldom approached. Abel looked upon them with no fear and an air of confidence that unsettled them. One of the gang members called out to the leader. "Reaper, I think this guy has a problem!"

Fondling the woman's shoulder, Reaper never turned to acknowledge Abel. He was whispering to the woman to give up the bag among other things. Her hands were at her waist, as she clutched the bundle like a baby. Trembling she sobbed silently waiting for the inevitable. Reaper continued his advances without turning around. "Then take care of him. He's interrupting my fun."

"Ok, Reap." The goon replied, still unsure. Abel had a calmness about him that made the gang members hesitate. Guns raised with fingers on the trigger, they could not figure out why this man was unafraid.

"No. I want Reaper to handle me." Abel said sharply. "Or does he just deal with women?"

"What!" Reaper yelled as he turned around clearly aggravated by the interruption and Abel realized his full size. He was hunched over the woman making his build deceiving. Bare chest exposed in his open jacket, Abel saw the zigzag of scares. He was no stranger to a fight and had the wounds to prove it. Stepping forward, Reaper sucked his teeth as he spoke. "You must not be from around here. This is none of your concern. Go on now before you get hurt."

Abel opened his mouth to retort in a similar sarcastic manner, but the words left him as he caught the eyes of the woman he had come to protect. She looked at him with a teary smile. It was Keera. They had grown up together, chasing game and learning the realities of their life in Gravope. Abel was witness to her transformation from a tomboy to the beautiful woman before him. According to her father, they had left the village in pursuit of a better life. It was rumored her father had acquired work at the Water Facility. If someone died, occasionally a person of little means could be in the right place at the right time to receive an offer. How did she end up here? Abel thought. This town was worse than Gravope by far.

"Abel?" Keera asked puzzled, unsure why he was in Bourdain. Abel could tell she was glad to see him regardless.

"Oh, look at this boys. They're sweethearts. Ain't that romantic." Reaper laughed seeing the fear in Keera's eyes and the determination in Abels'. "Hopefully there'll be something left when I'm done. Kill him."

Before his henchmen could react, Abel reached in his vest and threw two concealed knives. The first lodged in one of the thug's throat. He dropped the machine gun, clutching his neck while his eyes rolled to back of his head. Choking on blood he fell to one knee. The other gang member stared at the knife stuck in his arm at the shoulder. Abel's throw had missed its mark and his opponent was enraged. Grunting through the pain, the biker brought the gun barrel up to fire. They wrestled as Abel attempted to rip the gun from him, but Abel was caught with a blow to the face from his foe's free arm. Staggered, Abel was surprised by the brute's speed. Abel was being strangled from behind and lifted off the ground. He jerked downward using his weight to toss the biker over his shoulder. Abel lifted his foot high in the air and his boot left a permanent mark across his enemy's face. He spun in a crouched position to face Reaper just as the shot from Reaper's gun rang out over his head. Diving to catch Reaper under the arm, they tumbled to the ground. The leader was beneath him but far from being subdued. Suddenly, Abel felt his chest burn as the knife slashed across his chest. He jumped back holding his torn vest, blood sprinkled his hand. Thank goodness for the vest, he thought, or the damage may have been severe. Reaper was on his feet, blade in hand ready to charge.

"Looks like you got some of your blood on my knife." Reaper gave a sinister laugh. "I hope you got more to spare."

He crouched back to leap at Abel. Pulling the 9mm from the small of his back, Abel fired two shots striking him in the arm and leg. The gang leader crumpled to the ground. Abel walked over and pressed the gun against Reaper's head. The gang leader was sprawled out on the ground, eyes closed waiting to hear the trigger squeezed. Abel flexed his finger.

"No. Please." Keera intervened, grabbing Abel's arm. "There's been enough bloodshed."

Abel kicked Reaper, rolling him on his stomach and moved back to pick up his weapons. In the fray, Abel had forgotten about Keera and why he was fighting. She moved closer to him.

"You're injured." She said as she rubbed her hand across Abel's chest.

Abel looked down at his vest and wiped off the drops of blood. "It's nothing." He lifted his head and locked eyes with Keera. "Are you alright?"

There was a long silence between them. They stared at each other lost for words. Keera never realized how capable Abel was. Recalling their playtime together she knew he was quick, but where did he learn to fight? She surveyed the bodies around her. The leader was already dragging himself to his bike. He wanted no more trouble. Keera kneeled down to pick up the bag she carried. It was full of Xonox water. This was the treasure the gang was after. Had Keera's father procured a job at the Water Facility after all? Abel could not believe how she had grown. It was hard to take his eyes off her. This was not the tomboy he remembered.

Keera began to recount the events that lead to their meeting. "I was heading to the shop when those thugs attacked me. Normally I come with my father but....he's been unavailable."

Her eyes trailed off and Abel sensed something was wrong. Taking her hand in his, he comforted her. "You're safe now."

Suddenly, Isnor walked up. "Wow! Didn't know you had it in you. I may have a way for you to get home after all."

The moment between Abel and Keera was gone. Isnor patted Abel on the back beaming over the fallen gang. Keera shyly unclasped his hand. Abel was slightly annoyed. "What are you talking about?"

Isnor was oblivious to the broken mood as he spoke excitedly. "The Tournament. Every so often Warden, as he's known, holds a battle royal for sport. But he's also looking to recruit new talent. The winner receives a small crate of Xonox water."

"Warden?" Abel repeated the odd sounding name.

Keera chimed in as if she was reading Abel's mind. "He's a powerful man. People pay to enter his home to watch the tournament. This is how he's garnered favors, information, water and more importantly strong recruits. His army of mercenaries is the only force keeping this town from being overrun by the gangs." She pointed to the ruffians strewn about the ground.

Abel was starting to get the full picture. With the winnings from the tournament, he could buy the supplies he needed to get home and to reach Xonox. Maybe Warden could turn out to be an ally. Abel had fought many times growing up, but never for sport. His skills were honed through hunting and the protection of his family. Loun had warned against showing off or exploiting what he was taught. But what was the alternative? Sit back and wait for a ride home. Hope that everything would be fine when he arrived? He decided to take action. Maybe this tournament was the tune-up he needed for the battles ahead. Abel was convinced. "I need supplies and he seems to have them..." His voice trailed off thinking about what had occurred in the last few days.

Isnor misinterpreted the pause in Abel's voice. "Don't worry, nobody's ever died in the tournament. Although they have been severely beaten." Isnor hung his head and grimaced at the thought. "One guy swallowed his front teeth and another's eyes shut to the point, they were just slits." He demonstrated squinting his eyes. "And another. Oh let me tell you..."

"Please! My goodness." Keera scrunched her face in disgust at the graphic details.

Realizing he had gotten carried away, Isnor piped down. He really enjoyed the spectacle. The gambling and drinking was almost as fun as watching the gladiators. This was the first person he knew who thought of entering. "Sorry kid. I'm sure you'll do fine."

Abel waved off the apology, instead focusing on the task at hand. "That's the plan then. Take me to your leader."

CHAPTER 5
WARDEN

The journey to the Warden's domain was by foot. A three mile hike to the edge of town. Isnor insisted on going as a pseudo representative. Keera was also in tow. Curiosity had gotten the best of her. She heard stories, but never thought she would experience Warden's sanctuary. It was not known to be a place for lone travelers. But she could think of no safer place than by Abel's side. The town stretched into Warden's territory seamlessly. There were no markers to designate his property, just a transition from woods and dirt to pavement. Warden's home was an abandoned warehouse used for shipping goods in times long ago. Stepping out of the woods, the warehouse was impressive in its sheer mass. Small, ramshackled homes and tattered tents surrounded the foreground. The area was alive with activity with an open air market quality. People on the lot talked, laughed and traded as small children ran around. It was almost surreal to Abel, an oasis amidst the madness, people living so carefree only three miles outside of Bourdain. Why didn't everyone live here? Abel thought. Obviously Warden was well protected. Making their way through the crowd they reached the entry to the warehouse, more aptly described as a fortress. Warden's army were vigilantly patrolling the rooftop, rifles in hand. Their clothes were not uniformed, but a red emblem was emblazoned on the shoulder or chest of their jackets; A capital 'W' with arrows pointing upward on the ends and middle. As Abel tried to decipher the symbol an armed guard stepped in front of him blocking the warehouse door.

"State your purpose!" The guard sneered. His tone was abrupt and broke the easiness of the marketplace.

Abel returned his words in kind. "We're here to see Warden."

"Not today." The guard focused his attention on the market. "Try back tomorrow!"

Abel's eyes turned fire red, he was livid. He did not travel this far to be told to turn back. The thought of bull rushing the guard crossed his mind, but he feared for his companions' safety. What a waste of time, he thought. There had to be another way to get what he needed and he had time to figure it out.

"Forget it. Let's go." Abel spoke with disdain.

"Hold on." Isnor stepped forward. He placed his hands up near his face, approaching the guard slowly. "I am Isnor Profik a trader from Bourdain. This man is here to enter the tournament. We request to see the honorable Warden, scourge of the plains!"

"The tournament?" A gray-tooth smile spread across the guard's face as he looked Abel from head to toe. The doubt on his face was evident. "Why didn't you say that first and save me the trouble." The massive man moved to the side to allow passage. The group stepped through the doorway into the warehouse.

It was a city within a city. This was the inner circle of Warden's regime. The perimeter was lined with small living quarters, while above guards patrolled on a metal catwalk. There was a low buzz of activity throughout the building; an atmosphere in direct contrast with the hustle and bustle outside the doors. People had an air about them. They were superior to the denizens outside. Abel's group could feel the cold eyes on them as they made their way through the main entry. A sense of security had not quelled their apprehension towards strangers. Just as the situation was growing unbearable, a woman appeared with one guard at her rear.

"Greetings." Her manner was polite and easy. "Are you here to enter the tournament?"

The air tensed; clearly the wrong answer would spell trouble and a swift end to Abel's journey. Every patron in earshot froze in anticipation of the response. Arms were cocked over their weapons. Abel surveyed the hostility of his environment and decided to play this situation less aggressive. "Yes. I am Abel and these are my friends Keera and Isnor. Might the Warden be available to entertain an aspiring fighter?"

The woman smiled at his response. It was textbook on how to get an audience with the Warden. She was happy for Abel.

Many had died on the very spot he stood trying to portray toughness. The introduction was not the time for garish words. Save the ruggedness for the arena. The woman motioned her left hand high in the air with palm turned forward, signifying a greeting. But the group knew the gesture was much more. Guards lowered their weapons and the taut air drifted away. Those gathered around turned back to their business. For the first time Abel noticed that all the inhabitants were armored and bore the 'W' insignia. Warden was more than a modern day mob boss. Reaching him consisted of many layers and verbal intricacies. His success in the wasteland was predicated on the loyalty around him.

"Please. Follow me." She waved her hand beckoning for them to accompany her.

She turned her slim body gracefully, her head was covered except for the long, brown, knotted ponytail flowing down her back. Her movements were that of a hostess at a fine restaurant, belying the danger of the lair. The warehouse was a winding maze of structures, which narrowed and expanded the interior street. The configuration of the dwellings was deliberate, a way to halt intruders from reaching the heart of the habitat. Keera looked around wide eyed.

"This is incredible. I never thought there would be so many people here, so well-armed,   looking decently fed." She was clearly in awe of the volume of people and orderliness. It was commonplace for the Water Facilities to be pristine and sparkle with a cleanliness to which many were not accustomed, but here among the less fortunate. How did this man create a seemingly idyllic palace on the edge of nothingness?

Isnor shared her sentiment. "I've been here a few times for the tournament, but that was total chaos. I thought it was always like that. This environment is far more stressful."

"Don't worry old man." Abel quipped. "Stay close to me in case there's trouble."

"It's not my neck you should be worried about." Isnor responded gruffly.

Abel smirked, he knew Isnor would not take kindly to the comment. While Keera was expressing her naivety, he needed Isnor to be stout and aware. Who knows what would come of their meeting with Warden. When Isnor mentioned a tournament, Abel never imagined anything of this magnitude. He thought he would be wrestling on a cardboard box in the street. It was best not to show his concern.

The maze broke into an opening revealing a large half circle covered in sand with ascending benches around it. Blood, from previous bouts, stained the area. A maintenance crew smoothed out the sand in preparation for the next day. There were no trophies or plaques heralding the past winners. Just a desolate ring, emitting the bitter losses of the fallen and the triumphs of those that survived. Abel began to feel the weight of his decision. This was no sparring match. It was a fight for survival. Pondering the physical combat ahead and speaking to no one in particular, Abel said. "What's the prize for winning this thing again?"

"I have no idea." Keera surveyed the barren arena. "But I hope it's worth it."

"I told you. A case of water. Enough to buy passage to Gravope and trade for better weapons." Isnor reminded them. The group stopped and absorbed the distant battles of the arena, envisioning what lay ahead.

"Please. Come. Warden is waiting." The hostess called to the group.

"Yeah, I bet he is." Abel whispered to himself.

Keera leaned closer. "What?"

"Nothing, just getting my head ready." Abel responded.

"More than your head I hope." The merchant added.

Walking past the arena they approached an opening large enough to drive a car through.   There was a deliberate separation of public and private. This was Warden's inner sanctum. A few guards hung around the entrance smoking something with an unfamiliar smell. Cigarettes were far and few between. The guards paid little attention to them. They were led by the woman so they were safe. On the other side of the portal was another world. Women moved with purpose as young children scurried around. Abel noticed there were few women near the entry. Now he saw where the families dwelled, protected within the inner walls. All the women in this area had their heads covered signifying alliance to Warden. It was a primitive scene, almost tribal. The men hunted and protected the children, women and their leader. The children were simply the key to their future. Maybe if nurtured correctly they could be the key to turn the tides of injustice. At first glance, the women here were carrying out domestic tasks. More importantly they were symbols of lost beauty and simplicity cherished in this society. Who could question Warden's methods? Here was a thriving kingdom in a place where there should only be depravity.

Isnor let out a whistle. "I'm impressed."

Keera frowned at the scene. "I'm not."

"Doesn't matter." Abel interjected. "We're here for the water. Not a social experiment."

"Easy for you to say. Just don't ask me to cover my hair and get you a drink." Keera looked at Abel unsettled.

"Calm down. I'm sure it's by choice." He assured.

Isnor disagreed. "I don't know..."

Their escort rounded the corner into a large room with a long dining table. Seven people sat at the table, one stood off in the far corner. As they entered all eyes were upon them. Hostility instantly flared up in all but the man at the head of the table. He wore a robe of all white looking more akin to a prophet than the leader of an army. A smile widened on his face and his eyes flashed with danger.

"Excuse me sir." The woman bowed her head slightly as she spoke. "May I introduce a new tournament contestant, Abel." Rising to his feet, the robed man stood with his hands clasped. "Thank you Isabel. You have done well, you are excused."

She curtsied as she exited. "Warden."

Arms spread with a large smile and boisterous voice; his attire did not fit his tone. The robe adorning him was befitting a church leader, not the tournament host before them. Warden walked towards the group. "Welcome, welcome my friends. Your name again?"

Abel touched his chest first, and then introduced the group. "Abel. This is Keera to my right and Isnor to my left. We have traveled from Bourdain for your tournament."

"Very good. Keera, Isnor you do not fight, but please honor me by sitting and having a   drink." Warden said with a toothy smile.

Keera and Isnor apprehensively approached the table amidst false grins. Though Warden seemed genuine his comrades were not as trusting. As they took their seats a different woman brought out two cups filled with a brown liquid. From the smell it appeared that Warden dabbled with his own concoction. Isnor pounded his chest as he gulped down the drink. Wiping his mouth with the back of his hand, he raised his glass to the table. The men began to relax. Keera leaned forward and took a whiff, a small sip, coughed and sat back in her chair, eyes focused on Abel and Warden. Shaking Abel's hand like a diplomat, one hand over the other, Warden sized him up. "You're from Bourdain. I've never seen you. I know most of the young men there."

"No. My family is from Gravope." Abel said flatly still trying to figure out his host.

"Gravope." Now Warden was confused. "Word of my tournament has traveled that far. I'm at a loss."

"Sorry, not to mislead you." Abel continued. "But I never heard of you until yesterday."
Stepping back and unclasping Abel's hand, Warden had tired of the pleasantries.

"Well...What brings you?" With a low tone spelling trouble, Warden appeared ready to strike if the answer did not suit him. He respected Abel's bravery to seek him out the day before the event. But his brashness may get him killed before he began. Abel sensed the change in the room.

"My parents were killed by Xonox, I was knocked out and dropped in Bourdain two days   ago." He explained. "I want to use the tournament winnings to take revenge against Xonox."

A low chuckle emanated from the table at the thought of Abel going against the Xonox Empire with an old stumpy man and a young frail looking woman. Warden's face was blank. He admired the sternness in Abel's voice. A man on a path of revenge was a man with focused anger. Maybe Abel could be a benefit to him. "You want to fight Xonox? You have to win the tournament first. And I assure you, it's no cakewalk. Men come from all walks to compete. What makes you think you have what it takes?"

Isnor spoke for Abel. "I saw him disable two of Reaper's gang and give Reaper a pretty good beating too."

Before the words left his mouth Isnor knew he had spoken out of turn. Disapproving stares met his gaze from around the table. Warden quickly glanced at Isnor then back at Abel. "The gangs use numbers to overwhelm. They lack skills. Goll test him!"

Before Abel could figure out which person was Goll, he was tackled from behind. The man landed on top of Abel and punched him across the face. Abel spat blood onto the concrete floor. Goll was tall with a solid build, wearing a vest over his bare chest. He reared back for another attack. Shifting his body to divert Goll's second blow, Abel caught his arm between his legs. Spinning around, he arm-barred the attacker to the ground. The men at the table cheered. Even Isnor smiled at the spectacle, while Keera cringed, fearful of the outcome. Abel rocked back putting more pressure on his opponent's arm. The strain was evident as Goll grunted to break free, but he would not submit. Would he have to break his arm to prove his worth? Abel straightened himself ready to hear the cracking of bone. His robed host stopped the show. "Good. Good."

Warden patted Abel on the shoulder. Abel loosened his grip and fell back sprawled out on the floor. He hoped this was the last test. Goll got up quickly itching for payback.

"Have Isabel look at your arm." Warden commanded.

Goll's eyes seared with vengeance as he left the room. Abel's search was for water not more enemies. He would have to watch Goll.

"Should have let them finish." One of Warden's men shouted from the table with his glass raised.

"We'll save some for the arena." Warden grinned. "Good show. He caught you off guard and you turned the tables. I love it!"

Abel held his jaw. "Thanks. Glad you enjoyed it."

"No hard feelings, huh? We had to know if you were any good." The host exclaimed.

"Are you satisfied now?" Isnor said as he gulped down another drink.

"Competition is always a good thing as it forces us to do our best. Only the complacent are satisfied." Warden stared at the merchant. "The tournament is tomorrow. There are only a few rules. No weapons. You win by disqualification or by knocking a man unconscious or out of the ring." He walked back to the head of the table and gestured to Abel. "You and your group will stay here tonight as my guests."

A different woman entered the room dressed very similar to Isabel. Her red curly hair fell untamed beneath the head covering. "Naomi show them their rooms." Warden instructed.

"Make sure you have my water ready tomorrow." Abel said as he followed Naomi. "I'm not waiting around."

"Sure." Warden chuckled. "Love the cockiness Abel. But you will be tested tomorrow. Sleep well." Leaving the room, they could hear the group laughing and betting in the background. They were expecting a solid turn out and a good outcome.

The rooms consisted of four walls, a door and a salvaged bed. Isnor was given his own room. Abel and Keera were told to share a room with a single bed. Upon seeing the arrangements Keera protested. "Oh, no. This will not do."

"Sorry." Naomi confessed. "There is no separate room for you. Being alone here has its dangers."

Keera understood, but it did not subdue her anger. "It's still an outrage. You can't just assume..."

"Relax, I'll grab the floor." Abel said attempting to end Keera's rant. "Let's not cause a scene."

Keera paused for a moment. This was not the time to argue. She wanted to come along and supporting Abel was her first priority. "You're right. Except I'll take the floor. You have a tournament to win."

Keera covered the light from the crude lamp. The room was dark except for the light seeping under the offset door. She grabbed the tattered sheet and stretched out on the floor. Abel settled into the mattress hearing the springs shifting to support his weight. When was the last time he was in anything resembling a bed? Laying in the darkness Abel thought of his deceased parents. They were gone, but somehow he had found a new family. Where had Isnor come from? Dragging him from the streets similar to an elder watchman. Keera never explained what became of her father and why she was trading alone. It appeared she did not want to go back home. She complained, but stayed fervently by Abel's side. This ragtag group was his aid and under his protection. As he drifted off to sleep, he knew he would not let them down.

CHAPTER 6
THE TOURNAMENT

"Hey! Get up. It's time. Leave your weapons." Abel was awoken by the guard's voice in the doorway. The morning light outlined his body and illuminated the room. Keera lay still asleep on the floor. The guard looked at Abel then Keera. Abel knew what he was thinking. He jumped up and wiped his face with a towel and adjusted his clothes while attempting to wake Keera. She stretched herself and stood up. Abel offered her the bread left by the guard. He handed Keera his weapons, more for her safety than a fear of them being stolen. She wiped off her clothes as she stole a kiss on his cheek. "Good luck."

Abel held her by the shoulders looking in her eyes. "I'm gonna need it."

Abruptly Isnor burst into the room. "Let's go! No time for dallying. You left your weapons right? Ok. Did you eat?" Abel was unable to get a word in. He could sense Isnor's excitement and trepidation. "Here." Isnor shoved the bread in his hand and ushered him out of the room. Abel looked over his shoulder and shrugged at Keera.

The tournament was held monthly depending on the interest Warden received. It was exactly a month since the last gathering. He had finally gotten the pool of talent he strived for. The young and old, came from all around seeking their fortune. Winning the prize was only part of the appeal. Many past winners were brought into Warden's family if they showed loyalty. Combatants would compete numerous times before he trusted their skills. It was a training ground and the water was a small price to pay. Many traded the water before they left the building. Others pledged their winnings back to Warden as an oath of fidelity. It would be interesting to see how Abel would react if he won, Warden thought. Could he be persuaded to join the cause? Warden needed more good men who hated Xonox if his plans were going to reach fruition.

Brutal was the word to describe the experience. Abel sat holding the gash under his eye. It was one of the many wounds he received in the arena. The first bout consisted of his opponent attempting to kick him out of the ring. He caught Abel across the face almost knocking him out of the circle. Luckily Abel recovered and delivered a vicious blow to the man's temple ending the fight abruptly. His next opponent was cut from a piece of stone. Screaming words of a violent death he charged Abel. Using his momentum against him Abel literally threw the man to the outer sand. He lay motionless until his handlers gathered him up. It was the last scrap that really tested him. Abel squared off against a tough, young grunt that would rather die than submit. The pair grappled until Abel got the upper hand and choked him unconscious. Now the final match loomed. There was no advance warning of his expected opponent, nor did he care. This was his tournament to win, it was always his destiny. All that time toiling and training in Gravope. His father spoke frequently about the people rising up from the slums. The death of his parents would not be in vain. Revenge was at his fingertips. One man would not stop him from attaining his goal.

Hearing the cheers Abel knew it was time. He grabbed the torn vest on his body and threw it to the ground. Underneath lay his sweat soaked, blood-stained shirt. Removing the shirt, he could feel the tank top stuck to his body. Cargo pants clung to him in a shrunken manner. As he stripped down to his shorts he wiped the sweat from his eyes and hair. He could hear the crowd growing louder outside.

"Champions come forward!" The ring announcer called to the last contestants.

Abel walked from behind the concealed wall and the cheers erupted from the crowd. Earlier the area he waited in housed seven other fighters. As the day progressed he was the last one standing. On the other side was a similar holding area. Spectators stared from side to side as the two warriors approached. Betting and drinking was at its height. It was clear how Warden prospered. These matches were open to the townspeople and generated far more revenue than the cost of the prize. The common man was given a chance here. Be they fighter or gambler, all had something to gain. A welcome distraction from a hard life.

The fans were frenzied but orderly. Warden's guards kept the crowd in line, but there was also an air of respect. Something Abel had not seen from a group of this size. There was always fear of Xonox and his minions, but Warden had captured a different vibe. With the resources at his disposal, riots and uprisings seemed imminent. But beyond the gangs Warden was rarely challenged. His unique power was something to behold.

Abel spotted Isnor and Keera among the masses. Nodding fiercely, Isnor pumped his fist in support. Keera beamed at Abel's success. Her hands were together as if in prayer. She lifted one hand up and mouthed 'Go'. Abel winked confidently at the duo. Disappointment would be on his opposition's face in a few minutes. He did not come this far for second place. Stopping at the edge of the arena, Abel saw his challenger for the first time. To win the water, to continue on his journey to placate Xonox, all he had to do was defeat one man. Dressed in nothing but a pair of shorts and shoes, Goll smiled as he saw Abel.

His aggressive style and high tolerance for pain had earned Goll another shot. This was his third tournament and he planned to capitalize on the opportunity. Like Abel he was in pursuit of a better life. When Goll heard about the tournament he decided to compete and try to win favor. He was motivated by a chance to prove his skills and his desire to be a part of Warden's family. With Warden backing him there would be no limit to what he could accomplish or simply take. When Goll fought previously, small mistakes kept him from being the final Champion. Disqualified for using brass knuckles he had tucked in his shorts. It was not a gun, no one was killed, and how was he to know his actions would be frowned upon? He was knocked from the ring in his second stint for underestimating his opponent. This time would be different. He had something to prove and he could see Warden watching intently.

At the head of the ring, with his chair backed against the wall, Warden surveyed the contestants. Flanked by guards and servants on either side, his presence emanated royalty. He sat on a wooden high backed chair. His white robes hanging over the sides. A subtle movement brought him bread, drink and towels to wipe his face. Guards were at attention ready to quell any disruption. All of Warden's surroundings were sovereign. Yet there was no regality to his home. Besides the cleanliness it was a warehouse. The night sky peeked through the weathered skylights penetrating the roof. Sitting away from the commoners, he was a king among his subjects.

All eyes were focused on the referee in the center of the ring, Luchi. He was quick for his age; able to step in to break up dirty fighting and get out of the way of impending trouble. Luchi was in attendance at Abel and Goll's previous skirmish. He was excited to see who would be the victor with much higher stakes. He waved the brawlers to the ring. "This will be the championship match! The final contestants are Abel of Gravope and Goll from parts unknown!"

The applause reverberated up through the steel trusses, vibrating off the metal textured roof. Luchi gestured for the men to step to the center of the circle. The warriors sized each other up as the referee stood between them. Goll growled and sneered in an attempt to intimidate. Abel was unflinching; he stood statuesque knowing that he was near his goal. There could be only one victor. Goll did not stand a chance, Abel thought.

Luchi turned toward Warden as the crowd hushed to a low murmur. Warden stood and his guards flexed to attention. He raised his hands in the direction of the two combatants. The crowd vacillated as the words fell from his mouth. "Fight!"

Luchi stepped out of the way as they circled one another. Abel was in a defensive boxer's stance, while Goll stood broad chest with his hands to his side. He scanned Abel's defenses for a weakness. Letting out a primal scream, the man from parts unknown lunged at Abel in an attempt to tackle him. His style was unchanged from the previous encounter. Abel coolly shifted his weight to his back foot, caught Goll under the arms and flung him to the ground. The spectators erupted as Goll jumped up to wipe the sand from his face and mouth. Goll possessed a brutish technique, which normally wore his enemies down. Staying true to form he launched another straight forward attack. Abel was ready as he landed a right hook to the side of Goll's face. Shrugging off the blow, the unfazed two-time contender crashed body to body with Abel and used his leverage to wrestle him to the ground. Goll's ferocity had overtaken Abel's poise and he had little time to recover. A head-butt fell on Abel's right eye, followed quickly by two right hands to the side of his head. Leaning into the third punch, Abel absorbed the blow while maneuvering his right arm over Goll's head. Pulling his competitor down, he kneed Goll in the ribs to gain the upper hand. His adversary broke free as Abel prepared to deliver more damage. Determined to finish Goll off, Abel wiped the blood trickling from his eye as he gained his footing. Without warning Goll sprinted toward Abel. His tactics were getting old and predictable. How many times would he rush him? Abel thought. He needed to put this man down for good. Goll was so close it seemed he was going to run over Abel. In an instant, Abel slid under Goll and literally threw him across the ring. The crowd gasped as Goll floated through the air near the edge of the arena. With a thud Goll fell to the ground, his head and torso hung outside the ring. Abel turned his back, pointed to the ceiling and closed his eyes in thanks for the victory. The crowd was eerily silent. Was his victory so astonishing? He looked in Warden's direction and smiled. Warden did not move. His expression was stoic as he lifted a finger to point behind Abel. Turning around, Abel sensed something was wrong. The referee was close to Goll, with his palms flat and hands pointing into the ring. It appeared his opponent was not completely out of the circle. The match was not over. Goll staggered to his feet. Abel's face contorted, a quiet fury rushed over him. Running full speed at Goll he jumped in the air and extended his foot. Surprisingly, the kick was blocked. Abel felt the hard sand beneath him as he crashed to the ring. Goll was over him quickly grasping his ankles and yanking with all the power he could muster, attempting to throw Abel out of the boundary. Kicking free, Abel started to roll away. Goll let go of his leg and kicked him in the chest. Abel winced in pain, he braced as the next blow fell. The brute was behind him, choking him to his feet. There was no doubting the man's strength. The match had shifted to Goll's favor. Abel could see wide-eyed fans screaming feverishly. Sound was fading in and out. He struggled to remain conscious. Suddenly he spotted Isnor and

Keera in the crowd. Keera had her hand on Isnor's shoulder. Her head was down for fear of the outcome. Isnor held her in a comforting manner, but he was still shouting. Abel read his lips in slow motion. "Come on boy".

At that moment Abel recalled why he was fighting in this tournament. Not for glory, fame or to prove his ability. He fought for his family's memory. If he fell here, how would he avenge them? Summoning all his strength he forced Goll backwards. Even Goll was amazed at his sheer determination. Anyone else would have gone limp, let alone summon the energy to fight back. As Goll began to give ground he could feel the power welling in his foe. Goll's arms were growing weaker and his hold was beginning to slip from Abel's neck. With one final thrust, Abel was free. The crowd was raucous. In one smooth motion, Abel landed a right hand squarely on Goll's nose. The big man lumbered and fell out of the ring. Abel, exhausted from the bout, grabbed his feet and pushed his whole body out of the circle for good measure. Luchi ran over to Abel, grabbed his arm and extended it in the air. "Winner. Abel from Gravope!"

People were uncontrollable. This was one of the best matches witnessed in ages. Luchi led Abel around the circle stopping in front of Warden. He was impressed by Abel as he clapped slowly.

Abel glared at the would be king. "I'll take that water to go."

"Congratulations Abel, fine performance." Warden said as he continued clapping. "But you haven't won the water just yet."

Abel was outraged. His words shot fire. "WHAT? Are you not a man of your word? I defeated everyone before me!"

A hush fell over the people. No one addressed the Warden in that manner and lived. The clapping ceased. "Not everyone." Standing to his feet, Warden pulled off his robe to reveal an impressively sculptured physique for a man of his age. The pointed red 'W' was tattooed over his chest. 'Kill or Die' was tattooed on his right arm. Abel thought back to the room were he was first introduced to Warden. Two men bore an identical credo on the same arm. This was not a ragtag bunch of wanderers that pooled together for protection. This was a collection of men who formed a fierce brotherhood. This tournament was the initiation.

Warden stalked towards Abel. "Rarely are there first time winners of my tournament. Those who achieve initial success must fight me for the water."

In the distance Isnor surveyed the crowd and whispered to himself. "Is this new?"

"I come here. Fight through your whole gang. And when it's time to leave with the prize   you tell me double or nothing?" Abel spat out his words in disgust. "I only have two words for you Warden....BRING IT!"

"That's what I wanted to hear. No whining is allowed in my home." Warden smiled fiercely.

Abel assumed his fighting stance. How tough could Warden be? Abel thought. He sat around all day watching others fight and do his bidding. One solid punch would end this quickly. Luchi stepped timidly between them. His tone revealed even he was not privy to the seldom used rule. "Fight?"

Relying on his quickness, Abel lunged at Warden. With his size, Warden's speed was deceptive as he effortlessly ducked under Abel's haymaker. Off balance Abel pivoted to strike again. Unexpectedly, a piece of granite slammed into the side of his face. Falling to the ground Abel realized it wasn't stone, but Warden's fist. The crowd yelled their leader's name. Abel succumbed to darkness.

****

The room was larger than the one Abel occupied before the tournament. It was airy, sparsely decorated and a metal fan hung from the middle of the ceiling. The walls were covered with paintings. Light shone in from the window opposite the bed were Abel slumbered. Keera and Isnor hovered over him as he lay motionless. He had a tough bout, but it was the final fight that endeared him to the fans. Challenging Warden was one thing, living to tell about it was another. Still, Warden had Abel and his companions moved to one of the nicer spaces in his home. Access to natural light in the sleeping quarters was often associated with status in Warden's family. It was not clear what purpose Abel was to serve. The fact that he was still alive spoke to his value.

Abel's eyes fluttered open. His first image was of the heavenly Keera whispering encouragement to him. He closed his eyes to refocus and opened them to find Isnor hovering too close for comfort. Abel jumped back, pulling himself up on his elbows. He saw Keera smiling softly on the opposite side of the bed. Then it hit him. The tournament?

"Wait! The water!" Abel shouted through his hoarse voice.

He looked at Isnor and Keera hoping for good news. Keera shook her head slowly as Isnor grimaced and stared at the floor. Abel closed his eyes and lay flat on his back. Not only was the water lost, but now he was farther from home and his ultimate destination. Warden had stolen the victory he was so sure of a few days ago. This whole idea was a waste of time, he thought. It bore nothing for his efforts.

Isnor could sense the frustration. He felt responsible for Abel's current situation. In his experience as a spectator, Abel had what it took to win. He defeated all challengers before him save one. Was the rule real or something dreamed up by Warden to deprive Abel of the winnings? Warden was rarely known to engage in physical combat. What was so different about this situation? Why was Abel so special? Maybe Warden realized he could not convince him to join forces. Abel's anger stayed keenly focused on avenging his family. What is fair is fair though. He should get some form of compensation. Isnor finally spoke up. "You put on a real show kid. Everyone's surprised you got a swing on Warden. Sorry about the prize. I guess I never saw a first-timer win the thing. You definitely deserve something for your troubles."

Coming through the door with Luchi, Warden intervened. "And he will receive something for his troubles."

He tossed a bottle of water to Abel, who caught it instinctively. Luchi was carrying two bottles for Isnor and Keera. A third man entered unarmed, but was undoubtedly one of Warden's guards. He settled silently near the door.

"If I may, that was a great fight with Goll." Luchi said clearly astonished by Abel's skills. "Where did you learn your technique?"

Abel sat up on the bed so his feet were touching the floor. He cracked open the water and took a long swig. "My father. He was Special Forces in the old army."

"Yeah, those guys could really fight. The regular army was tough, but Special Forces were on a whole other level. I've seen them in action before." Luchi responded with wonderment.

"Really? When?" Isnor questioned.

Warden interrupted. "Luchi please. I need to speak with my guest."

"Excuse me Warden. Great fight Abel." Luchi nodded to the rest of the group then exited the room.

"What was that about?" The merchant wondered aloud.

Their host looked at each of them in turn. "Luchi has seen many things in his time. You should sit down and talk with him when time permits." Warden fixed his gaze on his last competitor. "How are you Abel?"

"Been better." Abel said as he rubbed his neck.

"It makes one a better person to have hardships and to have overcome those hardships only blaming oneself for mistakes made." Warden continued "Abel it's unfortunate what happened. We normally don't broadcast the first-timer rule. The fact is, few people get to the final round let alone win. And the rare ones that do refuse to fight me. They're too busy trying to gain my favor. You on the other hand chose to challenge me. I respect that. And believe me I don't respect many people." Warden's voice had a twinge of sincerity, but Abel was not so easily swayed by his explanation.

"That's how you show respect, by knocking someone out? Things really are done differently around here."

Warden walked closer to the bed. "I would be lying if I said I didn't enjoy it, because I did. But not for the reasons you think. A man in my position must set limitations on physical engagements. I'm not fighting the gangs directly anymore. I don't travel to trade with the Water Facility or Bourdain. My tournament is the only real connection to the outside world. It's how I gauge the plight and struggle of the common man."

"And recruit new talent." Keera snapped, unable to hold back.

Warden stopped his speech. Smiling at Keera he looked back at Abel and winked. "She's a feisty one. But I thought she knew better than to speak."

Taking another sip of water, Abel rose to his feet. His eyes had no fear as he stared at Warden. He had lost in the ring, but that was with a four challenger warm-up. Abel wondered how he would fare if he was rested. "Her name is Keera."

Warden raised his arms in mock appeasement. "Okay, okay. Keera, you're correct. But how else do you propose we fight against the corruption in this country? Do you have a better solution? Yes. I bring people here with the hope of fortune, but many find a fraternity that they never thought possible."

"Is that an invitation?" Abel asked smugly.

"No." His host said softly. "Unfortunately your display in the arena will not allow me to invite you into my fold just yet."

Isnor groaned. "Pity."

Ignoring Isnor he continued. "Indeed. But I know you, Abel. Or I should say I know men like you. And I know you do not want to leave empty handed. So I have a proposition for you."

"A proposition?" Isnor exclaimed, amazed at the man's gall.

"I'm listening." Abel said coolly.

"It would seem certain events have linked our paths." Warden started.

"Go on." Abel pressed.

"There is a man that goes by the name of Tommie Gun. As part of Xonox's circle, he was privy to classified information pertaining to Xonox's tower. Security clearances, number of guards, secret ways in and out, the whole layout. In the name of personal gain, Tommie defected. Before I could attain this sensitive information from Mr. Gun, he was discovered and forced to take refuge in the Grazen Woods." He purposely let the last bit of information linger.

"What are you saying Warden?" Isnor demanded.

Warden was still focused on the tournament winner. "What I'm asking is I need someone who can handle themselves to escort Tommie back to my home. Once here, I can analyze the plans and discover the weaknesses in Xonox's defenses. Destroying that House will weaken the remaining seven and pave the way for an uprising."

"You want Abel to go into the Grazen Woods! Everyone knows those woods are a death trap. No one ever returns." Keera was tense as she spoke, realizing the dangers Abel would face.

Warden attempted to calm her. "The tales of the Grazen Woods are exaggerated. People don't die there, they stay there to live off the forest. Never mind."

"What do I *get*?" Abel asked.

"You're not serious?" Keera said nervously.

"All the weapons you can carry and the use of one of my personal vehicles fully stocked." The host responded without hesitation.

"No. I mean what do I get." Abel reiterated, emphasizing the last word.

Warden whispered. "Oh. Yes. Unswayed. I see." The man who had built a kingdom on the edge of nothingness sought to sell him on the idea. "What if I told you I have a better offer than just water?"

"Better than water?" Isnor quipped. "Watch out kid!"

"Isnor. Some respect please. You are in my home." Warden reminded him and then turned back to Abel. "If you get Tommie and the plans back safely to me, you can keep the guns and I'll give you a case of water. Or..."

"Or what?" Abel asked impatiently.

Warden knew he had his interest now. "You can join me in the assault against Xonox. I guarantee you at least twenty soldiers under your command as well as anyone you want to bring in. Think of it Abel, with my resources and your fearlessness, Xonox will burn for all he's done."

Abel stared at the floor contemplating the offer. Keera was sure he should not take it and voiced her opinion. "Thanks, but no thanks. We've heard enough of your promises. How about compensating Abel for the four people he defeated in the arena. Don't listen to him Abel!"

She was beside herself and Abel wanted to assuage her fears. "Keera, calm down. Can we have a second, Warden?"

"Sure. I'll be outside." Warden stepped out of the room.

"Abel, we don't need his help." Keera spoke quickly sensing Abel's willingness to accept the offer. "What has it gained us so far?"

Isnor agreed. "She's right lad. Let's cut our losses."

"I understand your concerns." Abel chose his words carefully. "But I did not come this far to leave with nothing. Worst case scenario I can't find the guy and we have ammo and a car from the deal. But what if I do find him? Warden's right, I can do a lot more damage with his army behind me. This isn't your fight, so

I understand if you both decide to leave."

"We're with you whatever you decide." Keera leaned over and clutched his hand.

"That's right." Isnor put his hand on his shoulder.

"Good." He was glad they supported him. Their loyalty was more valuable than any of Warden's twenty men. Abel called out. "Warden!"

"Well..." Warden answered as he came back into the room.

Abel walked toward Warden. "Stock the car and don't skimp on the ammo."

Three days had passed since Abel competed. His wounds and pride were fully healed. Warden's people had taken good care of him. Keera and Isnor were by his side to ensure he reached full strength. As day broke, Abel geared up for the journey ahead. His vest and cargo pants were scrubbed to look like new. Warden provided boots, a compass, goggles, a machete, submachine gun, two handguns with all the water and ammo he could carry. This mission was too dangerous for Keera and Isnor. Abel planned to drop them off in Bourdain, which was slightly out of the way. The jeep was parked behind the warehouse. A red 'W' insignia was across the hood. It was fully fueled as Warden had promised. An M-16 with a grenade launcher was tucked in the back in case he got in a tight spot. Abel was ready for anything.

The trio climbed aboard and drove to the main gate at the side of the building. As they approached the exit, one of Warden's guards halted the vehicle. "Hold on."

There was no imminent threat, but the delay was odd. After a few minutes of waiting, Isnor piped up at the guard. "Is there a problem?"

Warden appeared from the side door with one unarmed escort. "No problem Isnor. I just think there was some miscommunication." He looked from the merchant to Abel. "This mission is far too hazardous for you and Keera. I would prefer you stay here as my guests while Abel is gone."

"Thanks Warden." Isnor stayed seated in the jeep. "We appreciate the offer, but I need to get back to my shop, Keera needs to get back home..."

"But I insist." The tournament host cut him off and motioned to the guards. "Help them with their bags."

"No..." Keera pulled her backpack to her chest as the guard reached for it.

"Hey, no need for that." Abel said with a steady voice, hoping to avoid a tussle that would injure his friends. "Isnor and Keera will stay."

"The heck we will." Isnor said infuriated at the request.

Abel grasped Isnor's shoulder. "Isnor. Warden's right. Who knows what could happen from here to Bourdain. I'll find Tommie Gun and be back in a few days. 'Till then food and drink are on Warden. He'll treat you as his honored guests." He eyeballed Warden. "Right?"

"You have my word." Warden smiled and extended his hands as a courtesy.

"If I find out different..." Abel warned.

Warden was tired of the banter. "I'll do my part, you just bring back those plans."

Abel stepped from the vehicle to help Keera out. She hugged him as he assured her everything would be fine. He shared a hearty handshake with Isnor. "Look after her and yourself."

"You're the one that needs looking after." Isnor said forcing a smile. "Be careful out there."

"I will." Abel replied strongly. He turned back to Keera and she grabbed his hand and placed one of her rings in his palm.

"For luck."

"Thanks." Abel stared at the silver ring; it shone through the scratches and dents it had collected over the years. Another symbol, he thought. He hopped into the jeep before his emotions got the best of him. Driving through the gate he glimpsed back to see Isnor and Keera being escorted back inside the warehouse. He had to find Tommie Gun now. Warden would undoubtedly treat them fairly. They would have the run of the complex. But if he failed to return or find Tommie, his friends' lives could be at stake. There was no windshield on the vehicle to halt the rushing wind. Abel pushed the goggles down over his eyes and accelerated towards the woods.

CHAPTER 7
GRAZEN WOODS

The jeep careened to a halt at the edge of the woods, Abel had reached his destination. He shut the engine off, pushed his goggles up and sat in the vehicle staring at the lushness of the trees. Tommie Gun was the needle and this was the proverbial haystack. Warden's instructions were to head to the middle of the forest. As Keera mentioned, few people returned from these woods. Supposedly, natives lived here but few ventured out. The young and old adventurers would enter these woods and never return. At least that was the story he heard time and time again. Were the natives the culprits or was there something worse deep within the brownish-green confines? Or was it fables used to keep children obedient? How many times were children threatened to be carried off into these very woods? Ironically his journey forced him to discover the true nature of what dwelled within the stoic evergreens. Abel was losing daylight. He needed to get his search started before the sun dipped. Grabbing the guardrail he jumped out of the truck onto the soft ground, the leaves crackled beneath his feet. He adjusted his vest, securing his blades at the same time. Each pistol was taken out, wiped off, magazine checked and pulled back to ensure a bullet was in the chamber before being slid back in the holster. The compass was sitting on the top of the bottles of water in his pack. He placed it in his pocket and walked to the back of the jeep where the M-16 lay. Hoisting up the gun, he could feel the full weight as he placed the rubber recoil pad on his shoulder and aimed in the direction of the woods. With two hands underneath the weapon, he tested the balance. It was a solid rifle, but would slow him down in the small jungle. He needed to be quick and agile if he hoped to find his target and come out alive. Abel scouted from his vantage point adjacent to a short hill. He could pick off any pursuers from this position if he was forced to retreat suddenly. Grabbing some fallen branches and leaves, he covered up the vehicle; the jeep's black paint mixed with the foliage creating camouflage. His concern over the vehicle being discovered and stolen was appeased. Holding the compass in his hands facing the wilderness, with the arrow pointing northwest, Abel walked into the unknown.

Abel yanked the machete from its sheath with his eyes focused on the compass's tiny north arrow. It was widely speculated that the woods were two-hundred thousand acres of dense, undriveable terrain. The area was thick with greenery and covered by a solid canopy above. As Abel crossed over birds shot into the sky. It was eerily silent beyond their flapping wings. Dry leaves crunched under his feet as he cut a straight path through the overgrown plants and tree limbs. For a land deprived of water, there seemed to be no signs of deterioration in this place. The area where he hunted with his father in Gravope was sparse in comparison. Coming to a clearing he wiped the sweat from his forehead with the back of his hand. He had walked for an hour straight, steadily pushing through the green barrier. He took out a bottle of water, took a seat on a rock and gulped down the contents. Through the thickness of the overhanging branches he could see the sun, but it appeared to be dusk where he was standing. Out of the corner of his eye Abel saw the shadow of a figure behind the trunk of the tree, watching him. He spun with his gun aimed at the spot. Had his eyes deceived him? There was nothing as he moved closer to the tree, with his gun extended. He could hear the leaves of the tree limbs rustling overhead. Looking up he saw a pair of eyes, human eyes, watching him through the branches. Impossible, he thought? Abel closed his eyes and shook his head refocusing on the spot. Nothing. Were his nerves getting the best of him? He had to be seeing things, he thought. Sliding his weapon into the holster he concluded it was fatigue. Since he left Warden's domain he had been moving nonstop. Isnor and Keera's faces flashed through his mind strengthening his resolve. Grains and bread, compliments of Warden, were wrapped in his backpack. He would have a quick snack before he continued. Sitting back on the rock he held the machete flat across his legs while he ate. His eyes may have lied to him, but his instincts told him he was being watched. Draining the rest of the water from the bottle he discarded it onto the ground. No sooner did the bottle hit the ground than a rush of wind poured through, shaking the tress and causing the animals to scurry. Abel swirled around with knife in hand looking in all directions. No one approached. Holding the machete in his right hand he inched over to the bottle, still keeping his guard up, and picked it up. The trees slowed to a sway and silence fell again. Abel took note. Apparently, the Grazen Woods were active and alive. No wonder unsuspecting explorers were consumed by it. Abel put up his hands to the trees without unclasping his weapon. Speaking to the perceived spirit of the forest in a low tone. "I'm looking for someone. When I find him I'll be out of here. I mean no harm."

Anyone passing by would have thought he was crazy, but like his father was known to say, 'Better safe than dead.' Abel believed in spirits and the Grazen Woods definitely possessed something. Grabbing his pack, he started to head west when he glimpsed a small glow off to the north in the distance. He had not noticed before, but it was starting to get dark. Was this a sign? He decided to take a chance and head for the light.

High above the trees Tequil watched the intruder. He was unlike the men who came before him. Alone, lightly armed and a little jumpy, Tequil was skeptical of the outsider's intentions. The forest was his people's home. Those that showed respect were allowed to pass through without injury. Those who did not were taken before the council and their punishment exacted without conscience. Tequil tracked the other men to a nearby location, but had sensed the presence of the foreigner who was heading toward the center of Grazen. Tequil was not alone in his surveillance. His brothers and sisters were among the branches and beneath the bushes. When the empty water bottle touched the ground they all shook, symbolizing the impending death of the intruder. But something strange happened, the man retrieved the rubbish and apologized. It was uncommon for out-dwellers to have this type of consideration. This man was different. Tequil shifted his weight on the branch and sprung across to the next out stretched branch, gliding across the canopy. His body was long and muscular, honed by years of living off the bark and sap of the trees. Only his torn jeans covered him, leaving the tribal mark on the middle of his chest exposed, a full moon with a broken arch behind it symbolizing an eclipse. The day that the earth was thrown into darkness when the Collective rose to power. Born in the forest, Tequil never ventured beyond the tree's shadows. All he knew were the elders' stories. The council believed that the Collective would be destroyed one day, but such a war would cause the annihilation of all around it. Until that day came, Tequil and his people fought fiercely for their home. Perched on the tree, Tequil moved silently as the wind. He needed to inform the council of what he had seen.

Abel had worked his way through the overgrown plants and was a few feet from the light source when he heard the voices. Ducking into the brush, he took cover near the group. Peering over the plants he could see two gang members sitting around a makeshift fire. As one of the members turned to secure his weapon, he was able to make out their markings. If memory served, they were part of the gang he encountered in Bourdain.

"Where the heck did Harvey get off to?" One of the gang members asked.

"Heck if I know." The other answered.

"He needs to be here when Sledge comes back with the rest of the guys."

Abel shrunk down. The rest of the guys? This was all he needed. More of Reaper's gang roaming around. In the last encounter, his surprise attack caught the group off guard. If he had to fight four or five armed bikers in the woods with light weapons, the outcome may not be in his favor.

"I can't wait to get my hands on the guy that attacked Reaper and disrespected
the crew." The biker punched his hand into his open palm.

"Seriously man." The other said with some clarity that contrasted with his leather clad, brusque appearance. "This has got to stop. We've already given too much territory to Warden. We can't have some nobody rallying the folks in

Bourdain."

"Don't worry brotha. When we get done with this guy, no one will disrespect us again." The two shook hands violently, brandishing their scorpion tattoos, one claw open and one claw closed on their biceps as he shouted. "We're going back to the old days and the old ways!"

Abel stepped back silently keeping his eye on the pair of bikers. He needed to work his way around and complete his mission. Once he got back to the Jeep, he had a biker gang problem solver in the trunk in the form of an M-16. As he backed up, he hit something solid. He thought, I don't remember a tree behind me? Suddenly he felt massive arms wrapping around him, lifting him off the ground. The assailant shouted towards the group. "Hey, look what I caught. We got a spy!"

Both members jumped up looking in Harvey's direction, guns in hand. "What the...? Bring him over here Harvey." The first Scorpion said. "Let's find out how long he's been listening." He pulled out his knife and wiped it across his leg. Harvey lumbered forward and Abel struggled to break free. Sliding his hand down his waist, Abel managed to reach his gun handle. Jerking his arm he squeezed the trigger trying to aim at the target. A shot rang out across the foliage, scaring the wildlife. Harvey released Abel as he let out a grunt. "Aaaargh!"

Harvey's boot smoked as he clutched his shin and fell to the ground. Diving for cover, Abel fired blindly in the direction of the remaining gang. Safe behind fallen trees, the gang returned fire with more powerful weapons than Abel anticipated. Shotgun blasts tore the bark off the tree from forty feet out. Waiting for a pause of shots, Abel fired around the tree. He could sense the level of his attacker's frustrations as the bullets from the automatic weapon sprayed his cover indiscriminately, stripping the bark raw. If their intent was to kill the tree they were succeeding. Abel waited for the firing to subside and emptied his clip in the gang's direction. Rushing to reload he let the empty clip fall to the ground and popped in a new one. He waited for the barrage to continue, but could hear the confusion as the gang was attacked from their flank. Abel was being assisted by an unknown ally. While the thugs were distracted Abel buried a bullet into one of the member's shoulders. The brute fell back dropping the shotgun. The second gang member turned towards Abel as the bullet pierced his leather cladded knee, he was helped to the ground by a shot to his arm by the unknown aggressor. The man stepped from the shadows of the trees to finish off the gang members. He coldly walked to each gang member, pulling the trigger one time for each fallen Scorpion. Abel searched the grounds but could not find the large gang member that attacked him. He must have lumbered off during the fray. Abel steeped out from cover to address his new friend. "Where...?"

"Oh, just passing through doing a little hunting. Saw you needed some help." The peculiar man replied.

"Yeah." Abel said still unsure what to make of the situation, Abel looked him up and down. He was older with graying hair and a grizzled beard. His clothes were all different shades of gray; a t-shirt, thick hunting vest and khaki pants. His boots were well used and needed replacement. As far as Abel could tell his only weapons were an old pistol hanging from his belt and a knife.

"You going to shoot me?" The man asked staring at the barrel of Abel's gun.

"No." Abel holstered the firearm. "Thanks."

"You're welcome." The man relaxed as he approached Abel. "What brings you to Grazen?"

"Actually, I'm looking for someone. I was told I would find him here." Abel measured his words carefully, searching the man for any clues of his intent.

The man's eyebrow cocked. "Oh. Where you heading?"

"To the center of the woods." Abel said feeling uneasy about his sudden interest.

"I've been there." The man sheathed his knife as he stared at the ground as if he was watching something. "Could show you the way?"

Abel was skeptical, but the man had shown his worth by helping him out of a tight bind. And time was of the essence, he needed to find Tommie Gun quickly. He extended his hand to the stranger. "I'm Abel."

He wiped his hand on his sleeve and returned the gesture. "Grey."

"You said you've been to the middle of Grazen?" Abel was

fascinated to meet someone that could survive in this environment.

"Yes." Grey said softly. "But you have to be careful of the Council."

"The what?" He asked unsure of the words uttered in the man's low voice.

Grey ignored his question, staring up at the sky. "It's getting dark. Let's get from the open. Plus these goons always have friends."

Abel followed Grey as he trudged deeper into the forest. He needed a break before he confronted Tommie Gun and was not expecting to get to the center right away. "Where are we going?"

"Right here." Grey stopped where the branches hung low and coverage was high, providing an ideal resting spot. "We'll rest here awhile and start again at daybreak."

Abel sat down on the ground and removed his pack. He reloaded his other gun and pulled the shaft. He offered water to Grey. They sat in dark silence gulping down the liquid. "So how do you know so much about the woods?"

"I've been in and out of here since I was young." Grey said focused on the darkness in front of him.

"How was it? You know. Before the Collective." Abel liked to ask that question of older people. It was his way of piecing together the history that was lost to him. His father had told him the story of the rise of the Collective, but a new voice always added a different wrinkle to the tale.

Grey leaned back and read the stars in the sky nostalgically as if they could tell the story. "My father lived in the town of Bourdain, but it was different from how you know it today. It was a thriving suburb. Before the Collective came, water was growing scarce. People got by accessing creeks, finding wells and sharing the resources. If you discovered a creek, folks would come from miles around to get a taste. Then, someone got the bright idea to purchase the land and charge for the use of the creek, pond or well. It was a cheap way to regulate overexposure to a water source. Few complained because the cost was low. It was just the beginning. Some rich entrepreneurs decided to purchase the lakes, too polluted for human consumption and the ocean fronts, not consumable due to the salt. At first no one opposed the acquisitions. Many thought these men and women could find a way to bring an affordable water source to the masses. Soon, the lawyers moved in and expanded the waterfront property law to extend two-hundred miles from shore as opposed to the previous law of two-hundred feet. Fences started going up around the beaches and great lakes. Only people of status were allowed near the water. Trespassers were being shot on sight. No water for washing and no fish. Riots ensued; everyone realized their folly. By then it was too late. The government and military collapsed under the economic strain. The most powerful families held a summit high in the Rocky Mountains, dreaming up the Morphesizer. They promised this would be the answer to humanity's prayers. The gates would be removed and water would flow again. Many were doubtful. Over a one year period, with architects, engineers, scientists and craftsmen working twenty-four hour days, the machine was built. It was held as the solution to America's problems and perhaps the world. It was to be unveiled on the west coast as a gift to the human race. At the time, the Collective was a non-profit organization, so water prices would fall back to the early twenty-first century costs. The main philanthropists who spearheaded this dream met again to commune and congratulate one another on their success. At the end of the gala, a jumbo private jet left headed towards the west coast carrying the richest people in the country along with their socially conscious peers. The two jets escorting the aircraft dropped behind it and fired two missiles a piece. There were no survivors. The pilots were eventually apprehended and executed, although they maintained their innocence. The nation mourned, but was given hope as the Morphesizer was commemorated. Fronting the project was a man not known for his generosity, Yual Mordal. He became the head of the House of Saran, the richest man in the country and promoted the machine with Quitteri Croman and Victor Xonox. You know the rest. They monopolized water production and thrust us back into the dark ages. My family retreated to these woods to live off the land. They swore to defend it against intruders.

Abel was silent letting the story sink in before he spoke up. "My father told me of the machine's intention. I never understood why the terrorists destroyed that plane. Those people were the hope for our society."

"The real question is not what group, but what men." Grey

reminded.

"My father spoke of the Xonox rumors." Abel said retrospectively. "I guess I never cared enough to ask more questions."

Grey was not surprised. "Few people speak of Xonox or the rumors."

"Until a few days ago, he seemed like something that mothers dreamed up to scare their   children." Abel sat back against a tree trunk. "But now, for the first time I understand how real a threat he is. He's why I'm here. I need to find a man named Tommie Gun."

"Tommie Gun? Strange name." Grey said dully.

"He's supposed to be in this forest. He used to work for Xonox." Abel revealed.

"Oh, I understand now." Grey said, his voice growing lower. "We'll find him."

"I appreciate your help Grey. You seem to know this forest well. How can I repay you?"

Grey laughed, raising the bread in his hand. "You can provide a real dinner next time."

"That's a deal." Abel smiled as he put his hands behind his head satisfied he was on the right path.

The forest was dark and still. It was impossible for Abel to see his hands in front of him. Only the dull glow from Grey's small pocket light penetrated the night. Abel slid down from the rock he was perched on, closing his eyes as he put his hand over his weapon. Grateful as he was for Grey's assistance, he was still leery of the stranger. How did he manage to take out the gang so effortlessly? He could make out an outline of Grey and hear him nibbling on the bread they shared. Abel could see the white of Grey's eyes staring off into space it seemed unlikely that he had dispatched of three gang members just a short time ago. His nature was docile or even harmless. Abel faded off to sleep confident in his ability to thwart any trickery. He had a long road ahead and rest was a necessity.

CHAPTER 8
KEERA

Two days had passed since Abel rode off in search of Tommie Gun. There was no word from him or sign that he would be coming back. But Keera knew in her heart that he would be back. He had to come back. She could not imagine living out her days in this place. True to his word Warden was a host of hosts. Food, wine and laughter flowed freely. Every night she and Isnor were the guests of honor at Warden's table. Isnor seemed to have made friends, boasting, toasting and gambling with Warden's inner circle. She was not sure if he was displaying common courtesy or really admired how Warden lived. In the mornings they would be summoned from their rooms for breakfast. The morning meal consisted of the leftover meat from the night before. If Warden was not a king, he surely lived like one. Warden and his cohorts would ramble on for hours about distant battles, faded memories and the excitement of the last tournament. Only his inner circle, who had battled at Warden's side in the gang's infancy, could jest about Abel almost catching Warden with a solid punch. They said he was a step slow. If Abel had not fought four combatants prior, Abel would be sitting at the head of the table and Warden would be out searching for Tommie Gun and fighting off killer bushes. Everyone got a great laugh at Warden's expense. Even Isnor joined in.

In the afternoons, Warden and his circle would venture over to the arena for in-house battles and training. The contestants were mainly disgruntled members of Warden's army. This was the way disputes over money, titles or pride was settled amongst Warden's people. The battle that day was between two of Warden's Sergeants. A bet was wagered and lost, but someone had refused to pay. No matter who was right or wrong the outcome was mediated in the circle. The ring was the final decider. To the victor went the spoils. Occasionally a rowdy person from the market would be brought in and taught the error of his ways. Warden did not allow his followers to abuse their power. But if a youngster wanted to test his mettle Warden would oblige from time to time, usually to the young man's detriment. In that instance, the fights were normally stopped before they got out of hand. The rabble rouser would be cleaned up, offered a couple bottles of water and sent on his way. Now he had a story to tell his friends. He had 'fought' in the 'tournament'. Nothing was farther from the truth, but Warden loved the notoriety, another commoner with his name on his tongue spreading his lore. Shortly after the in-house matches concluded, Warden would strip down to his pants and ask for challengers to test him. If no one volunteered he would get a couple of his guards to participate. Unable to match Warden's quickness and power, the bout often ended with them strewn about the ring. On this day, Warden taunted the inner circle. He chastised the group concerning his perceived 'lost step', inviting them to test the validity of their statements. He pointed at Isnor to step into the circle. Isnor stood up on the bench with a defiant look. The group around him grew silent. Isnor took a swig of his drink and laughed. "No thanks. I think I'll wait for Abel!"

Laughter erupted around him, Warden even chuckled slightly. Then, quickly composing himself he breathed in deeply with his hands close to his body. His legs were set apart even with his shoulders. His left leg slid out as he stretched into a low position with his arms extended. Slowly he pushed his hands in and out as if collecting power. In the blink of an eye, he flipped backwards, kicked upwards; leg swept, spun around and came up blocking and parrying an invisible foe. His speed and precision belied any lost step. The people in the complex looked on and marveled as Warden continued to fight his intangible opponent. Warden rolled forward, popped up, started running and performed a flying kick across the ring. Stopping near the edge of the circle, he brought his hands back together and calmed his breathing before bowing to the audience. Everyone clapped in recognition of Warden's display of skills. Keera wondered, did the clapping come from awe or fear? No doubt Warden was impressive, but how many times had he done this same routine and his people fell over themselves with praise? Maybe they did revere Warden. Or was it something else?

At dinner, Keera was the sole woman allowed to dine at Warden's table. Women came in and out to serve the table, but ate in a separate area with the children. She had not noticed the arrangement until the second night and was appalled by the situation. She sat in her seat fuming, refusing to eat or drink. Isnor leaned over and lifted his cup towards her, motioning for her to eat. Keera kept her mouth taut. Warden noticed she was not partaking of the meal. "Keera, is the food not to your liking?" Warden addressed Keera in a soft tone. But Keera did not return the gesture in kind. Her reply was acidic.

"No! This place...You're a tyrant! Why do these people bow to you? You're nothing but a mercenary!"

Before anyone at the table could react to the severity of the comments, Warden sat back in his chair and bellowed a throaty laugh. "You see why I like her." Warden spoke to no one in particular, lifting his hand toward Keera. He called out to one of the women serving food. "Naomi!"

"Yes Warden?" The woman quickly answered.

"Please escort Miss Keera to the women's table. I think she has had enough of us for one night."

Naomi motioned to Keera. "If you please Keera."

Keera stood up without a word, her eyes burning red and fixed on Warden. She followed Naomi out of the room. Isnor watched her leave the room. He continued to drink, but was concerned for Keera's safety. If he could find a chance to step away, he would check on her. For now he sought to smooth over her words. "She just misses the boy. That's all."

"They say the butterfly that brushes against thorns will tear its wings." The smile was gone from Warden's face. "Still...Her spunk intrigues me."

Isnor gulped down his wine. It had only been two days since Abel's departure. Isnor felt he and Keera had another a week before Warden's hospitality would wear thin. At any moment

Warden could decide to dispatch of them both. Or worse, keep Keera as his prize. Isnor shuddered at the thought. Forcing a grin, he lifted his cup again. He thought about Abel and a speedy return. Don't fail us now boy, he thought.

Isnor knew how dangerous the Grazen Woods were. He had ventured there once a few years ago. Five of his associates had gone in to hunt game despite the warnings from the villagers. Only he and another survived. They swore never to speak of that day. He rarely thought about those encounters. He just remembered the trees having eyes, the shaking of the tress and the chaos that ensued. Isnor took a drink to dull the memory. Abel was tough, but even he could not fight a forest. He took another sip and told himself that Abel would be back any day now. That was the hope he held onto until Abel's return. Since Abel's departure, Isnor had not stepped foot outside of the warehouse or felt the direct sun. It was eat, drink and be merry all hours of the day. Though Isnor knew, anytime your movements are restricted you are imprisoned. There was no question that he and Keera were Warden's prisoners, to be released when Abel came back with the right person and the right information. Isnor was a gambler, so having the odds stacked against him did not sit well. If Abel did not hold the wild card this situation could turn bleak for the duo. Isnor summoned a laugh at one of the men's jokes and his eyes caught Warden. It was as if Warden was reading his mind. Warden raised his cup to him, confirming Isnor's fears. Isnor returned the gesture, but neither man smiled. Time was standing still and running out at the same time. Isnor hoped he would not have to do anything drastic. He was getting too old to fight young men's battles.

Keera followed Naomi to a small room near the back of the remodeled warehouse as they walked past the dining area. The room was small, but spacious with a large piece of mirror hung on the wall. Secured by crude brackets, it was surprisingly intact except for the broken edges. Below the mirror was a makeshift desk with a purple cloth over it. On the cloth sat brushes, combs and other vanity items. Naomi pulled out the chair and motioned for Keera to take a seat. Keera stepped slowly to the desk, she had never seen such a large mirror or hand carved hair styling tools. Keera thought back to her childhood, sitting in her mother's lap staring out the bedroom window as she combed her hair. The comb was old, missing half of its teeth. Her mother always said she would trade for a new one, but the time was never right. Keera sat down and Naomi picked up the brush. Standing behind Keera she began to softly glide the bristles through Keera's curly hair. Keera felt herself relax as she looked at their reflection. Glancing up at Naomi she began to see her for the first time. She was petite, but her eyes had an inner strength. Keera had viewed her only as a servant, thinking her life was miserable. It seemed she was wrong. The gentleness of Naomi's hands told the story of a woman who avoided the ruggedness that this world possessed.

"How does that feel Keera?" Naomi asked as she worked to straighten her curls.

"Good." Keera said. "I didn't know all this was back here."

"We have access to more than you think." Naomi smiled as she placed her hand on Keera's shoulder. "You are a pretty woman Keera. You know it is dangerous to travel alone. Or are you and Abel..."

"I'm alone." Keera corrected. "Abel is just....a friend"

"I see." She continued combing her hair.

'We grew up in Gravope together. But I hadn't seen him for years." Keera said, her voice trailing off.

"Oh?" Naomi continued stroking Keera's curly locks.

"Yes. He saved me...Well, helped me with that biker gang in Bourdain."

"He is quite a fighter." Naomi acknowledged.

"You should have seen him. He was so quick. So fearless, not at all how I remember him." Her eyes widened in excitement as she remembered how Abel had come to her aid. Naomi smiled as Keera spoke. Keera saw her and began to blush. "Anyway, I was glad he was there."

Naomi felt the tension drift from Keera and she knew she could probe for more information. "Is that why you accompanied him here?"

"I guess." Keera fumbled through her words. "It was all happening so fast. I don't know."

Keera stopped talking and contemplated Naomi's question. She never asked herself why she had come. First she was just afraid. But then. She stopped her mind from drifting. Her only concern should be Abel's safe return. "So tell me Naomi."

"Yes Keera." The two woman chuckled.

"Why do you serve a tyrant?"

Naomi stopped combing, smiled and bent down to look at Keera. "Is that what you think?"

Keera turned to look at her new friend. "Yes. He separates the men and women, lords over everyone like a king and takes unsuspecting travelers hostage."

"You are the best treated hostages that I have ever seen." Naomi pointed out.

Keera had to laugh. "You know what I mean."

Naomi proceeded to tell Keera the story of Warden's arrival.

"Before Warden came, this area was very similar to small towns on the outskirts of the city. Small amounts of water or food and overrun by gangs. This warehouse was abandoned and very rundown. Townspeople came from all over seeking refuge. Soon the gangs followed. They began to harass and extort the inhabitants until they practically ran the town. The biggest bike gang, the Scorpions, was headed by a man named Diablo. They began to grow in power and their ability to terrorize. They looted, demanded protection pay and had their run of the area from here to the Grazen Woods. More young men and women fell into their ranks, opting to side with the people in control instead of rebelling against them. The alternative was a life of desperation as all we had was taken from us. All that was left were the old and the weak, too tired to fight a small army. The herd had been culled and with it any future hopes. I remember when I was younger, how my father tried to protect my brother and me from the mercenaries. Many times he was forced to give up what small rations he had. Often he would comfort us, while we shared a bit of food and a few ounces of water, telling us things would get better. He would rarely eat saying that he was not hungry. But as I got older I realized there was very little to go around." Naomi paused as the emotions welled in her.

Keera put her hand over Naomi's wrist. "I'm sorry."

Naomi composed herself. "Thank you. Where was I?"

"You were saying things were getting worse."

Naomi continued. "Yes. Then one day a man came to this area. He was unlike any we had seen. Traveling alone is rare now, but especially in those days. No one knew where he came from. Carving a small spot near the warehouse, he hunted and traded for what he needed. All was well, until the Scorpions pulled into town for their weekly pillage. The masses were so accustomed to the routine they collected the bulk of their food, water and offered it with little resistance. The Scorpions collected everything in large sacks worn on their backs. There were only three bikers, but more could easily descend on the town. It was a typical raid until they spotted the man we know today as Warden."

He was dressed in white, with boxer pants and a loose shirt. He rested lazily against the warehouse staring at the sky, disinterested in the terror the gang was causing. One of the gang motioned to the other two thugs and they approached Warden. The group crowded him as the main member spoke, kicking Warden's leg. "Hey, we need half of whatever you have there."

Warden responded half in a daze. "What...?"

"Food and water now!" The gang member yelled angrily.

Warden looked at the lead member coldly. "Look. I think you've taken enough. Be content with what you have."

The Scorpions were struck by his casual manner. Most of the people were too fearful to raise questions. The leader addressed him again. "Are you crazy or something? Do you know who we are?"

Warden was unresponsive just staring forward into the sea of concrete before him.

'I don't know if you know this, but..." The biker tapped his biceps to show Warden his scorpion tattoo; a black scorpion with one claw open and one claw closed. "We run things around here. If you don't start handing over that stuff, you're gonna be in a world of trouble."

Warden's facial expression was unchanged. "A wicked man often brings himself into trouble by giving his tongue too great a liberty." The gang was dumbfounded by Warden's reply, but slowly determined they had been insulted.

"That's it! Let's end this guy." The lead biker reached down to grab the defiant man. Warden jumped up, grabbed the back of the thug's head and slammed his knee into the leader's face causing teeth and bone to snap. Before the man's head was out of his hands, Warden spun around and delivered a skull shattering elbow to the other gang member. He pulled the gun from the goon's holster as he fell to the ground. The third gang member was in shock at how quickly his comrades had been downed. Warden punched him square in the chest with his open palm. As the man slid to the pavement Warden approached with the weapon. The last Scorpion gripped his chest and his eyes widened as Warden leveled the pistol.

"Death is the broom I take in my hand to sweep the world clean!"

The shot rang out across the desolate lot. All three bikers lay about the ground. But there were no cheers for Warden, only trepidation.

"What have you done?" An old man shouted feebly. "Now more will come. You can't fight them all!"

The man was weak from lack of food. Fear was etched across his face from so many years of telling himself things will never change. Warden walked over to a fallen gang member and removed his holster, strapping it to his waist.

"I'd rather die fighting, than die wanting for food and water."

The old man quieted down. He thought Warden was foolish. Others in the town shared the same sentiment. They rushed to collect the dead rogues, placing them and their bikes on the edge of the land. The people braced for retaliation. Their anxiety was palpable. By the following day the roar of eight bikes could be heard nearing the camp. The gang rolled into town in search of their missing brothers. Warden strode out to meet the leader. The townspeople gave the oppressors a wide berth, staying clear of the calamity as much for their safety as to signify they were not aligned with this lone warrior. Warden was unarmed as he stepped in front of the leader's bike while the Scorpions dismounted. Similar to the previous bikers, the leader was large and eager to pick a fight. His muscles tensed as he rose from the bike staring at Warden behind the dark shades covering his eyes. He wore a helmet painted red, with horns curved up on either side. In case the symbolism was not obvious, 'Diablo' was etched across the face of the helmet at an angle in red. "Where are our brothers and our water?" He demanded scanning the town.

Warden stood stoically. "I'm sure we can come to a

resolution."

"A resolution?" Diablo reared his head and gave a deep laugh. "No one stands behind you my ignorant friend. We make the rules here!"

Warden was unwavering. "We will keep what we hunt, trade and find. Your group will have to find another town to loot."

The gang leader looked back at his men. "This guy is insane." All the gang shared in a laugh. Every so often some lone person would rise up against them and they would have to set an example. This would be no different. Diablo pulled a small sword from his motorcycle. "It's been a long time since someone dared to stand against us."

"I'm unarmed." Warden held his arms out.

Diablo grinned. "Good. Let's have some fun guys." The seven bikers began pulling out bats, knives, pipes and other forms of hand to hand weapons.

"Thus honor lies broken at the feet of the unjust man." Warden's voice carried softly over the wind.

"Broken, bruised and battered." Diablo raised his sword high over his head and swung it down upon Warden. All the townspeople grimaced expecting to see Warden cut in two. Warden dodged Diablo's blow and brought his right arm behind the man, using his momentum to send Diablo crashing face first into the concrete. The gang was shocked by his speed. Diablo was the biggest and toughest of the Scorpions. To see him dealt with so effortlessly gave the gang pause. Warden took the sword from the gang leader's hand. He stood slack holding the sword to his side in a non-threatening manner. The gang eyed the upstart as they gripped the various weapons in their hands. It was dead silence except for the wind rustling through the trees in the distance. One of the gang members let out a primal yell. The rest of the gang responded with a resounding cry of 'Scorpions'. It was seven to one and Warden should have been easily crushed under the numbers. But it was Warden who overwhelmed his foes with his sheer skill and ferocity. Warden dug into the first attacking member with the sword and crushed the larynx of the second. The people watching covered the children's eyes as other's looked on with awe and reverence. As quickly as he engaged the first biker, the fight was over as he slashed through the last man standing.

Warden paused, took a rag from his pocket and wiped the blade clean. He walked over to Diablo's motorcycle and took the scabbard that sheathed the sword. The people were stunned as he made his way back toward the warehouse. One man had dispatched of eleven gangsters in less than twenty-four hours. But there were more to come and the people were still dismayed. Warden grabbed his water from his bag and took a long drink. No one said anything. Finally one of the elder men spoke up as he pointed a stubborn, wrinkled finger at Warden.

"Do you know what you've done? You've condemned us all. They will not rest until they have revenge. They'll be back in greater numbers. Probably double or triple the men!"

Warden sipped his drink, hardly listening to the frightened old man. "I guess we all have to fight then. That's if you want to be rid of them?"

"Who are you?" The old man replied angered by the newcomer that had upset their peaceful balance. "Who are you to tell us? They will seek payback and they will have it. Most of us are too weak to fight them."

The crowd murmured in agreement. Warden sized up the crowd and the old man was right. Most of the young people were deceased, part of the gangs or too afraid to fight. "I see your point, but if a few of you take a stand we can beat them back."

The old man threw his hand in the air in disgust. "He's mad!" Some of the warehouse dwellers nodded in agreement. The elder had the crowd behind him. "You downed...what, eleven men? There are hundreds in their ranks. You and ...what...twenty able bodied youths best them all? It's not possible!" The crowd was agreeing with the old man and the anxiety was beginning to rise. A sense of impending doom washed over the people. Warden knew he had to sway them to his side.

"You are one of the eldest survivors here. Your words do not fall on deaf ears. But if twenty among your rank will stand with me, we will conquer the gangs. For men ought to either be indulged or destroyed. For if you merely offend them they will take vengeance, but if you injure them greatly they are unable to retaliate. We will injure the Scorpions greatly and end the plague upon this town."

Even the talkative old man was without a response. Young

men and women started stepping through the crowd stopping near Warden as a show of unity.

By the time the goons returned in greater numbers as the elder man had predicted, Warden had a small army at his back. Many of those young fighters gave their lives, but the Scorpions were decimated. Half their forces were lost that day. They retreated, allowing Warden to rebuild this area as his domain. He worked to renovate the warehouse and began to hold the tournament a few years later to attract new recruits. It's amazing that a lone man would empower so many people by standing against evil and corruption." Naomi put both hands on Keera's shoulders. "Now do you understand?"

"Yeah." Keera said mockingly. "You traded one warlord for another."

Naomi patted her shoulders. "You are a hard one to convince."

"Really. I understand. I feel that is what Abel is trying to do. He's taking a stand against Xonox."

"That is another matter entirely." Naomi searched to change the subject. "What would you do if something happened to Abel?"

"I don't know." Keera admitted. "I pray he's protected."

"Tell me truthfully, you have feelings for him?" Naomi inquired.

"Maybe." She replied in a low, soft voice.

"I knew it." Naomi clasped her hands together excitedly. "We're going to get you made up so when he comes back he'll never want to leave you again."

Keera was clearly uncomfortable with the suggestion. "I'm not sure."

"Trust me." Naomi assured. "I know the way to men's hearts."

Keera knew Abel cared about her and protected her, but she was sure his need for revenge trumped any deep feelings he held. "I don't think Abel is concerned with such things."

Naomi persisted. "There is a direct line to every man's heart and I'm going to show you the way to Abel's."

Keera shyly nodded her head in agreement. Her friend clasped her hand with excitement as she moved with intent. Naomi would ensure that Abel had left a young woman with Warden, but would come back to find the woman of his dreams.

CHAPTER 9
TOMMIE GUN

Abel awoke feeling tight and uncomfortable. He attempted to stretch his arms as the sleep crowded his eyes. To his dismay his arms were stuck in place. Worse yet he could feel the rocks and grass rushing below him. To Abel's surprise he was caught in a net being dragged across the greenery by the very man who saved him earlier, Grey. Abel reached for one of his pistols, but they were conveniently missing. Grey had his back to him as he casually pulled Abel through the brush. Abel could see his backpack slung across Grey's shoulders with his blade protruding out. There was one weapon that Grey had not discovered. The handle dug into Abel's flesh as it banged against the rocks. Now, if he could just reach it. Feeling the weight of the net shift, Grey turned towards him. "You're up. Good."

"What are you doing?" Abel said in a commanding tone, hoping to slow down the man to enable him to reach his weapon. "I thought we had a deal! You need to let me out of here Grey or..."

"Or what?" Grey spun around his eyes wide and red. "I've got your weapons...I'm holding the net....And by the way. I do know Tommie Gun. He's a friend of mine."

Abel sought to explain the confusion. "Listen Grey. I'm trying to...."

Grey interrupted. "I know what you're trying to do! But we'll see what the Council thinks!"

"The Council? Wait."

"Yes. How do you think I know these woods like the back of my hand? We're going to a dinner in your honor. Don't be surprised if you end up over the fire!" Grey looked down upon Abel with a wildness that had escaped Abel the previous day. His eyes were hollow and deadly. Nothing Abel said would sway his actions. Abel struggled to reach the gun in the small of his back. This relationship needed to come to a swift end.

"No use struggling. I've got all your firearms." Grey turned and started pulling Abel again. Abel strained to reach the weapon as the land rushed under him. Without a word, Grey stopped in his tracks. He was motionless for a few seconds, then his head slumped down. Lifting his head and looking back towards Abel out the corner of his eye, he gagged on his own blood. The net dropped from his hands and he fell back with a thud. The dagger was lodged in his chest as he fell on top of Abel. Bewildered, Abel lay frozen until he heard the laughter.

"Good shot Harvey!" The biker exclaimed. "He never saw it.'

"That's definitely one of the guys that attacked me and the others." The voices grew closer as Grey's body was pushed to the side, revealing the aggressors. Harvey, the biker with the vicious bear hug, was hovering over him with two fresh gang members. They say bad luck comes in threes, Abel thought. He could see the knife wound patched up on Harvey's neck. No doubt a beauty mark from Grey. Harvey bent over and pulled at the net bringing Abel face to face with him. "You cost us two of our guys the other day and we're gonna take it outta your hide."

Abel fumbled for the gun handle as the brute held him up with one arm. "Be careful. Your boss tried the same thing and look what it got him."

"Wait a minute? You're the guy from Bourdain?" Harvey scowled.

"Yeah. What about it?" Abel responded his fingertips touching the cold, steel of the gun.

The biker was incensed. "You got a lot of lip for a dead guy!"

"That's funny, 'cause I was about to say the same to you." The barrel of the gun slammed into the bottom of Harvey's chin. Abel squeezed the trigger and Harvey's luck finally ran out. The two goons dived for cover. Abel rolled away, quickly untangling himself from the net. Shots began to ring out over the forest. Abel could not place his attackers. The forest began to shake amongst the confusion. Abel clutched his weapon with his back to a tree. This was the most excitement he had encountered on his entire journey. He was starting to believe the lore of the Grazen Woods. He was here less than one day and there was chaos all around him. The forest began to settle, but Abel was still focused on any sudden movement. He could hear a low murmur near Grey and the fallen gang member, an indecipherable language in a faint tone. Leading with his gun in his right hand and a knife in the left, he stepped from the protection of the tree base. There was no sign of the remaining bikers, just a lone figure knelt over Grey's body. The man was kneeling as he whispered to Grey's stiff body. He closed the hunter's eyes and without moving from the fallen man he addressed Abel.

"He's dead."

"I know." Abel responded with his weapons at the ready.

Where did this guy come from? He thought? He had appeared out of thin air just like Grey and he was not dressed like a biker. Holding the gun and knife tightly, Abel stopped in his tracks unsure of the man's intent. If this was a friend of Grey's there could be a misunderstanding. Abel could see the well-worn blood stained knife in the man's left hand. Abel had forgotten about the two bikers. There was no sign of them, as if the forest had swallowed them. The man remained still as his eyes scanned over Grey. He was long and muscular, with short cropped blonde hair that was matted to his head. His sleeveless vest, pants and boots were black. The black tank top he wore was of little contrast to the outfit. Abel noticed the vest casting a shadow over the tattoo on his arm at the shoulder. The man spoke again.

"Were you traveling together?" This time he locked his eyes with Abel's and his glare burrowed through Abel's head. It was clear he sought retribution for his comrade's death. Abel measured his words. "Grey assisted me with the gangs yesterday. Today he ensnared me. The gang caught him by surprise."

"Where were you headed?" The man asked his eyes fixed on Abel.

"Just passing through." Abel said

"You weren't going to the center of the forest by any chance?" He asked.

"Possibly, who wants to know?" Abel was growing tired of the stranger's questions. He needed to decide if he was going to fight or let Abel pass. Keera and Isnor lives' depended on his quick return.

"I'm asking the questions here." The man said.

Abel stared back, his eyes unblinking. The tension was stifling and this game had worn thin. "Looking for a guy named Tommie Gun. You know him."

The man twitched slightly as Abel spoke, indicating he might know Tommie Gun. "Know him..." The man tensed and Abel braced for his response. "...I am him."

The knife was thrown so quickly, it was inches from Abel's face before he deflected it with a loud 'ping'. As swift as a cat, Tommie was upon him with another knife in hand, while he batted Abel's gun away. Abel was on his back with Tommie rearing back to plunge his dagger into his chest. Abel swung his blade short to gain some room, catching Tommie's wrist on his forearm. The blade was dangerously close to Abel's eye. Abel dropped his knife and they stayed frozen in place until Abel twisted and kneed Tommie in the ribs. Abel sprung to his feet as Tommie jumped back stunned by Abel's strength. They sized each other in a short semi-circle. Abel could see his gun lying among the leaves. He leaned back to retrieve it. Just then Tommie launched himself at Abel and they fell to the ground in a tussle. Abel gained the advantage, crashing his knee into Tommie's chin. Tommie staggered back trying to gain position. They circled one another panting like beasts. Tommie adjusted his jawbone, Abel cracked his knuckles. The two combatants danced around waiting for an invisible bell to sound. Instead, the silence was broken by a whizzing sound through the air. A metallic disk dropped between the two foes.

"Crap..." Tommie sprung backwards behind a thicket of trees. Abel did not wait to decipher the threat, he instinctively sought cover as the blast erupted searing the back of his hair and clothes. Lying face down in the mud, he could hear someone striding through the woods.

Standing in the smoke filled clearing, The Mountie scanned the forest for Tommie Gun. Stepping over the bushes he found Tommie, still dazed from the blast. Grabbing a handful of

Tommie's shirt, The Mountie pulled the man toward him. "Hey Tommie. Long time. Where's the plans?"

Tommie replied with a bloody toothed grin. "Hey Mount. Didn't expect you so soon."

Holding Tommie with his left hand, The Mountie slapped Tommie across the face with his right. "The plans. Now. I promise you a quick exit from this world."

Tommie spat the blood from his mouth. "No can do Mount."

The Mountie reared back to slap Tommie again. A large branch fell from the tree canopy and landed near the mercenary forcing him to look up. The trees began to shake with violence, almost condemning The Mountie's actions. Dropping Tommie, the mercenary pulled out his Luger and stared into the woods. Suddenly, a sharp stick shaped like a spear ricocheted off The Mountie's back shoulder armor. He turned to face an unseen opponent. His goggles scanned from infrared to zoom trying to detect the attacker. Another spear zipped out of the trees landing at his left foot. As he stared at the primitive spear sticking out of the ground, another hit his hand knocking away his firearm. The Mountie focused in the direction of the thrown spear and opened his coat, revealing the metal boxes. Abel knew this was his opportunity. He leaped at The Mountie and kicked him in his armored chest. The offensive attack caught the hired killer off guard. That was something that never happened to him. Abel followed with a combination of punches that stunned the bounty hunter. Victory seemed imminent for Abel as he pressed the assault. Shaking off the blows, The Mountie decided to spin the fight back to his favor. Pulling a pistol from his arsenal he fired two shots wildly, uncommon for a man with deadly accurate aim. One of the bullets caught Abel across the cheek. Abel retreated near Tommie and The Mountie refocused intent on eliminating the aggressor. To his surprise and Abel's relief, a hail of spears fell from the woods. The Mountie fired into the trees. Something, a combination of man and beast, screamed out from the branches. Yet the spears fell without ceasing. At least if the mercenary was not being injured, he was distracted. Abel turned to Tommie. "I'm here for the plans. Not for you. Warden sent me."

"Warden?" Tommie understood. "Why didn't you say so

earlier. Could have saved you that butt whoopin.'"

Abel grimaced at Tommie's timing. The Mountie was occupied, but they were not out of danger. "Follow me. I've got a truck nearby."

"Yeah. Right. I think my people have this under control." The pair rushed through the thicket. They glanced back to see The Mountie knocking away spears and firing round after round into the midst. Abel thought, he might be the first outsider actually saved by the forest dwellers. It probably helped to be with one of the men connected to the enigmatic tribe that dwelled within. He looked over at Tommie and made a mental note to probe him for information later. For now he was glad to see his jeep in one piece.

"Let's get out of here!" Abel shouted as he started up the vehicle.

"Back to Warden's place?" Tommie asked. "He's gonna love what I dug up."

"Yeah Warden's. But first I need to make a little detour." Abel said as he pulled away from the forest.

"Where? What could be more important." Tommie wondered after all they had been through.

"Gravope!" The last day had been a whirlwind. Battle after battle. Abel knew for sure the legend of the Grazen Woods was no myth. He could not have prepared for all he encountered. Extenuating circumstances and a bit of good luck had allowed him to come out of the forest unharmed. The missions that lay ahead would be easy in comparison. Abel pushed down his goggles and hit the accelerator. Grazen rapidly faded away into the background. He was going back to where his journey began. Maybe he could find solace in seeing the town and his home again. Maybe if he was lucky, he could find the man who betrayed his family.

****

Gravope was unchanged in the days Abel had been gone. He had set out to avenge his parents and the path had taken him around towns and places he only heard about in stories. It was good to see his home and the people still surviving. The townspeople were on edge and scurried with suspicion when the black jeep rolled through the borough. He could not blame them. An unfamiliar jeep with two rough looking men riding about would make anyone question their intentions. Abel thought how he looked; goggles over his eyes, face speckled with dirt and his clothes sullied and stained with blood. Tommie dressed in all black and in a similar state was an equally imposing figure. Abel rolled through the stares and murmurs stopping in front of his home. Unimpressed with the surroundings, Tommie questioned the reason they were in Gravope.

"This is what we drove out here for?"

Ignoring Tommie, Abel climbed from the Jeep. He walked past the house, by the small fence, to the hidden well. Just as Abel thought, sealed with a large piece of metal bolted to anchors on the ground. Painted in red on the face of the metal was the all too common double 'XX's'. Abel tightened his jaw as he swallowed the bitter taste of revenge. He walked through the back door of his parents' home to find it dirty and in shambles. It was a sight he never experienced in all his years living there. They were poor, but his family prided themselves on their cleanliness. Abel spotted the bucket he often used to get water. It was cracked and the handle was missing. Abel could see a faint light seeping from under the bedroom door. Probably from the front window, he thought. Abel closed his eyes as he touched the door, imaging his parents in the room; laughing, talking and sharing stories on how things use to be. He knew it was just an unfulfilled wish. The door creaked as he pushed it open, pivoting off the hinge. He could see the mattresses all over the room, a broken lamp on the floor and the shattered window pane. How horrible it must have been for his mother. Laying there helpless, dying from a disease easily cured by one of Xonox's doctors, unable to aid her husband and son. Abel bowed his head in frustration. As he looked at the floor, a glint of metal caught his eye from under the mattress. He knelt down on one knee to get a closer look. It was a charm his mother often wore when she wanted to 'look nice' as she would say. She said the jewelry livened up her clothes as well as her spirit. Abel would always laugh, thinking nobody noticed anyway. But his father would notice. He was the one who gave her the necklace. Abel grasped it in his hand and held it tightly, as if it had the power to bring his parents back. He brought the charm to his mouth and kissed it vowing his vengeance. "Mother, Father, I will not rest until Xonox is brought to justice. You have my word."

Abel stayed knelt holding the necklace with his eyes closed for a moment longer. Then he stood up, placed the charm in his pocket and went out the front door. To his surprise, a small crowd had formed outside the house. Abel recognized many of the townspeople by face, if not by name. The crowd grew silent as he approached. Grise was among the crowd, but only the town merchant, Aaron could muster his voice. "Abel we are all terribly sorry about your parents. They were…great people. This life is cruel to us common folks. We barely have food. How can we fight him?"

Abel appreciated Aaron's words, but he also sensed his fear. A fear that Abel lost the day he awoke in Bourdain. "Him? You mean Xonox."

The people were shocked that Abel would say his name. Few spoke Xonox's name, for his retaliation was legendarily swift. Abel's boldness astounded them. Aaron attempted to diffuse the situation. "Slow down Abel. You've had enough trouble."

"Trouble." Abel's trembled with anger. "You haven't seen it yet..."

Tommie cut Abel off before he could finish his thoughts. "Yeah, I have something that's going to have the big dog scratching for a while. Y'know what I mean."

Aaron was confused by the choice of words, but got the gist of Tommie's meaning. "Surely you aren't thinking to challenge him and the House of Vancrew?" Aaron surveyed the jeep, Tommie Gun, and then Abel. "We know you have been through a lot. Come stay with me awhile. Bring your friend and we'll talk this through."

Abel listened with little inspiration to Aaron. He knew the man meant well. Suddenly, he noticed a familiar face in the crowd. A name he had not forgotten. Pushing through the people Abel yelled his name. "FORSUM! You dog! You traitor!"

Forsum put his hands up gesturing his innocence as Abel continued to advance. Realizing Abel was beyond reason, Forsum took off running down a side street with Abel not far behind. Forsum was always quicker than Abel when they were younger, but eluding Abel proved difficult this time. Forsum ducked and dodged, nearly collided with an older woman and jumped over boxes as Abel moved closer. As Forsum slid to turn a corner, Abel bull rushed him into the side of a house. Taking Forsum's shirt in both hands, Abel pulled him to his face. "Give me one reason I shouldn't kill you right now!"

Half choked, Forsum spat out a reply. "Abel...It wasn't me..."

"It wasn't you! You didn't sell my family out to Xonox?!"

"No." Forsum choked out the response as the shirt tightened around his neck from Abel's grip.

Abel held Forsum and stared into his eyes. "What did they give you for my parent's deaths?" He tried to understand what led a childhood friend to betray him.

A distinct voice spoke from behind Abel. "It wasn't Forsum, Abel. I'm the one to blame."
Abel turned to see Grise standing near him.

Still clinching Forsum, he could not believe his own ears. "No...It can't be you. My Father trusted you with his life."

Grise hung his head in shame. "I know...Your Father said tell no one of the well. But I had to tell my wife, Liona. She was the one that notified the Water Facility Manager and ultimately Xonox."

"Why Grise?" The pain on Abel's face was evident. Grise was like an uncle to him.

"She sought power." Grise started. "She hoped it would elevate us out of Gravope. She was wrong. They sent a case of water to our home. That was all, a case of water for my friend's lives." Abel was now facing Grise, Forsum all but forgotten.

"Where is she now?"

"I took care of her." Grise said.

Abel reiterated. "No. I mean, where is she?"

Grise knew what Abel was implying. What Abel did not understand was the matter was already resolved. "Abel....She is no longer of this Earth."

Abel paused, sensing the loss that Grise had suffered due to his wife's hunger for power and status. It was all a vicious game structured by Xonox and the Collective. The poor hungered for status and many destroyed all they had built to obtain it. In this instance, there were two broken homes. Meanwhile, Xonox dwelled unaffected in his ivory tower, basking in the wealth of absolute power, acquired on the backs of the downtrodden. Abel placed his hand on Grise's shoulder. "They will be avenged my friend."

There was a still silence. The men hung their heads honoring the dead. Tommie finally interrupted the tribute. "Hey, I don't mean to break up the reunion, but we need to get going to Warden's before The Mountie or Xonox's spies track us here."

Abel looked at Tommie and shook his head in affirmation. Turning to Grise and Forsum. "We could use some more bodies for this. People we can trust. Either of you up for it?" Grise nodded his head in agreement. Forsum wearily raised his hand. Abel smirked at the contrasting responses. Tommie, unamused, slapped Forsum's hand. "He's raising his hand. Are you kidding me? You aren't volunteering to be the designated driver for a road trip, this is series business kid!"

"I can handle myself." Forsum said sheepishly holding his bruised hand.

Abel stared at Forsum and thought about what he was bringing him into. Like Abel, he had lived his whole life in Gravope isolated from the severe dangers that lay outside. Was he ready for the challenge? Abel was not sure. But what he was sure of was Xonox's reign had to end. He knew that he wanted to be part of the force that brought him down. Though Warden offered him direct command over his soldiers, he needed people that he could trust around him. Would Isnor fight when the time came? Abel could not say. But Grise and Forsum would be at his side to the end regardless the outcome. With that rationale, Abel began making his way to the jeep with his two allies. Tommie gritted his teeth and growled under his breath before taking up the rear.

CHAPTER 10
UPPER HOUSES

Xonox stepped from the elevator. He was finally going to engage the party goers. They had been in his home for the last day. The events for Pheona's birthday were always two or three day affairs. This was nothing compared to the week-long gala she held for her twenty-first birthday last year. As he walked down the short hall he straightened his tie. Dante ceremoniously dusted lint from the shoulder of his suit. The suit's blend of gold and the rarest silk threads touched off with the Vicuna cloth gleamed under the soft white light. His gold, pave-set diamond buttons sparkled as he moved toward the door. Xonox motioned for the two guards to open the doors, and he made his grand entrance into the ballroom.

As Xonox entered the music and chatter died down to a murmur. All of the House of Vancrew was there to honor his daughter. Many had stayed overnight in the guest quarters on the lower floors, so as not to miss his eminence. There was a mix of the upper crust, servants and performers. Bodyguards stood in each corner of the room, while others roamed through the crowd staying alert of any suspicious actions. Drink and food flowed so the guest wanted for nothing nor had the need to ask. A singer crooned softly next to the piano player on one side and on the opposite end a juggler tossed knives in the air to amuse the small children. There was no concern for the man's skill the knives he juggled were akin to his life. If one knife slipped or touched the floor his fate was decided. A man and woman who were moments ago dancing furiously paused to show their respect. Xonox had his private painter sitting at a large canvas etching the moment in time. His talents with pastel colors were known through the town and people marveled at his evolving depiction of the celebration. This was the House of Vancrew. This was Xonox's family. Similar to most families, most of the people in the room would step over his dead body to gain more power. The ruling class lifted their glasses and bowed their heads to Xonox honoring their king. He caught the eye of Nere Hilson, the third to the House of Vancrew, who nodded his head as a gesture of thanks. He saw the swift retribution that Xonox doled out on anyone who disrupted his home. Hilson knew that Crispus was a distant memory. His allegiance to Xonox was strengthened and he was assured if he ever came against Xonox his plan best succeed. There was nowhere to seek forgiveness in this realm. Hilson learned that Xonox's influence had a far reach.

For Xonox the worst part was the men and women vying for Crispus' abandoned position as fourth to the House. He also pondered what to do with the Crispus family. By law he had every right to dispose of the family and anything that resembled the Crispus name. Unfortunately, his daughter was smitten with Crispus's son, Juda. Xonox intended to drop Juda into his shark tank on the fortieth floor and see if the boy drowned before the sharks ate him. The rest of the family would have shared a similar fate. His last discussion with Pheona made him rethink the strategy. Instead he would essentially sell the family to whoever took over the fourth spot and incorporate them into his court. Daeph, Crispus's mother, was a wise, shrewd woman. Her council could have some value. A part of Lilia, Crispus's wife, would be destroyed but she may be more thankful her life was spared. Crispus's daughter was a quiet beauty, though she was young she could be a valuable asset to him. If Juda ever found out that Xonox killed his father he would have no choice but to seek revenge. If the son was like the father, Xonox figured he had little to worry about. Crispus's poor attempt to kill Hilson made him wonder of the boy's ability. Xonox laughed to himself at the thought of fearing this boy, then quickly contemplated letting him swim with the sharks, then reasoned that he had come up with the best solution. Why destroy an entire family for their father's ignorance? Besides he could easily change his mind if things did not go as planned. Xonox made his way to the front of the room. He spotted Edon Stylez, his second in the House of Vancrew. Stylez raised his hand to acknowledge him, but Xonox could not stop and commiserate, he had to address the crowd then speak with his daughter. As he neared the front of the room Pheona approached him. Xonox kissed her on the cheek as they embraced. They both acted as if the earlier argument had not occurred. He had trained her well. The warmth and smiles between them belied the conflict over the handling of Crispus. He turned towards the filled room and the servants froze in place. In mid-pour one of the attendants lifted the bottle ever so slightly to discontinue the elixir's stream. Xonox addressed his court.

"I want to thank you all for coming. There is food, drink and entertainment for all. What more could we ask for in this life? We are the fortunate ones behind this great city's wall, high above the desolation beyond. We have been tasked with a great responsibility to usher in this new world, this new age, into something greater. I would call it a golden age, an age of wisdom. All among us has succeeded and thrived due to our intellect and sophistication. Let us not forget our courtesies to one another. For if we lose that, we are no better than the animals that dwell among the outer plains." The First of the House of Vancrew paused allowing the gallery to mimic his sentiment. "As you know we are gathered here to honor my daughter Pheona on her twenty-second birthday. I have watched her grow into the smart, strong and beautiful young woman that stands before you. One day soon, she will be the head of this family and possibly the head of the House of Vancrew." The crowd applauded vigorously. "Again, thank you for coming. Enjoy the splendors of my home and remember, 'Wealth is the result of a strong mind'." He took a glass filled with sparkling wine from a servant's tray and raised it. "To the House of Vancrew."

The nobility raised their glasses and spoke in unison. "To the House of Vancrew!"

Xonox lowered his glass turned to Pheona and the festivities continued.

"Father. Thank you for everything." Pheona said. "About our last conversation…"

She was interrupted as her father motioned towards the

young man standing by her. "Who is your friend Pheona?" It was all for effect. Xonox was well aware of the name and rank of every person in attendance. It was his sole purpose to know who was in his presence. His survival rested on understanding what they were thinking and their motives. He accrued power by staying five steps ahead of his aggressors and they feared him.

Pheona introduced the man obviously unsettled by Xonox's perceived intentions. "Father you remember Juda, Crispus's son."

"Yes. Young Juda. A pleasure. How are you enjoying yourself." Xonox inquired as he squeezed Juda's shoulder.

The First's eyes were met with trepidation as Juda summoned his courage. "Mr. Xonox. It is always an honor to be in your presence. My father always speaks highly of you sir."

"No need for formalities tonight Juda. Your presence speaks volumes." Xonox intoned.

"Thank you sir." The man replied with a slight bow.

"Are your mother and sister with you?" Xonox questioned.

"My mother had to step away. She...she had some concerns she had to deal with."

"Oh?" Xonox eyebrows perked up as if he was about to hear some disturbing news for the first time. The pressures of the evening were obviously wearing on Juda. His voice trembled as he spoke. "My father has not returned home. There has been no word from him or his aide."

Xonox and Pheona eyes caught momentarily while Juda stared at the floor searching for his words. He knew as well as they that his father would not be returning. It was unlike his father to disappear in the night with half of his personal guard and send no word to the family. Juda knew something was wrong. He was young, but he could sense the danger that his family was in. If his father died or was killed in an honorable manner, as the head of the Crispus family, he was next in the line of succession and would carry on the family dealings. But Juda had seen people disappear before and watched as families were torn apart. Words escaped him. Xonox tried to give him false assurance. "Crispus is a smart man. He normally thinks his actions through before he acts them out."

"You're right. Thank you for your sincerity." Juda said hopefully, searching for a ray of hope.

"Of course." Xonox patted the young man on the shoulder while searching the room to conduct other business. His words were truthful to Juda. Normally his father carefully crafted his plan of attack. Unfortunately his overzealous ambition had been his downfall. He cultivated his family so well in the course of civility he forgot to train those around him in the art of impropriety. Xonox walked a short distance to engage Stylez.

"Xonox." The Second of the House remarked. "You have outdone yourself. This is a marvelous feast."

Xonox grabbed his hand and exchanged pleasantries. "Your son Edin's birthday was quite the event. I could not let you outshine my home. We must play our parts in this game of ascension." The two men shared a laugh as the fire of competition burned behind their eyes. Stylez naturally vied for Xonox's position through his show of wealth. He could not match Xonox in violence and corruption, therefore nothing was too outrageous or gaudy for Stylez. The more attention the better. His home was several stories lower than Xonox, but it was trimmed in gold inside and out. The ballroom was an ice rink of highly polished gold. He employed servants and guards in an attempt to stay on par with Xonox to the point of overcrowding his home. So when Stylez hosted a two day gala for his son's sixteenth birthday, Xonox was expected to hold a week-long event at his home at enormous expense. All expected for someone in Xonox's position. His Second was skilled in the art of conversation and his charm was alluring. Where Xonox ruled with impunity, using his massive wealth to inspire loyalty, Stylez gained friends and influenced with his. He was loved by his peers and servants. Many in the House of Vancrew felt he should replace Xonox on personality alone. But there were those who were entrenched with Xonox, mainly the Collective heads. It took a certain combination of ruthlessness and false grace to run a house within the Collective. Let alone the ravenous House of Vancrew. They were aware that Stylez was not without sin. No one rose in the Collective without washing their hands in blood. But Xonox possessed the resilience only rivaled by Mordal and Croman, the leaders of the first and second Houses. Propelling themselves to the status of sovereign rulers had led them down a path of lies and destruction. Rebellions were crushed, people left to die of dehydration and constantly lording over the masses to protect their kingdoms.

Xonox was known to use gangs and mercenaries to keep the townspeople in line. The gangs stole from the people and kept them discouraged. He supplied them with water and supplies for their loyalty. Mercenaries were for more powerful foes, dispatching of a rogue gang leader or permanently silencing one of the fallen elite. He knew the ability of his organization and was adept at inciting terror around him. Stylez might be more loved, but he would never sit atop the Collective. That was Xonox's destiny only. Lost in thought he barely listened as Stylez described the large diamond he recently acquired for his wife. Dante approached him slowly, touching his shoulder and whispering in his ear. "Sir, you're needed in the comm room." Xonox nodded his head.

"Forgive me Stylez. We'll continue this game of whose diamond is bigger another time. I have a pressing matter to address."

"Is this finally a crack in the armor?" Stylez's voice dripped with sarcasm. "I mention the acquisition of a small diamond and you rush out of the party post-haste. Surely a rare red diamond won't come between friends." Stylez chuckled as well as some of his underlings around him. Xonox was accustomed to this sport of one-upmanship, but his attention was focused on real concerns. His tone was distant as he responded looking through his guest.

"No Stylez. I'm sure the diamond you speak of is the one my wife wore to many parties. I recently parted with it as it was a painful reminder of my wife's unexpected death. The diamond may be rare and beautiful to behold, but it was ultimately of no value to me. Enjoy the party."

Xonox left the room with the grace he had entered. He was neither bother or annoyed by Stylez comments, but their back and forth had lost its luster. Stylez and the other guest within earshot of the conversation were stunned. Xonox never mentioned his wife, especially at a time of celebration. It was a bad omen. Stylez would sell the diamond and offer his apologies to his host at the next opportunity.

Xonox stepped through the double doors leading to his communication room. Within the small foyer a smooth, steel double door was tucked behind the wood finished wall. The doors shut and locked behind him. On cue the lights dimmed as the room turned pitch black. Infrared blades of blue light scanned over his body. The whole process ended as quickly as it began. Once his identity was confirmed the lights illuminated and the steel door slid up. Xonox crossed the threshold facing a matte black wall with two stairs ascending on either side. Placing his foot on the right stair treads he watched the embedded lights slowly brighten and run up the stairs and along the railing. As he reached the top of the stairs he could see the short cantilever bridge extending out into the large room. The central control area was at the end of the span and large screens curved around in a semi-circle. Xonox proceeded down the middle of the bridge until he reached the end. Sitting in his custom chair he looked at the screens above. He slid his palm over the sensor in the arm rest as the screens flickered from black to blue.

Xonox spoke aloud. "Mordal, House of Saran."

Xonox leaned back in the chair and straightened himself toward the middle screen. He had an inkling about the call but would not give away his thoughts. The Collective held their weekly meetings to discuss strategy, production and all inter-House problems between them. This meeting had been called by Yual Mordal the head of the first House of Saran. All was not well among the Houses. The masses were in constant rebellion, especially against the lower four Houses. Water was being hijacked, guards killed and the people prayed for the great tower homes to come crashing down. Normally such things did not affect the House of Vancrew directly, but he knew that if Houses six through eight did not hold, it would be a matter of time before all the Houses started to crack, crumble and fall like so many dominoes. Some of the lesser regales suggested more compensation to the poor and downtrodden. This compromise was not the answer. The Collective had risen to an elite level and Xonox was not going to relinquish his control so easily. Neither would Mordal or Croman. They agreed harsher restrictions were needed and every act against the Collective would be punished with death. Public execution was the only way to tear the fight out of people's hearts. What amazed him the most was the resistance of these savages beyond the city walls. Many were half-starved, deprived of decent water or living conditions but they persisted.

Some force propelled them to live and ultimately question their fate. Xonox had proposed a long time ago to round up those not under his immediate domain and dispose of them. In the early days of the Collective he eliminated any who stood against him. He would wipe out detractors all-round the city until there was nothing left if he could. Xonox envisioned a Godly utopia, a clean, efficient city with only the morally high-class at its pinnacle. Mordal and Croman agreed with his plans, unfortunately it was put to a vote and the remaining five voted against it. They argued the vagrants were needed for labor, hunting and other menial tasks. Now these beasts of burden were the obstacle to the Collective's glory. The lower houses were almost pleading for help to keep the masses at bay. Each House had its unique proficiency, otherwise Xonox would let the weaker Houses fall and reunite under one strong leader. Initially the Collective was broken down into eight Houses by territory. Families took over the areas where they could harness power and thrive. Were eight Houses still needed? Xonox wondered. Were three? Xonox's thoughts were interrupted by the screens transitioning from blue to the vivid faces of the Collective and the voice of Yual Mordal.

"Let's bring this meeting to an open."

CHAPTER 11
THE FIRST OF FIRSTS

Yual Mordal, The First of Firsts as he was widely known, imposingly covered the center screen. Two guards were at his back with a red 'Y' over an 'M' emblazoned on their chest. The emblem abstractly resembled a wine glass sitting on an inverted three legged table, a symbol of Mordal's refined culture. His face was etched with lines of wisdom, while his brow and beard were jet black with the hair on his chin coming to a sharp point. Mordal wore a matte solid white silk shirt with a red robe trimmed at the vest and sleeve with gold. Covering his balding head was a headdress garment of the same material, with the gold band running across his forehead. He wore the garment as a crown. It was his right as the most powerful man among powerful men. His regal appearance was a stark contrast to his abrasive demeanor. Mordal embodied ruthlessness. If he ever had feelings for anyone, it was never shown. His eyes were black, dark orbs of petrified coldness, devoid of any emotion or compassion and that is how he led the Collective. Every move was calculated to his advantage to inspire fear. Mordal's home was almost two times higher than Xonox's residence and was filled with his large family. Mordal was known for taking a new wife every few years, while still married to the old ones. He was on his tenth wife and expecting his thirty-sixth child. His motto was, 'Power is in the strength of one's family'. And he had family in abundance. The wives were each given a floor with their children and Mordal groomed each child in leadership, combat and his brand of honor. He often traveled with his two sons Yuon and Yued, respected as two of the best hand-to-hand combatants in the area. His daughter, Yonice, ran his day-today affairs including the water distribution and production. The wives wanted for nothing, the first wife being honored the same as the tenth. Mordal had insulated himself in the center of a family that he taught and trained. Their loyalty was unquestionable. These layers of family kept him in power. Some in the Collective frowned upon Mordal's lifestyle. How was a new utopia to sprout out of the seeds of adultery and bigamy? These terms were long forgotten in the Collective bylaws, but it was a subtle reminder that all were fallible.

Mordal's marriages were not always consensual. Some women of lesser families were just taken from their homes. Compensation was rendered to families inside the Collective, death to those outside. Who would stop Mordal? He took what he wanted and those who complained against him did not complain for long. Recently Mordal had taken one of his former servants as his eleventh wife. She worked for years within his home as his seventh wife, Azerel's, assistant. When he saw her young supple figure beneath her evening gown at one of his many parties he whispered his affections into the ear of one of his aides. His personal guards visited her small one level home within the walls of the city. She lived a modest life with her husband, a guard of the Water Distribution Facility. On that night Mordal ordered for everyone in the house to be murdered. They went to the home and took the life of her husband, mother, uncle and sister. Unbeknown to Mordal, the husband had switched duties with another guard. The man they killed was a friend of the family. When the husband, Ferris, came home to an abandoned house he was stunned and confused. Was there a robbery in his home? Where was his wife, Seria? What of the family? One of the locals, who watched Mordal's guards file into the home, informed him of the atrocity. For most of his life Ferris had served the House of Saran without question. Unspeakable acts were carried out in the name of Mordal so he could preserve his life and carve out some type of existence. It all had been taken from him in an instant. Mordal had taken enough. A few days before his wife was to wed Mordal, Ferris stormed the house with thirty well-armed and well-trained dictractors who shared his sentiment and sought to end Mordal's tyranny. The House of Saran guards were surprised; they never expected a fellow guard to attack them so brutally. No one realized Ferris was alive until that moment. His army cut through sixty of Mordal's base guards before they were halted at the twenty-fifth floor. The group had broken into two parties to search for Seria. Ferris was aware of the layout and her possible whereabouts from Seria's descriptions of the House over the years. He found her in a gallery cowering with other servants. She was not yet Mordal's wife and still had duties to attend. As he entered the room, he shot two guards. Each received a bullet from the pistols in his hands. They slumped hard to the ground. He grabbed Seria under her arm and lifted her to her feet.

'Ferris..?" She said in shock. "What are you doing here…He'll kill you…"

"Only death could keep me from you." Her husband replied and she could see the warmth in his eyes. They quickly embraced and Ferris led her into the hall leading towards the elevator. Halfway down the hall the elevator door opened and Mordal's personal guards poured out. The few fighters with Ferris were getting mowed down. Ferris fired back dropping guards as they advanced. His rebellion was falling around him. The situation was turning dire. Backing towards the stairs Ferris convinced himself that he and Seria would have a better chance fighting their way out floor by floor. He had plenty of ammo and hoped the other group would meet up with them. Ferris backed around a corner and fired again. Letting go of Seria's hand he pulled out his comm device. He spoke into it, but the comm crackled back with static silence. The last man on his team fell in front of him. He had to get to the stairwell. Dropping the comm he clutched Seria's hand as he fired at a guard catching him in the arm. As the guard fell another took his place firing at Ferris with a precision that made him believe they did not want to hit his wife. He looked back at her and could see the fear in her eyes. She held his arm with both hands. Ferris turned towards his enemies spraying the hall and inching towards the stairway door. Suddenly, he felt his back explode with a wave of fire. He lurched forward, his weapon falling from his grasp and losing his hold on Seria's hand. He crashed to the floor unable to move. His vision went blurry, he could hear his wife screaming as if he were in a vacuum. Five guards were coming from the gallery where he found Seria. They surrounded him quickly while one of the guards pulled a delirious Seria off his back and carried her away. The lead guard touched the communicator on his arm to call Mordal.

"The leader is down sir, but still alive."

He could feel the footsteps of the guards from the elevator as they moved in to encircle him. His gun was in reach, but his arms were unresponsive. A slow grating voice came over the personal guard's comm. "And his group?"

"They've been neutralized sir." The Captain of the guard stated as he watched for any movement from the fallen attackers.

"Seria?" Mordal asked.

"She's been taken back to the gallery and on to the aide's quarters." The guard's leader informed. "What should we do with the infiltrator?"

The comm was silent for a moment and the guards looked at one another. Whatever the order this man's life was forfeit. "You know what to do Captain." Their master answered.

The Captain motioned to another guard standing in front of Ferris. The guard kicked Ferris in the ribs to turn him over and see his face. His pistol was aimed at Ferris's head. Ferris choked out his last words looking straight at the guard. "It'll be your wife next time…"

Seria heard the single shot as she was dragged down the hall. Her husband was truly dead. She heard rumors of how Mordal chose his wives. She thought they were part of lies told by people to fuel the trepidation inspired by Mordal's name. It was all too real for her. She witnessed first-hand the heinous act of the Collective. Now she knew why Ferris never spoke of his work. She closed her eyes thinking of the way things used to be and how her life had changed forever. A few days later she was wed to Mordal.

It was far from the end of Mordal or the Collective's problems. The small rebellion had brought challenges to his iron-fist rule. The people no longer trembled at his name. They were more aware of the evils within the House of Saran. Though Mordal's army was strong and could easily dispatch of the city inhabitants, the masses were starting to unnerve him. The uprising was a source of embarrassment for him and the main point of why the heads were meeting.

"As you all know a rogue guard led a band of rebels against the House of Saran. It was crushed but not before much bloodshed.

These peasants had the audacity to invade my home. Per the Collective protocol the men were killed as well as their families." The room was deadly silent as Mordal spoke. Xonox could sense the revenge taken on those involved and their families did not satiate Mordal's appetite for blood. This was not the time to break the order of the Collective, which stated no one spoke until the First was done speaking. Once Mordal concluded, the head of the second House would speak and so forth. Mordal continued.

"In more pleasant news, I've recently taken a wife and she will be a great addition to my House. Power is in the strength of one's family!" Mordal paused, looking straight ahead as he spoke. "Mine was not the only recent insurrection. The House of Iossec fought a lengthy battle in the city of Farmorh." Mordal looked slowly at each Collective member. "These people are not satisfied with the luxuries they are provided. They have become more brazen with the passing time. It is imperative to rethink our previous agreements. I propose the annihilation of all outside the city walls excluding the gangs and mercenaries. We'll use them to hunt down the stragglers." Mordal let his point linger through the minds of the assembled. "Croman and Xonox of the House of Janus and the House of Vancrew undoubtedly agree with me. Time is of the essence. We must reach an agreement before these people get out of hand. What are your thoughts Croman?"

Quitteri Croman wore a crown of thick white hair. His gold cloth shimmered as it clung to his body. Known for his obsession with the sun, his face and arms were tinged orange. He was a stocky man, those around him joked he was out of shape. What he lacked in physical prowess he more than compensated for with superior intellect. In fact he was considered one of the most brilliant minds in the Collective. Where Mordal was the financial titan and Xonox possessed extraordinary vision, Croman was the chief designer and engineer. His skills were unparalleled. Yet his capricious nature left him spending unhealthy amounts of time in direct contact with the sun. The top four levels of his home were constructed similar to a cruise liner ship deck. When he was not tinkering with a new gadget, he spent his private time swimming and sunbathing. His obsession was not a pastime, but more a religion. Croman pledged himself to the only God more powerful than money, the mercurial orb in the center of the universe.

Croman revered the sun's beauty and the capacity it possessed for destruction. How could something that gave life, simultaneously take it away? The contrast fascinated him. As he had mastered salt water, turning the liquid into something consumable by humans, he longed to harness the sun's power. The Morphesizer was an invention collaborated on by him and his colleagues. His next project would be his alone and would usher in the supreme reign of the House of Janus.

There were rumors of secret projects hidden within the depths of Croman's home. Small devices that shot a concentrated beam of light capable of penetrating a three-inch thick piece of steel. Others in the Collective speculated on the purpose of Croman's hobbies. His creations could be for manufacturing and production or they could be for darker reasons. No one knew except for Croman and his highest ranking aides. Croman was an ambitious man and would not be content with his current status. His actions had to be monitored.

Croman nodded his head in acknowledgement of Mordal. "Yual, I have many thoughts as well as questions and answers. In this equation these murderous beggars are the unknown. I love solving for the unknown or in this case x-ing out the unknown. I'm very much in favor of their termination."

"I knew you would be." Mordal said.

"What I do not favor is the execution of innocent men and their families. Men who have pledged their allegiance to us. It weakens our overall strengths and should not be allowed to persist with impunity." Croman adjusted in his chair to face Xonox. "Don't you agree Victor?"

Xonox despised the way Croman addressed everyone by their given name. Mordal found it amusing on the occasions when Xonox mentioned the affront. Croman spoke as if they were boys in his classroom. His tone was condescending and needed to be corrected. As capable as Croman was, he needed to be taught manners and the respect afforded Xonox's status.

His voice resounded with annoyance. "I agree Croman, as long as the man or woman you refer to are completely innocent. In my House ignorance and incompetence equate to death."

"So you admit openly Victor, amongst all the Houses. You have no regard for the principles that established us." Croman shouted back.

Xonox responded sourly, not appreciating his contemporary's tone. "Make your accusations plain. I have no time for games."

The head of the House of Janus did not delay. "My wife's first cousin, Gerrius Crispus, your fourth in the House of Vancrew was found dead on a stretch of road halfway between my House and yours. His life ended by a single execution gun shot in the middle of a swirling war zone."

"And your point?" Xonox countered.

"Are you denying your involvement with the death of Gerrius outside of your walls? The breaking of a law that has always been upheld by all here. Persons of position will not be killed by other persons of position outside the city. You deny this?" Croman was growing infuriated.

Xonox remained on an even keel. "I deny nothing…"

"So you admit breaking the Collective law?" The Second of the Upper Houses accused.

"I admit that if someone in a certain position conspires to kill someone in a greater position, he had better succeed." Xonox said sternly with a hint of a warning.

"As if your hands are clean!" Croman shouted unable to contain himself.

"It's not about the attempt, but the disgrace of the failure." Xonox rebuked. "A poorly planned coup is the aggressor's downfall, not that of the attempted upon. I'm sure your House is not without reproach." The debate was not going as Croman predicted. He refocused on the other point of the argument.

"Where is Gerrius's wife and family?"

"They are well, though I have every right to sell them to the highest bidder. Gerrius is no longer of this House or this earth." The Third of the Upper Houses said matter-of-factly.

"I want them sent to the House of Janus immediately!" Croman demanded.

Xonox could sense the fire brimming under Croman's words. He decided to see if he could push Croman further to see if he would actually threaten him. "And what is your compensation?"

"Compensation?" The master engineer was irate. "I'll bring you up on charges of killing an honorable man!"

"I thought all the honorable men died long ago." Xonox quipped.

"Watch yourself Xonox." Croman warned. "Words kill men."

"No Croman, men kill men. Words are their master."

Croman and Xonox were locked in an icy stare. The two men were considered friends once. Their relationship devolved as Croman's lack of attention to the overarching problems of the Collective persisted and Xonox's unwavering nature grew. Croman mistakenly underestimated Xonox's desire for the second House. Xonox had set his sights much higher. He had nothing against Mordal, but it was time for one sovereign leader with complete control over the Collective. Xonox would be that leader.

Yual Mordal ended the stalemate between the two Houses. "Xonox, you will respect our laws. Without them we would fall into chaos. You will send Crispus's remaining family members to Croman as a show of good will."

"Always Mordal." Xonox held Croman in his gaze a while longer before turning to look at Mordal. "There are four surviving members of Crispus's family, his wife, Lilia, his son and daughter, Juda and Litrice, as well as his mother Daeph. Because of the transgressions that occurred in my house I have the right to strip them of their positions and leave them begging in the streets. But Croman's curt words have touched something withered and frozen within my soul. I'll send Juda and Litrice to the House of Janus at once. They will be accompanied by my personal guard, so to ensure no ill befalls them as it did their father. They both are bright and beautiful young regales and should do well in your house. Actually my daughter has taken a liking to Juda, who knows what may come of that. But I will be holding on to Daeph and Lilia a while longer. Lilia will be incorporated into my second, Edon Stylez's, home. We all know him as a gracious man and she will flourish there. Daeph will stay in my home as one of my personal advisers. They will both live out their days in excess wanting for nothing." Xonox looked casually around the room at the faces staring back at him on the screens. Then he focused his eyes intently on Croman. "Unless… for some unforeseen reason the Crispus family becomes an enemy to the Xonox family. Maybe there is an attempt on my life, or one of my aides is poisoned, or I slip awkwardly in the shower. Then all of his family and conspirators shall know the pleasure of pain and cruelty."

Xonox sat back in his chair satisfied that his threats were made plain to Croman. He would give him Crispus's children, but any action against him would spark a civil war amongst the Collective that no one wanted. The lower houses in the Collective sat nervously waiting on Croman's response. It was clear that Croman was in shock. Xonox's words reeked of war and left him speechless. The sweat beaded on his forehead as he contemplated his retort. It was blasphemous for Xonox to address the head of the second House of Janus in such a manner. Croman's accusations were planned to bring Xonox's true intentions to light. Once again he had strung Croman along and twisted his words and came out of the fracas unscathed. He knew better than to continue down a destructive path with Xonox.

Mordal sealed the deal. "Then it's settled. Croman, prepare to receive Crispus's children within a day. Xonox, make sure the children's journey is uneventful. There will be no second chances."

"Understood, Mordal." Xonox stared back at the First. "Before I forget, congratulations on your wedding."

"Your congratulations are received. Are you concluded?" Mordal said grimly.

"Yes." Xonox answered. "I turn to Lifretent from the fourth House of Agress."

"Thank you Xonox." Diteri Lifretent stated enthusiastically. "Not much to report, we've had little trouble. Everything is running to optimum capacity. Our water production is strong. I turn to Gratsun from the fifth House of Deira."

"Our status is similar to Lifretent." Lotha Gratsun summarized, her long, gray hair falling over the stark black suit she wore. "The peasants are placated and our city is thriving. I turn to Kasmine form the sixth House of Iossec."

"Mordal, Croman, Xonox and other distinguished heads." Eltioc Kasmine spoke hastily, his eyes red and withdrawn, sunken into the sockets from worry. "The House of Iossec has had many issues in the last few months."

The heads of the Collective were well aware. Mordal brought his hands together as he stared at the head of the sixth House of the Collective. "All have heard, elaborate Kasmine."

CHAPTER 12
RISE OF HOUSE IOSSEC

Kasmine's voice trembled as he spoke. "The House of Iossec has been under a horrific siege. I want to thank all the heads that sent supplies and reinforcements to allow our House to stand."

None of the Houses were accustomed to being attacked at length. His fine white robe appeared to be unwashed and wrinkled. It was uncommon for a man like Kasmine who prided himself on his attire. He was an aggressive man who never backed down from a challenge. This strength was also his greatest enemy as he often irritated the men in the Collective with his uncompromising attitude. He was slender and lean, hiding his age gracefully. At a young age he aspired to be the head of a House in the Collective. He began in a privileged capacity in the seventh House of Toessar, his family many rungs down the ladder of succession. The effect of his peculiar and particular nature allowed Kasmine to excel at his studies and he was capable of applying his knowledge to real world problems. As a young man he ushered in the Order of Division among the families in the House. Too many lower families were mixing with the wealthier class. Kasmine subdivided the families into distinct classes of wealth and instituted marriage protocol based on status. His methods are still applied by the reigning head of the House of Toessar, Joesteon Phoeltro. Following the restructuring of the house, Toessar began to double its production and the city of Frontamioum prospered. Shortly thereafter Kasmine was requested as an aide to the former head of Iossec, Milred Transt. The House of Iossec had fallen into disorder and disrepair. Word of Toessar's renaissance had spread as well as the influence behind it.

Transt was a man of substantial means and speculated to be over eighty years old. His inability to connect with his people had incapacitated the growth of the House. His surviving sons and daughter were little help in setting Toessar back on the right course. While his sons chased after the women in the city, his daughters gossiped about the latest trends and fashions. Kasmine quickly grew from Transt's aide to his right hand, single-handedly willing Iossec back to a place of prestige among the Houses in a few short years. Transt's children showed no interest in the affairs of the House, acquiescing to Kasmine and Transt's father-son relationship. It was to no one's surprise when Kasmine was named the heir to the House of Iossec on Transt's death bed. All seemed supportive of his decision. By that time, Kasmine was married to Felise, Transt's daughter. He was widely accepted as a member of the family. Many of Transt's children looked to Kasmine for advice and guidance. He was the driving force behind discussions of moving Iossec into a position to be the fifth house of the Collective. His rule over the house was imminent and seemed to be without question except for Dalsha Transt. Dalsha, Transt's third wife, the first two died of mysterious illnesses, was infuriated to hear the news of Kasmine's impending ceremony. She was grooming her only son Ralston to be the next heir. Dalsha questioned her husband's state of mind when the decision was made. She said he was old, weak and his thoughts were unclear. Transt's aides assured her the discussions of Kasmine's rise in the family had taken place over the last few years before he had grown ill. She was not alone in her feelings of betrayal, Transt's second and third in succession thought they were more qualified to lead the House of Iossec. For an outsider to come in and be selected was not unheard of, but Kasmine's meteoric rise was an oddity. Dalsha sought to turn one or more families to her side, making promises of greater access to the Transt family wealth and positions as aides to her son.

Ralston Transt was a young man in his early twenties, when his father died, he had little time to grasp the ramifications before his mother began promoting him to take over. His father was his mentor and Kasmine was a big brother. Many times he had confided in Kasmine on issues he could not discuss with his siblings. Tall and wiry, with a muscular build, Ralston spent as much time sharpening his mind through his studies and the political dealings of the Collective as he did honing his body. Ralston was seen as a young version of Kasmine, but while his mother wanted him to stake his claim for the head of the House, he was not ready to lead.

On the day of Kasmine's inauguration, all the families gathered together in his home to witness the passing of the responsibilities from the old to the new. Transt's former aide, Wisen, now Kasmine's aide, read aloud the short bylaws of ascension within the Collective. Upon completing the reading Wisen turned to Kasmine and handed him a red medallion passed on to each new leader. Applause erupted throughout the House. Each family came forth to pledge their loyalty and honor Kasmine. It was a small ceremony with the heads of the higher thirty families waiting patiently to greet their First. Dalsha intermingled with the families and lined up to supposedly show her support. Her actions were unnecessary since she was already a member of the Transt family and by law now a member of the Kasmine family. All around the house tensed when she and young Ralston approached. As expected she was less than gracious and spoke with a defiant tone. She spat on Kasmine's shoes and asked aloud how this bastard had been allowed to become the head of the great House of Iossec; he had brought dishonor to the House and the Transt name. All in attendance were bewildered by her accusations. The families that were present knew Kasmine and his upbringing, his father held favorable standing in the House of Toessar. Beyond Dalsha's lies was the more grievous offense; her outburst in public and blatant disrespect for Kasmine was punishable by death. As her tirade continued she asked who would stand with her against this abomination. The ballroom was silent except for the low murmurs of outrage for her behavior. Kasmine looked sternly at Dalsha, he had hoped they could reach a common ground behind closed doors. She was a hard woman to talk to, but he reasoned that once the ceremony was concluded she would have to capitulate. Dalsha continued to rant about her son being the true head. Kasmine looked down at the red medallion in his hand and squeezed it. This was his first true test. He watched Ralston try to calm his mother as she frantically went from person to person. Kasmine met the eyes of his aide, Wisen, and made his decision. Wisen nodded towards the guards and they quickly seized Dalsha, bringing her to the center of the room before Kasmine. Dalsha struggled to break free of the guards on either side of her. She straightened herself as Kasmine began to speak.

"Dalsha, you are respected as Transt's widow and a part of the Kasmine family, but your insubordination will not be tolerated. Your actions have brought you into violation of the Collective heir to a House protocol. If you do not cease...you know the consequences."

All eyes were focused on Dalsha. Her offenses were serious, even if Kasmine wanted her to recant, only her pleas for leniency would bring her mercy. Dalsha had no intention of backing down now.

"Transt was old and senile at his death. You must have tricked him into handing over the reins of this great House. I will never honor you as the head. My son Ralston is the true head by right."

Ralston intervened. "I'm not ready." He spoke with a quiet strength, while trying to placate his mother and the situation. "Kasmine was named. My time will come."

Dalsha was unswayed. "No Ralston your time is now. I denounce this ceremony and demand my son be elevated to the first of the House of Iossec!"

"Dalsha, I have known you for many years. You've raise an intelligent young man. Ralston will be one of my trusted aides soon." Kasmine spoke slowly and measured his words. "But if you continue this treachery against this House and against me I will institute the highest penalty."

"I'd rather die than serve one second under your lineage!" Dalsha's mouth frowned with bitterness as she spoke the words disgust.

Ralston stood with his hands on his mother's shoulders speaking quietly to her, hoping she would see the error in her actions. He was destined to be the head of the House of Iossec, just not today. The guards had stepped back as he tried to console her. Ralston knew the kind of man Kasmine was, they would come to a resolution. After this ceremony, he would speak to Kasmine in private.

Kasmine could see the hatred burning in Dalsha's eyes.

Transt never spoke of any agreements involving Dalsha or Ralston, but it was clear she felt slighted to the highest degree. Did Transt tell her Ralston would rule at his death? Was this promise made during more prosperous times? No one would ever know since dead men tell no tales. Dalsha's actions had left him little choice. Kasmine waved his hand back and forth toward the guards as he turned around to look out the window behind him. The Houses jutted towards him, towering a few levels below. He could see the insignificant people scurrying below. They had no idea of the adversarial political battles that occurred high above their simple lives. It was always his dream to rule a House in the Collective. Iossec had grown at a substantial rate in the last twelve years. He desired to elevate the House from a lower to an upper tier in league with Mordal, Croman and Xonox. His plans were set in motion and he expected in less than ten years the House of Iossec would be situated as the fifth House. How would this, his first official act as the First, affect his calculated aspirations? Ending the life of Milred Transt's widow, while her young son watched her being dragged off. What would the other families say? He had every right, he had given her every out. Heavy was the head of the man who wore the crown. The guards snatched her up and restrained Ralston. Dalsha swore her vengeance as she was hauled off kicking and screaming.

"No you can't just take her!" Ralston punched one guard across the cheek. The man fell backwards into one of the guests. Ralston started towards his mother. He swung at another guard and missed. The guard landed a solid blow to his sternum knocking the wind from him. As Ralston was doubled over three more guards grabbed him and the main guard knocked him unconscious. Ralston's body hung slack from the arms of the guards holding him.

"Take him to his room and watch him." Kasmine ordered. "I want no harm to come to the boy."

The years passed by and gradually the incident with Dalsha was forgotten. Ralston had retreated to his room and was rarely seen amongst the family or throughout the house. He was allowed to skip mandatory dinners and events. Kasmine decided to tread carefully with him after ordering his mother's death. He reasoned that time would lighten the blow and Ralston would be the asset to the family that he envisioned. Others in the house, including Wisen, told Kasmine to send him to rest with his mother. Kasmine would not hear of it, he wanted no innocent blood on his hands. Besides he had more pressing concerns. From the moment Kasmine was crowned there were small uprisings throughout the city. Each small skirmish was reducing the Iossec's production and keeping him from challenging for the fifth House.

It was the third anniversary of Dalsha's passing and Kasmine was receiving reports of Ralston's strange behavior. He requested combat training with the Sergeant of the guard at all hours of the day and could be found on the gun range on the eleventh level as if obsessed. Kasmine was so preoccupied with the small battles sprouting up around the city, Ralston's whereabouts were of little concern. On the fourth year, the son of Milred Transt requested an audience with him. Was he finally coming out of his shell and searching to be a productive member of the House? Kasmine wondered. He was in his mid-twenties and had not taken a wife let alone shown any interest in women. Kasmine had recently traveled to the fifth House of Deira and was impressed by the many elegant, cultured women there. If Ralston desired, Kasmine could find him a suitable match.

Kasmine stood on the balcony outside of his council room. His aides were informing him of the latest attacks against the House. Every day it seemed the rebels grew bolder and more reckless. What surprised Kasmine the most was their coordination. The attacks were swift and targeted crucial areas of the building they assaulted. It was all too much for him to assess. He constantly worried about the Water Facility. He ordered double patrol around the building and doubled the guards. He turned to look into the council room. His aides and assistants sat gathered around the solid white table, a large italic cursive 'K' etched into the center. At the head of the table 'Kasmine' was inscribed in the stone. Each advisor had his name etched into a stone tile, laid into the table. Their names were not permanent, but gave each a sense of their belonging while realizing the tile could be easily replaced. All were trusted advisors, but he wondered to himself was this rebellion merely coincidence or a coup against his reign? He walked towards the glass wall as one of his guards pushed the glass door in for him. As he crossed the threshold he could hear the murmur of conversation. There was obvious concern over the citizens' increasing boldness. Some of his advisors pressed for public executions. Others thought it was time to part with some crumbs to appease the masses. Kasmine agreed with those who wanted to root out the rebel leaders, publicly disgrace them and then show lenience by extending a hand of compassion to the less fortunate. Maybe through generosity Kasmine could turn the upheaval to his favor. Cleary a protracted war would not benefit any member of the House of Iossec. The conversation began to die down as he took his seat at the head of the table, his white suit blending neatly with the clean marble. It was symbolic of his pristine nature which he strove to convey. Conversely, his city was being torn apart, essentially soiled, and that weighed heavy on him. Kasmine clasped his hands together as he sat back in his chair. His eyes flashed the seriousness of the situation.

"As you all know, the city has been under attack by the dregs of society. They perform the tasks that are unbefitting to men and women of our caliber. We have suffered minor losses as our ground sergeants and guards have kept these ill-equipped rebels at bay. What we have lost is roughly five-percent of our work force and more casualties are expected unless we can find some way to placate these people. I've doubled the Water Facility guards and issued a decree that all detractors will be dealt with swiftly. Before I issue an order to start going home by home, shack by shack and executing anyone suspected of these terrorist acts, I want suggestions from this council."

An aide spoke up. "We must deal with this problem immediately before the other Houses see us as weak and unable to maintain our city. I say door to door patrols are the answer. This city must fear the Kasmine name!"

"And to what end?" Another aide asked. "Killing innocent people will only fuel the fire. We have to isolate the leaders and assure the conspirators they will be rewarded for their cooperation."

"Or, we remember why we rose to power in the first place." Wisen said with clarity. "This is not a democracy. We must rule over these people with no empathy or there will be no end to satisfying their needs. Today its extra water, better living conditions, more food. Tomorrow they will be living amongst us.

Is that to be the fate of the House of Iossec? A bastion of incivility, littered with the morally inferior?"

A hush fell over the room. Wisen was respected for his age and wisdom. He was a steadying force in the House aiding Kasmine, Transt and the leaders before them. His words were never truer. Kasmine stood to his feet with his hands firmly on the table.

"Then it is decided. We will take back this city with the power and strength that built it. I want all Captains of the guards to be notified. We will start an intense sweep of the area. Anyone not proclaiming undying loyalty to this House is to be executed immediately at the discretion of the commanding officer. We will have this city under control in less than a week. What is the next order of business?"

The men collected nodded in agreement. One of the aides answered Kasmine's last question. "Your son Ralston has requested an audience before this council."

"Bring him forward." Kasmine straightened himself to receive his adopted son.

Ralston stomped into the room in all black, escorted by a single guard. His attire was akin to a prisoner of war more than one of the high born. His boots echoed across the polished marble floor. His face was stoic, with a body hardened by his training, hardly the look of the boy Kasmine took under his wing a few years ago. The loss of his mother caused him to withdraw and turn inward. There were whispers of Ralston being a potential threat. Kasmine was advised often to send him to join his mother. But Kasmine was hopeful, expecting time to heal the wound from his mother's death. It was this idealism that made Kasmine a good leader and simultaneously clouded his decision making on more serious matters. Ralston stopped and stood at the end of the table opposite Kasmine.

The first of the House of Iossec addressed him. "Good to see you son. You have grown strong over the years. I pray for many more good years to come. To what do I owe the honor of this audience you've requested?"

Ralston placed his fist over his heart to show honor. Kasmine and his aides returned the gesture. Everyone lowered their hands as the tension began to subside. Ralston spoke slowly, looking past Kasmine to the city beyond.

"I've grown in this House and been afforded all the luxuries that come with it. From my birth I was destined to rule the House of Iossec. Then my father Milred Transt died. Then I..I lost my mother Dalsha. I must express my appreciation to you Kasmine. Other men in your position...well I know I would not be given the chance to stand before you today. With that said, I mean no harm to the Kasmine Family."

Kasmine was glad to hear the somber tone. Maybe there was a chance to make amends and put the past behind them, he thought. "Thank you Ralston, your sincere words are a mark of your maturity and how you have grown over these last few years."

"Don't thank me yet." Ralston refocused his eyes on Kasmine. He wanted to look squarely upon him as he revealed his true intentions. "The reason I am here. The reason I requested an audience. I can no longer be a part of the Kasmine Family. I am a Transt by blood and I will always be a Transt. I denounce the name Ralston Kasmine and reclaim my true name Ralston Transt. I denounce the death of my mother Dalsha Transt. As my father Milred Transt was the true leader of the House of Iossec, I stake my claim as its true heir. I will take back what is mine."

Kasmine sat back in his seat as his aides looked on in shock. No one ever dared to denounce the House of Iossec and threaten the head in the same breath. Unflustered by the unexpected outburst, Wisen leapt to his feet. "This is blasphemous you cannot speak against your leader in that manner. The penalty is death!"

The council murmured in agreement. The guards stepped forward two on each side of Kasmine and three behind Ralston. The scene was surreal to Kasmine as he thought about his treatment of Ralston. From the day of his mother's death he was blessed with every opportunity. Though it was Kasmine who had his mother executed for treason, he often looked to Ralston as a son. He was starting to see how foolish he had been. Still, he tried to appeal to Ralston in hopes that another Transt's life would not be ended by his hands. Kasmine gathered himself and used the chair's arms to steady him as he stood up. He began to walk toward Ralston with guards in tow. The guards around Ralston were nearly shoulder to shoulder awaiting their Sovereign's orders or a sudden move by the antagonist. "I know you have carried a burden over these last years that no one can understand. You must find a way to move forward son."

"I'm not your son." Ralston's words cut like a knife. "I never have been. Never will be."

"Purge your soul and power will find you Ralston. That is what we believe." Kasmine reminded.

Ralston responded shrugging off the enlightened words. "The strength of your will is the source of your power." The usurper recited. "That is what my real father believed."

"Ralston. Take a moment to think." Kasmine reasoned. "Think about what you are doing. What you are saying. The entirety of this House is yours under my rule. You may still rule yet. My sons, your nephews are only infants. You must find another way."

"There is no other way." Ralston's eyes were cold black orbs.

Kasmine knew then he was lost. "There is always another way. Guards!"

The guards restrained Ralston. Kasmine approached and placed his hands on the side of Ralston's face. He could feel the defiance radiating from him. Kasmine pulled his head forward and kissed him on the top of his hair. The moment was tender as Kasmine stepped back and viewed his protégé from head to toe. What could have been? He wondered, if not for the impatience and greed of his mother. In his heart he always suspected he would part with Ralston in this manner. Kasmine held him a while longer then slid his hand down to his shoulders. He could feel the aggression slipping from Ralston.

The hold on the young detractor was loosened. Ralston's face grew calm. He too reflected on the blessed life in the house and how everything changed on that one day many years ago. Ralston could fall in line and accept his lineage in the House of Iossec. He could become a trusted aide to Kasmine or eventually have his on family. Ralston looked up at Kasmine and for a second contemplated rescinding his denouncement. What was he doing? He thought. This man had treated him well. But the image of his mother being dragged off haunted him. It covered over Ralston's thoughts. The image was crystal clear as if it occurred yesterday. It was seared into his brain and could not be forgotten. The only way to erase it was to honor his mother and fight for what she believed. The doubt passed and the strength welled in him as he struggled to break free of the guards. Kasmine could see the subtle change within Ralston. The inner turmoil he faced. But once again it was out of Kasmine's hands. He turned his back to Ralston and started towards the balcony. "Strip him of everything save his clothes and throw him outside the wall. Hence forth Ralston Kasmine is no longer a member of the Kasmine Family or the House of Iossec. Ralston Transt will live out his days as a vagabond in the streets."

Wisen leaned toward Kasmine and whispered. "Sir. Is that wise? The boy has disrespected this council and…"

"It's done. Guards you have your orders." Kasmine stepped onto the balcony and the glass slid closed behind him. Wisen looked back at Ralston then back at the aides seated around the council. The guards were holding Ralston and looked towards Kasmine's back. Wisen walked toward the guards. His lack of confidence in Kasmine's decision was evident.

"You heard your orders. Throw him to the street, if he tries to come into any House of Iossec…shoot him."

"I expected more from you, Wisen." Ralston scowled as he was lead out.

Wisen returned the resentment. "As I of you, young Ralston."

The five guards barred Ralston's hands and escorted him out of the room. He was led to a service elevator where the group crowded in. Two men positioned behind him, two on either side facing towards him and the squad leader facing Ralston. Their uniforms were unchanged from the days his father was the first of the House, stark white with a thick red stripe running down the side of their arms and legs. Red helmets, gloves and boots with black visors stopping at the bridge of their noses, covering their eyes. The distinct difference was the white 'K' outlined in red instead of a 'T'. How easily these people changed their alliances, Ralston thought. He looked from the letter on the guard's chest to his face. The guard in front of Ralston was the only one without a helmet. He was an older man, clean-shaven with his years of service clearly etched into his face.

"If you ask me they should have killed him." The squad

leader said to his team.

"You still can." The son of Milred challenged undaunted by his current predicament.

"You'll wish we did at the end…traitor." As the word left his mouth the sergeant punched the prisoner in the stomach. The other guards joined in, punching and kicking Ralston to the floor of the elevator. Before the door opened they composed themselves, straightening their helmets and wiping the red fluids from their gloves. The door opened and Ralston was dragged down the corridor with a guard under each arm, his legs dangling behind him. As the door closed servants rushed in to clean up the elevator cab. The sergeant walked down the hall acknowledging the guards positioned in the hallway. The exterior door was pushed open and Ralston was thrown awkwardly into the back of a waiting truck. A short drive to the opposite side of the city walls, the fallen prince was kicked out of the truck bed onto the ground. He rolled over onto his chest. His face was bludgeoned and his left eye swollen. The blood mixed with dirt, painted shades of red and brown onto his black uniform. Two guards jumped from the truck. One was armed, the other with a key in hand. The guard pulled Ralston up by the arm restraint as he grunted in pain. She unlocked the device, dropping Ralston back to the ground. Ralston's head was down but he could hear the footsteps coming towards him. The shiny black boots stopped near his face, and then the tip of a boot moved under his chin pushing his head up. The sun was behind the Sergeant and the glare caused Ralston to squint.

"I was told to give you rations when we released you." The Sergeant paused taking his foot from under Ralston's face. He looked at Ralston withering on the ground and the thought crossed him to put the man out of his misery. How long would he last outside these walls? Then again, he thought, orders were orders. But maybe he would help speed up the process. "Here's your rations."

One of the guards stepped forward and flung a bag onto the ground then proceeded to stomp and mash the bag until it was flat. He opened it and dumped the contents over Ralston. He then handed a bottle of water to the sergeant. The sergeant kicked Ralston to turn him over on his back and poured the water into his face. "I've followed my orders. Now you know how the scum feels outside these walls."

The Sergeant spat on Ralston, then climbed into the truck as it headed back. Ralston laid flat on his back in the dirt. He wiped away the food and water turned into sludge across his face. Looking to his right he could see the city walls and the guards positioned at the entry. They would surely shoot him if he attempted to go into the city now. He had no food, no water and some would say little hope of survival. He turned his head to look up at the sky and slowly whispered the Transt motto.

"The strength of your will is the source of your power." A smile spread across his beaten face.

CHAPTER 13
RALSTON

Kasmine sat in his personal study reviewing the inner workings of the House of Iossec. He went there to retreat away from all his responsibility and look at the House with a critical eye. There were two rooms; the first was off a side hall from his main room. Two L-shaped couches lined the walls. In the middle of the room sitting on a pedestal was a bust of Kasmine, sculpted just last year, his stone bust etched into a Romanesque pose and harkened to the days of their generals. The walls contained a painting of the Kasmine family on one side with him positioned in a chair with the family around him. The other wall held a picture of Transt and his family. Kasmine always showed respect to his predecessor. Hardwood floors ran from the entry door to the secondary door with two guards on either side. More guards milled around in the hall. Behind the metal door Kasmine stood in front of the computer screen which covered the entire west wall. On the opposite side was a table with six chairs. To the north was a glass wall with the sun screened by an exterior structure. Kasmine held a long solid black stylus in his hand roughly two feet long. He touched the top right corner of the screen with the edge of the stylus.

"Eye level". He said. The document slid down in front of him. He looked at a word on the screen. "Enlarge".

The words began to enlarge from that point. Kasmine had studied these figures for a few days and he needed to find a way to propel Iossec to one of the upper Houses if he ever hoped to gain power. The efficiency with which he ran the House allowed for the rapid ascent. Now he poured over data trying to figure out how to cut anything that was not absolutely necessary while increasing the production. The door slid up and Wisen walked in. "I hope I'm not interrupting."

"You are." Kasmine responded without looking at his aide.

Wisen knew what he had to say trumped Kasmine's displeasure with the imposition. "I have urgent news sir." Kasmine continued to study the data, unfazed by his intrusion. "The Water Facility was attacked."

Kasmine stopped and slowly turned towards Wisen. His eyes were noticeably larger. A major production loss at the Water Facility could be catastrophic to his data. He composed himself as Wisen continued. "The rebel attacks have grown more fierce and coordinated over the last few days. It's as if someone is leading them."

"What was the damage at the Facility?" Wisen asked, calculating what loss they could absorb, if any.

"It was minimal." His aide stated. "Production is down by fifteen percent, but will be back to full capacity in a few days. The rebels are ill-equipped to cause any major damage, let alone hold the Facility. My concern is who's leading them?"

"Your concern should be getting that Facility back to one-hundred percent operation." Kasmine's tone was sharp. "We need that facility if we have any hope of surpassing the House of Diera. That is our main concern. These rebels are nothing more than an annoyance."

Wisen was similarly perturbed by the rebels, but they had grown from more than a small irritation. "I agree Kasmine. But we need to be more aggressive about stomping them out. If rats take over an area we don't just wait until they've run out of food and starve. We find the nest and exterminate them. That is what you've proposed."

"Are you saying we have traitors in our midst?" Kasmine questioned.

"No…maybe…my main point is you have to rule in a way that inspires terror and lets these aggressors know they will be stamped out." The aide hastened to make his thoughts plain.

The first of the House of Iossec held the stylus in his hands considering his most trusted confidant's words. "I don't want to shed innocent blood to root out this evil."

Wisen reminded him of their position. "Sometimes blood,

innocent or otherwise, has to be spilled for the greater good of the House. You of all people know that Kasmine."

"That's enough Wisen." The point was made and Kasmine needed to act swiftly. "I'm sending patrols door to door in the city. We'll round up any survivors of the Facility attack and make sure they are questioned before they are executed. That is all."

"As you command Kasmine." Wisen bowed his head and backed out of the room. If he had not known before he realized now, Kasmine had no idea what was ahead. If he thought this rebellion would be easily squashed, he would be sadly mistaken. For now Wisen acquiesced, but he knew he needed to prepare for the danger to come.

Two nights later, Kasmine was awakened by Wisen and asked to meet in the personal study. Wisen seemed to be in a bit of a panic, which was out of character. Kasmine sleepily sat down in his chair. He looked out the window and he could see smoke billowing from the house of his second in command, Giless Lenfree. Kasmine sat up in his seat as the computer screen flickered on showing images of rebels being killed outside his home and inside on the main floor. "What the hell is happening?"

His aide rapidly brought him up to speed. "There was a full-scale attack by the rebels early this morning. Every home in Iossec is under siege. Just through superior force they are being kept at bay on the main level here, but the under houses are not faring so well. Some of the men who are part of the attack are former guards. The underlying theme is they are discontent with the current conditions, lack of water, how they live, what they eat, what they wear.

Kasmine was livid. "After all we've done for them they still complain."

"As I said before." Wisen stood, staring down at Kasmine's distraught mass. "Rats who have gone wild. Now their disease and filth is spreading through this great city."

"We have to stop them Wisen. I don't care about the cost. If they take even one building our status will be diminished in the eyes of the Upper Houses." He finally understood the magnitude of the assault and he realized he should have heeded Wisen's earlier warnings.

"The guards are doing what they must to ensure that does

not happen." Wisen looked at the monitor. "Sir, you have an incoming call."

Kasmine looked toward the screen. He leaned forward trying to speak with confidence, but his voice revealed his hidden fear. "This is Kasmine, First of the House of Iossec."

Giless Lenfree's slender face appeared on the screen. He was Kasmine's second and normally in a good mood. Today his clothes and hair were disheveled and the lines of worry crisscrossed his face. Kasmine could hear the screams and gunfire in the background. Giless gave a half-hearted greeting. "Kasmine, First of the House of Iossec, I have news concerning the rebellion."

"My friend," Kasmine responded. "No need for pleasantries, speak freely. The quicker we understand this threat the quicker we can contain it."

Lenfree explained. "They struck in the middle of the night killing half my guards and staff. Right now rebels are taking control of my home floor by floor. I don't know if I have the manpower to stop them. The other Houses are under similar duress. If you have anyone to spare…"

"How many are there Lenfree?" Wisen asked.

"More than anyone anticipated; former guards, former servants, and some people from the adjacent city of Sinsabae. We're being overwhelmed." Lenfrce hung his head. "Without any aide it won't be long before we're overtaken."

"We'll do everything we can to get extra guards there." Kasmine assured him, then he turned to his aide. "Wisen, are we making progress pushing back the rebels? We cannot let Lenfree fall."

"We have them under control, but we must make sure this House is secure before we aid another." Wisen stated. "Lenfree do you have any other information that can help us understand what we're dealing with?"

"I do." Lenfree looked at the floor.

"Tell us Lenfree. We don't have time to guess." Wisen demanded.

"I know who's leading them." The second stammered out. "I know who's leading the rebels."

"What?" Kasmine was surprised by the revelation that the rebels had a leader.

Lenfree continued. "He's leading this assault personally. That's why they're taking floors so quickly."

"Who?" The aide inquired.

"One of my guards on the lower level. He confirmed it." Lenfree looked at Wisen, then at Kasmine. He wanted them to understand there was no mistaking the one responsible for the assault.

Wisen was growing weary of his guessing game. "Lenfree if…"

"It's Ralston Transt." Lenfree blurted out.

"Ralston!" The mentioned of the name confused Kasmine. Surely the boy was dead.

His second saw the look of discord on his face. "I'm sorry Kasmine. I didn't want to believe it. But it's true."

"We have to put an end to this." Wisen reasoned. "Where is he now?"

"He's on the ninth level and steadily advancing." Lenfree confirmed, exhausted by the thought. "By my calculation he'll be on this floor in the next few hours."

Wisen, not Kasmine responded to the new information. "Then we need to take drastic measures."

"Yes. I knew you would come up with something Wisen." It was clear to Lenfree that Kasmine was still in a state of disbelief.

"We may have to blow the building." Wisen said in a calculated tone.

"Wait…what…blow the building?" The second responded, discouraged by the aide's strategy.

Wisen turned toward Kasmine. "That's the only way we'll be sure he's dead, Kasmine."

"No…you can't blow the building. My people, I have some family on those floors. There has to be an alternative. Kasmine, think about what you are doing." Lenfree pleaded to no avail.

Kasmine was still in a trance after hearing Ralston's name. He should be far from the city or dead by now, how was he leading a rebellion against him? He thought. This did not happen overnight. Ralston was planning this all along. Wisen and the rest of his aides were right. He should have killed him when he had the chance. Kasmine was determined not to make that mistake again. "Lenfree you've been loyal to the House of Iossec and always heeded the commands of your First."

"Yes Kasmine, but…" Lenfree's words were cut off as Kasmine expanded on the severity of the situation.

"Then get everyone you can to higher ground. Ralston's uprising against our House ends today."

"Yes…You're right Kasmine. He's on the tenth floor per my reports. Do what you must." Lenfree put his fist over his heart. "It has been my honor to serve as the second to the House of Iossec."

"You and your family's sacrifice will not go unnoticed Giless." The screen went dark. Kasmine straightened himself in his chair as he addressed his aide. "Wisen, find Sergeant Bilyar. Tell him to grab two men and head to the armory. I want all three of them to meet me on the council room balcony with FPB's in hand. Make sure the shooters selected can aim straight. We have a clear shot to Lenfree's home and we may only have one chance."

Wisen put his hand on his leader's shoulder to reassure him. "This is the right decision."

The First answered as boldly as he could muster. "We don't have much time."

A few minutes later Sergeant Bilyar and two snipers were standing on the balcony holding large silver tubes under their arms. The weapon had a long shaft similar to a rocket launcher, but the operation was different. Bilyar walked over to a case resting on the balcony and opened it to reveal four, six inch diameter metal balls. He rubbed his hand over the top of the cylindrical mass before he placed his weapon on the ground. Angling the shaft, Bilyar slid the ball delicately into the tube. He waited to hear a locking sound. Instantly the FPB, or Force Propelled Bomb, started to whir as it calibrated the closest target. Bilyar picked up the FPB placing his right hand on the back end under the trigger and his left hand focusing the barrel towards the tenth floor of the Lenfree home. The two guards followed the same exacting procedure one at a time until they were all standing with the weapon facing over the balcony.

"Make sure to aim for the tenth floor." Kasmine commanded. "That is where the forces are concentrated. It's a preparation area for the entertainment floor above."

"Good sir. These here will tear through those walls like

butter." The Sergeant tapped the side of the FPB, then looked back at Kasmine. "Awaiting your order sir."

Kasmine looked out to the House of his second. He could see the smoke and hear the gunfire around the city. What had become of his city? So calm, clean and set to elevate to a higher status, who would have thought a Civil War would tear down all he created? Losing Lenfree's home would devastate morale and even cause a drop in their position among the Collective. How could he have been so blind as not to see Ralston for what he would become? He was more of a corporate leader; he diagnosed information, clarified data and kept a firm hold on energy production as well as consumption. Maybe this type of leadership was not for him. The bloodshed was more than he could stand. He still saw Dalsha's face on nights when no stars covered the sky. His ears would ring with her screams of treachery. Would Ralston haunt him too? "Fire!" The words rung from the base of his throat.

The three metal balls sailed through the air effortlessly as the trajectory sent them crashing through the glass windows on the tenth floor, through the wood board walls. The first crashed into a kitchen area landing in front of Lenfree's guards attempting to flank the rebels in the main room. The second one thudded off one of the rebels backs sending him slamming into the opposite wall. While the rebels engaged in close quarter fighting to take the floor, the third bomb smashed through the wall and slowed in the middle of the group. All the fighters froze. One of the rebels looked back at Ralston. He turned from his opponent, leaping toward his general shouting. "We must protect Ral..."

The explosion shook the twenty-one story building as debris shot out from every opening. Floors dropped down upon one another weakened by the blast. The building rumbled and creaked as the structure began to give way. The home swayed from side to side on the verge of collapse, then slowly leaned to one side and stopped. The fighting below subsided as the rebels attempted to get from under the building. Kasmine watched as the Lenfree's estate leaned toward his home. He had not expected so much destruction. If the house toppled causing a domino effect there was no telling the amount of damage. Kasmine turned backed to Bilyar. "Sergeant, I applaud your efficiency."

"Thank you, sir." Bilyar said through a wide grin.

"Not as accurate as we would like though." Wisen observed.

'No sir. They never are.' The Sergeant agreed.

"War is never accurate Sergeant." Kasmine noted as he stepped through the door into the main room.

Wisen gave Bilyar further instructions. "Sergeant, no time to gloat over your success I need you to get down to the main level. Round up your best soldiers and push those dogs into the street. I want to know the minute the building is cleared. We'll start cleaning the streets and going house to house to reinforce those under the most severe assault."

"Yes sir. You two grab the case and follow me." The squad quickly disappeared through the room and down the service elevator. Sitting at the head of the table, Kasmine had activated the monitor and was watching the battles rage through his home and right outside the ground floor doors. The rebels continued to fight unabated by the destruction they surely heard and witnessed. Kasmine hoped the loss of Ralston would mean an instant cease and desist. Instead the rebels seemed more determined. Wisen walked over to him and placed his hand on his shoulder. He could feel the First of the House trembling with fear. Wisen made no effort to hide his concern. "I thought the fireworks would have slowed them down, but it seems we're dealing with something greater than we anticipated."

"I see that Wisen." Kasmine said clearly agitated.

Wisen knew he had to reinstill confidence in his battered leader. "What I'm saying Kasmine is you are the First of the House of Iossec. We are backed by the most powerful families in this country. Our resources are virtually unlimited. All you need to do is lead and command. These filthy mongrels will surely fall. Their faith in a lost cause will never defeat our power."

"You're right. I know you're right. It's just…" Kasmine was lost for words. The events of the day had shaken the foundation of their city as well as his core convictions.

"No. You are the leader, you are the First. Your commands are the people's desire." Wisen insisted.

Kasmine was still not convinced. "We've never been attacked like this, Wisen. Not like this…"

"Uprisings always occur." The aide reminded him. "You

think the masses are happy with their status in life? You think they don't desire a greater life, a greater purpose, just as we do?"

"I never thought…they've just been…just been tools to build an empire. I never thought to ask a mule if it longed for a better life." Kasmine encircled his right hand toward the floor as if one of the vagrants were in front of him.

"And you won't ask now. We'll beat them back into submission. They'll be too fearful to ever cross Kasmine again." Wisen spoke with authority, something Kasmine was unable to do at the moment. He was without words. Wisen spoke the truth, but did little to subdue the impending dread growing in him.

Wisen continued to advise. "You have to call Mordal and request a special meeting. The heads of the Collective have assisted in the past, but they need to know the severity of our current situation." Kasmine quietly switched on the wall monitor and spoke aloud. His voice quivered as he called out the name.

****

That was the current state of the sixth house of the Collective. Guards fighting day and night with the rebels, forces split between the city and the Water Facility. Xonox wondered how it had gotten to that point. Was it the inside leadership of young Ralston Transt or was it the lack of leadership by Kasmine? Or did a combination of both lead to the sixth House being on the verge of falling to the last house? Maybe Kasmine's intense desire to elevate the House of Iossec caused its inevitable decline. Resource production was not the only way to raise a House in status.

Blodware Falsteri from the House of Ultirum, the eighth house, was finishing his report. He committed what men he could to aid Kasmine. Every member was aware the fall of his city would cause a ripple effect through the Collective.

Yual Mordal spoke. "It seems a vote is not necessary. There is a consensus that anyone that is not essential to our Houses must be eliminated and driven to the outer cities. We must round up all agitators and publicly execute them. This will be a warning to those who think of coming against us. Let what is happening at Iossec be a lesson to all of us. We cannot let these transgressions go unpunished. Are we in agreement?"

The group answered and nodded in affirmation. Kasmine's troubles had brought a growing problem to the forefront. The people were no longer happy with scraping by as they watched the Houses continue to grow in wealth and excess. They had to be broken if the Collective planned to keep the status quo. There was no question the men and women assembled had no intention of relinquishing even a fraction of what they accumulated.

"Then we all know what to do. Starting today and hence forward anyone thought to be suspicious of treason against a House will be put to death immediately by the order of the First of each house. We will not allow these miscreants to defile what we have built." Mordal asserted. Each person agreed in silence. "This meeting is concluded. The best to each House; Saran, Janus, Vancrew, Agress, Deira, Iossec, Toessar & Ultirum. Especially Iossec."

"Thank you Mordal. And thank you all for your support." Kasmine managed in a low tone.

"You are part of this family, Kasmine." The First of Firsts affirmed. "You should expect nothing less. All of you can sign off, except Xonox. Can I have a word?"

Xonox perked up from his daze. He knew why Mordal requested a private conference. His mouth involuntarily turned up in the right corner in a half smile. "I'd be honored." The individual screens went dark until there was only Yual Mordal left.

"I'll make this brief Xonox. Croman was right. Per our established bylaws you were to let Crispus go once he cleared your city limits."

"I don't let murderers go free." Xonox replied challenging Mordal and the outdated laws.

"You don't let innocents go free." Mordal scowled.

"Neither do you." The First of the House of Vancrew recalled.

Mordal retorted with an air of superiority. "You don't have to remind me Xonox. We've all made sacrifices to get where we are today. It's allowed us to be blessed with unlimited resources. But we also follow rules. And if we don't, I can assure you we will both see this great empire we've built crumble."

Xonox was unimpressed by his speech. "I understand how it works. I'm one of the reasons we're here today. You, I and

Croman." Stressing the 'and' as he spoke.

"I agree you were a large part of our success and Vancrew is the third House. Don't forget where you've come from Xonox. And don't forget where you're at." The First warned.

"Nor you Mordal." The Third said unflinching from the perceived threat.

"Oh, I never forget. That's why I'm 'The First of Firsts'. You can sign off Xonox." Mordal signed off abruptly before Xonox could respond, making sure he had gotten the last word. Xonox stared at the blank screen. His eyes burned red. This was not the first time Mordal had asked for a private conference to scold Xonox then ended the communication brazenly. His elbows rested on the arms of the chair and he brought his hands up to his face. Fingers crossed, he touched the bottom of his chin with extended index fingers and whispered to himself. "My time is coming Mordal."

CHAPTER 14
THE RETURN

The black jeep sped across the landscape as the trees and terrain disappeared. Abel eyed the gas gauge and the needle continued to plunge below empty. He knew he was running on fumes. The detour to Gravope was more costly than he thought. He mashed the pedal and the vehicle propelled forward. The dirt accumulated on his goggles as the dust swirled around the group. The water had run out on the way to Gravope. They were lucky to trade for a few bottles from Aaron. He was happy to take the large machine gun off Abel's hands. It would fetch the merchant a fair price.

Tommie Gun sat by his side, turning his head as granules from the road blew in his eyes, talking non-stop since they left Abel's home town. He told Abel what was on the plans and his last few years in the House of Vancrew. He was one of Xonox's personal bodyguards, therefore he was allowed access to all levels of the House. Forsum who had been relatively quiet and slumped down in the back seat sat up when he heard 'Xonox's personal guard'. As many of the people in Gravope, he was at the same time fearful and fascinated by Xonox. "How is that?" Forsum asked.

Tommie Gun turned back to look at Forsum a little annoyed by his interruption of his conversation with Abel. Tommie's eyes scanned him from head to toe. Where Abel had a lean, muscular build with a look that told you he was on a mission, Forsum looked frail as he held what appeared to be an old sniper rifle between his legs. His arms protruded from his shirt, long, thin and devoid of color. Abel swore he was a sharpshooter, but his face held no trace of a man who had killed anybody or anything.

Tommie doubted he would be of any use against Xonox's army. "How's what?" Tommie responded gruffly.

Forsum followed up a little more enthusiastically. "How do you get to become one of Xonox's personal guards? I mean, just being a guard at the Facility is an honor."

"An honor?" Are you listening to this Abe?" Tommie turned his attention to Abel as Forsum sunk back in his seat. "You sure we don't need to do a U-turn and drop this guy off." The rogue contorted his face disapproving of the naivety expressed by his new companion. "An honor."

"I'm curious too. And I'm sure Grise wants to know." Abel said without taking his eyes off the road.

Riding next to Forsum, Grise had hardly made a sound since they started out to Warden's camp. He sat stoically, broad shouldered looking straight ahead, dark sunglasses covering his eyes as the wind drifted over his short dark hair. His arms rested in his lap with his left hand holding the wrist of his right. He had fallen into some kind of combat position, patiently waiting to meet the Warden. He heard the stories of the tournament and knew the reverence Warden enjoyed among the small outlying cities. What Grise did not share with Abel were the rumors surrounding Warden's true origins. Was he just a simple wanderer who saved a town from outlaws, or was there more to his story? He would find out soon enough. Either way, he was responsible for Abel now. Grise rotated his head and grunted in response to Abel.

Abel cocked his head in Tommie's direction. "See. We all want to know."

"It's not for the faint of heart." The hardened man looked back at Forsum. "Could give you nightmares." Tommie smiled and Forsum could see the dirt seeping into his cracked tooth. He sat back further in his seat. "Alright then, if you really want to know." Tommie said. "The quickest and easiest way to get into Xonox's House is to be taken as a prisoner. And that normally leads to dying in some creative way as I've rarely heard of anyone who left those cells. Well, I ended up picking a fight with some guards outside of Xonox's home. I was giving a good beating to the first three or so, then another five more joined in and stomped me good. The guard I initially attacked pulled out his gun to shoot me, but luckily one of the Captains knocked it away." Tommie recounted the tale.

"No I have a better idea." The Captain said. "Let's have some fun with this one." He ordered the other guards to pick Tommie up and drag him to the holding area on one of the lower floors. The cell he was escorted to held the dregs of the city and surrounding area. Many of the prisoners were affiliated through gang ties or necessity. Tommie was tossed in the cell exhibiting the same vigor that had spawned the fight.

"I beat the crap out of you guys and I'm rewarded with free room and board. Thanks. Send Xonox my love." He grinned from ear to ear as he spoke to the Captain, unfazed by the blood smeared on his lips. The Captain began to step out of the doorway looking around at the men in the room. "Fresh meat boys."

The inhabitants grumbled and growled like wild animals some stood from their seats as they eyed Tommie. "Here's a little something to make it interesting." Reaching behind his waist the Captain pulled out a small hunting knife. He held it in front of him and the singular light bulb in the center of the room reflected off the blade. It dropped to the floor as it made a ting, clank sound. The Captain closed the door. Tommie counted nine men in the cramped twenty foot by twenty foot cell. They began to crowd him. For one of the few times in his life he was without words. He lunged for the knife as he felt the first blow land on his back.

The next morning the Captain made his way down the long corridor to the last cell door where Tommie had spent the night in the company of people who had nothing to lose. It was eerily quiet. Normally he would hear the prisoners mumbling about breaking free or what they could do to please Xonox. The door was solid steel with a key code entry. He gestured to the night watchman to open the cell. He placed his hand over the reader on the wall near the door. The panel turned a bright blue, then faded as the door clicked acknowledging the guard. He pulled the door open. The Captain had seen his fair share of battles, his status in the House assured that. Even as a seasoned veteran he was unprepared for the scene. Men were strewn about the cell, their bodies contorted in awkward positions. The light was faint and he could see the limp feet or arms of some men as their bodies protruded from the dark corners. The floor was damp and stained red. In the middle of all the mayhem, stretched out and face down was the man known as

Tommie Gun. His left arm was tucked under his body with his right arm lying flat next to him. The Captain turned to the night guard who stood in the doorway. "How did this happen? Who did this?"

The night guard was speechless, his mouth was agape and he was visibly shocked by the unexpected carnage. Then his eyes grew large, his lips trembled as he stared past the Captain. Before the Captain knew what happened, Tommie Gun was upon him. His face and clothes blood-stained red. The knife was under the Captain's chin. He could feel it nick the skin at his throat. The Captain froze in place expecting to meet the same fate as the prisoners. Fortunately for him, Tommie Gun had not gone through all that trouble just to kill him. Tommie spoke into the Captain's ear, his hot, foul breath washing over him. "I just did you a favor Captain. Now you owe me one."

There are many ways to become a guard to a House. You can be randomly selected, placed in servitude to pay off a debt or simply given to the house at a young age to bring prestige to a family. Then there were extraordinary circumstances where someone had proven their worth in a conflict and could be nominated by another guard, this was how Tommie Gun found himself standing in front of Dante, Xonox's top aide. The Captain recommended Tommie, noting his prowess as a fighter. To save face, the part about the knife under his neck was left out. To be a guard under these terms Tommie had to prove his loyalty to the House of Vancrew. His test, bring back the head of one of the Legion gang leaders, Bull. The gang was situated halfway between the House of Vancrew and the House of Janus. The Legion was a combination of several gangs coming together for survival. Bull controlled one of the factions and lately the gang was attacking convoys randomly. Normally Xonox would use one of his mercenaries or send a portion of his army, but with the uprising and the tension between him and Croman it was best to send someone else to make an example.

Tommie was dropped off late at night on the edge of the Legion's camp. He was told to get back the best way he could. The truck sped off into the night leaving Tommie with limited weapons and supplies. He walked towards the camp trying to figure out how he would determine which man was Bull. Two days later he rode back into the city on a motor bike clutching a bag in his hand. He was allowed to meet Dante on a lower level where less important visitors were entertained. He picked the bag up and shook the contents onto the floor. Dante looked down at the severed head and realized why they called him Bull. His head was huge, with bulging jaws. A large gold ring looped from one nostril to the other. His hair was pulled back in a thick red ponytail. The only thing he was missing was the horns. From that day forward Tommie was a guard. Soon, through some planned untimely deaths, he was one of the personal guards that roamed the building floor by floor allowing him to collect all the data he needed. All along his plan had been to sell the information he gathered.

Tommie concluded his story. "Now, here I am heading to Warden's with you."

"That's how it happened?" The skepticism was evident in Abel's voice.

"From my mouth to God's ear. I swear." Tommie said holding his hand over his heart.

Forsum questioned the story. "So you just walked into the gang's camp, cut off their leader's head and came back without a scratch."

"Not quite." Tommie said, with no intention of clarifying what he meant.

"When you put it that way it seems more unlikely." Abel stated as he turned his focus back to the road.

"Who are you to question me?" Tommie shouted looking around the vehicle. "What have any of you done? What?"

Abel took his right hand off the wheel and lightly punched Tommie on the arm. "Calm down Tommie. We're just messing around."

"Seriously? What?" Tommie was still heated.

"Hey." Abel pointed ahead. "We're here."

As they approached the warehouse, the expanse of the structure spread out before the group. It was larger than Abel remembered. He was on foot the first time, he thought. They could see the people milling about the front of the complex and Warden's men perched strategically along the rooftop. He could see one of the men looking through a pair of binoculars to confirm their identity. Another of Warden's men used the scope on his sniper rifle as they drew closer. Abel hoped he was trying to confirm who was inside the jeep before firing. After all they were expecting two men and Abel had come back with a jeep full. The black vehicle rounded the building and came up to the gate entry where they were halted. Abel pulled of his goggles as he addressed the guard. "What's going on, is there a hold up?"

"Just stay there." The guard answered gruffly. "Warden's being notified of your return."

"Somebody tell Warden I've been out here for four days, I found the man he asked for and I'm not in the mood for games." Abel was irritated by the treatment.

Another guard stepped from the side door inside the gate. "Tell him yourself. You've been cleared. But leave your weapons in the truck. All of you."

Abel grimaced at the guard. "No Problem."

"You gotta love this guy huh?" Tommie said. "He's got security like crazy but he's worried about the three of you coming in here causing trouble."

"Don't you mean four?" Forsum asked.

"Warden knows they'll be no trouble from me. I expect you to project the same sincerity if you want to make it past dinner." Tommie patted Grise on the shoulder. "That goes for you too big guy. I don't think Warden likes the strong, silent types."

Grise brushed Tommie's hand off his shoulder. "Worry about yourself."

Tommie lifted his hands and backed up. "Ok. Don't be so sensitive. That doesn't play well in a place like this. Just warning ya."

"Good advice Tommie. Everyone be alert. This should be a formality, if not..." Abel's advice was cut short by the guard.

"Warden is ready."

The group walked through the doors squinting as their eyes adjusted to the dim light. Abel was first through the door with Tommie, Forsum and Grise following close behind. They walked through the staging area where Warden fixed and modified his vehicles. Each of Warden's technicians stood near a vehicle or weapon staging bay with their eyes locked on the group as they passed. The room opened into a larger dining hall with tables pushed against the wall. In this space they were greeted by roughly twenty of Warden's guards with weapons exposed. They stared menacingly at the group, itching for a reason to use force. It was not the greeting that Abel expected. Even Tommie was starting to wonder about their host's intentions. They were all unarmed and obviously vulnerable to whatever Warden had in mind.

Abel stood stoically looking defiantly into the eyes of each man, waiting for any sign of hostility. He still had the 9mm in the small of his back just in case. He was sure Tommie and Grise had followed Abel's stealth and tucked away a spare weapon. Forsum stood to his right. Abel looked over and could see the concern growing on his face. He would find out quickly if he had made the right decision bringing his childhood friend along. If the situation turned messy, Forsum would be forced to fend for himself. Smartly, he was positioned between the two men from Gravope. Grise stood tall, arms by his side ready for what would come next. Tommie, on Abel's opposite shoulder, had a strange smile on his face, as if he had been in this situation before, maybe more than once. Tommie calmly scanned the room as he caressed the point of the hidden knife sticking out of his sleeve and resting in his palm. Abel relaxed his stance and placed his hands behind his back, hand in palm as a soldier would do. He wanted to position himself for quicker access to his weapon. One thing he knew for sure, they would go down fighting. As the room grew increasingly silent and the group continued to face off, a booming familiar voice parted the guards. "Abel, my friend! You've made it back. With Tommie Gun no less. When I was told, I couldn't believe it."

To Abel's surprise Warden was dressed similar to his men with camouflage pants and flak jacket, underneath he wore a white tank top. The prophet robe was gone. He was unarmed as far as Abel could tell, wearing the same wicked smile across his face.

"I never had any intentions of not coming back. Hope I didn't disappoint you Warden." Abel responded.

"How could I be disappointed? The principles of living greatly include the capacity to face trouble with courage while accepting disappointment with cheerfulness." Warden said with his arms spread wide towards the group. "I ask you to find one man and you come back with three. And so quickly. Did you have any troubles?"

"I found more than Tommie in those woods." Abel

answered. "There was a man out there…half-man, half-machine. He was looking for Tommie and he destroyed a good chunk of the forest."

"A man you say?" His host was intrigued.

"Yes." Abel scanned the room of guards. "With advanced weaponry I've never seen before. Some type of high-tech goggles. I was able to surprise him and get the upper hand for a while, but he eventually turned the tables. His marksmanship was impressive. Have you heard of such a man, Warden?"

Tommie Gun interceded. "Warden's heard of him before. They've all heard of The Mountie"

A hush fell over the compound. Warden and his followers knew well of whom he spoke. He was an instrument of destruction often sent out at Xonox's whim. His presence showed the value of the information that Tommie had obtained. Warden knew their paths would cross soon. He enjoyed the thought of testing his skills versus a renowned mercenary.

"So now you know what I had to go through to get Tommie back here." Abel said making sure Warden would acknowledge that he had accomplished more than he was asked.

"This must be some sort of sign, young Abel. Few people have seen The Mountie's face and escaped his bullet in the same day. Xonox's defeat is surely at hand. That is if you have the information I need?" Warden directed his last comment at Tommie, but Abel answered for him, placing himself in front of Tommie. "He does. But do you have what I need?"

"Yes. Yes. You were promised your own personal army to take on Xonox. Together we will fight side by side to victory." The host reminded. "Water and revenge will flow in abundance." The fighters around him lifted their weapons and cheered.

"And for that I thank you Warden. You are a man of your word." Abel said.

Warden stared at Abel, he was smart to protect the data. "My word is all I have Abel. And it's worth more than all the treasures you could imagine."

Abel looked around the room. "Where's Isnor and Keera?"

"They have been taken care of and enjoyed more privileges than any outsider before them." Warden responded.

Abel was not appeased. "I'd like to see for myself."

"You question me?" The self-proclaimed king laughed. "Has your adventure to the Grazen Woods made you so bold or has it made you so foolish? Give me the data drive and you will lay eyes on your friends."

Abel was growing tired of Warden's game. He slid his hand from his back revealing the gun. Warden's people stiffened. Warden had instructed his guards to bring them in without weapons. Clearly he intended to dictate the terms of the arraignment. Abel showing up with two more men besides Tommie Gun was also unexpected. Not only was Abel armed, but Tommie held a knife in each hand, the large man near Abel had somehow snuck in a sawn off shotgun that he held at waist level. Warden did not know what to make of the last man in Abel's troop. Either he was very skilled or he had been thrust into the wrong situation. Nevertheless, Warden did not plan on killing them, he just wanted to exercise his authority. Abel had made that difficult. That is what he admired about the young man, but one day he knew his brashness would get him killed.

"That wasn't the deal Warden."

"Abel. Take a moment and assess your current situation. I see two guns, two knives and one man who is woefully unprepared. On the other hand my men outnumber yours five to one. Is this really the time you've chosen to try and gain the upper hand?"

Abel surveyed the room and looked back at Warden. He was unmoved by Warden's words. "I've had worse odds."

"I doubt it Abel." Warden surmised. "The opponents you've faced thus far have been inferior."

Abel gripped the handle of the gun tighter. "Except The Mountie."

Warden took little notice of the young man's threats. "Abel, you don't need to be so fierce and bluffing…if you already know I can't be intimidated."

Abel looked from Warden and his men to the people following him. This was not how he wanted it to end. He could not fight Xonox from the grave. He relaxed and concealed the weapon in his back. Tommie looked at him with a confused expression. "If you cannot be honorable in this place." Abel reasoned to his host. "How can I expect different in battle?"

Warden turned away from Abel and walked towards his men. He contemplated killing them and taking the data from their cold bodies. But Abel had impressed him. He was sent on a suicide mission and somehow succeeded. If Grazen did not kill him then he may still be of use against Xonox. "Men, lower your weapons and put them away. Abel and his friends are guests in this house. They are to be treated as such."

"Are we guests Warden? Or am I to lead a faction of your forces to victory in your name?"

Warden understood what Abel meant. "You're right Abel. You're right. From hence forth you are officially a member...no, a ranking member of this humble clan. With all the rights afforded that position." Warden shouted to the men. "To Abel!"

"To Abel!" The words resounded from the warehouse ceilings. Then they all spoke their battle creed in unison. "Kill or Die!!"

Warden walked towards Abel. "You've impressed me Abel. Xonox has much to fear."

"I appreciate the honor." Abel said graciously.

"I know it was a long journey so we'll speak more when you are settled." Warden waved his hand and from the crowd stepped Isnor. Abel moved to greet his friend.

"Isnor." The two shared a hearty handshake. "You're looking good kid, had us waiting a bit though. I'm getting too old for suspense."

'There was never a doubt." Abel said. "You should have known that."

Isnor surveyed Abel's group. "I'm surprised you had any luck with this ragtag, dirty bunch."

"Hey, you give any of these guys a decent scrub and a loaded gun and the results will speak for themselves." Abel assured.

"I'll take the loaded gun, but I'll pass on the scrub. The name's Tommie Gun. But my friends call me Tommie Gun."

"So you're the guy Abel needed to find. Didn't make it easy on him I see." Isnor noted.

Tommie played along as there was a more relaxed air in the atmosphere. "As much as I could. He helped me outta that scrap with The Mountie, so he's okay with me."

Abel introduced his friend from Gravope. "This is Forsum."

Forsum grabbed Isnor's hand, as he sensed the tension leaving the room. "Nice to meet you sir."

"Sir?" The merchant was indignant. "Call me that again if you're trying to make enemies boy."

"No…I…no…" Forsum turned red as he released Isnor's hand.

Isnor patted Forsum on the side of his shoulder. "It's okay. Really. A friend of Abel is a friend of mine."

Isnor looked at Grise inquisitively. "And this is?"

Abel's protector stood broadly. "Here with Abel."

Isnor looked at Abel. "Doesn't talk much I see."

"No. But he's good in a fight."

"You left to find one man and brought back a little army. Smart thinking." Isnor winked at Abel.

"I got lucky stopping in Gravope." Abel responded flatly.

"Gravope?" Isnor was taken aback. "Your parents. Are they…"

Abel glowered. "Gone. But their memories have been laid to rest. All that is left is for Xonox to answer for their deaths."

The merchant grabbed his arm and pulled Abel toward him. "He will."

"Good. You're getting reunited." Warden had allowed the reunion to carry on long enough, it was time to conclude their business. "Four days is a long time. Now that all that is out of the way we need to get down to business. Tommie the data drive."

Tommie reached into his pocket to pull out the drive. Just then a woman walked through the crowd, silencing the men with her gentleness. The sweetness of her perfume lingered in the air as she neared the group. With all the posturing and fighting for water to survive, it was easy to forget about the softer side to this life. She stopped halfway between Warden and Abel's teams. She extended her hands elegantly beckoning for someone unseen to step forward. The men were docile and quiet as another woman appeared passing cautiously by the small army. She was dressed similar to the first woman with a red colored cloth over the top of her head, the brown hair flowing behind her as she approached. Her dress plunged tastefully at her breast, with a flat wooden necklace lying softly on her skin. The dress hugged her hips as it tapered past her knees. Men closed their eyes as she passed, her sweet aroma sending them to places in their minds they thought forgotten. What she lacked in grace, she made up for in a bold presence that propelled her toward Abel. Her eyes flittered with self-conscious doubt, but as the quietness grew louder so did her confidence. She ran towards Abel, no longer capable of the restraint Naomi had taught her. "Abel, you're back!" Keera threw her arms around Abel's neck and hugged him tightly.

Abel hugged her, unsure what to think. Keera was so beautiful, even more so than the vision of her he carried with him the last few days. He loosened his hold on her as she continued to grip his neck. Then he began to wonder. When he left she was completely against Warden's way of life. How was she indoctrinated so quickly? Was she okay? He thought. Did something happen while he was gone? Keera could feel the tenseness in Abel. She let go of his neck and grabbed his hand. Keera looked him eye to eye, as if to say everything was fine. "Come with me." She said.

"Yeah...Ok..." Abel uttered. Keera led Abel down the corridor she had entered from as everyone watched. Tommie watched them walk off and spoke out loud. "No wonder he was in such a hurry to get back. Didn't know he had it in'em."

Forsum agreed. "Abel's full of surprises."

"I see." Tommie stated as he watched the pair walk off.

Grise grunted as Abel disappeared down a corridor. Tommie handed the drive to Warden.

"I'll give him some time." Warden said as he accepted the data. "He's earned it. We will all need to meet tonight and go over this information. I need to formulate a plan quickly before Xonox realizes what we have. Naomi, show these men to adequate quarters."

"Of course Warden." Naomi answered. "Please follow me." She turned around to lead the men to their lodging area.

"With pleasure." Tommie responded eyeing the elegant woman. "Whoo. I would follow you anywhere." Naomi turned around and smiled at Tommie; she was used to this sort of gruff behavior from the men. She found the best way to deal with it was smile and stay focused on her task. Warden always ensured their safety.

As if on cue Warden spoke up. "Manners, Tommie, manners."

"Right." Tommie said still transfixed on Naomi. "I'll help her get the good china out. We're guests after all."

Keera held Abel's hand as they navigated the maze of halls reaching an opening. From that point the compound started to look familiar to him again. They walked into a room that Abel knew well. He had spent three day in it recovering from the tournament. Keera walked to the back of the room before she turned around.

"So, I leave for a few days and you're one of Warden's hand maidens? What happened?" Abel smiled as he spoke.

"Don't make fun Abel." Keera blushed.

"No seriously you look…you look beautiful." The last tournament winner searched to express himself.

She playfully slapped her hand against Abel's chest. "You're just saying that because I'm wearing Naomi's clothes."

"No, I'm not." Abel put his hands on Keera's shoulders and looked at her intently. Keera started to blush again, her shyness coming out. She pulled back slightly from his grasp. "Stop it. Why are you looking at me like that?"

Keera's ring hung around his neck on a chain, tucked into his shirt. He pulled out the ring, clutched it in his hand and kissed his fist. "Because I was hoping I would make it back and I did." He opened his hand showing the ring to Keera. "This belongs to you though. It brought me all the luck I needed."

"No Abel." Keera said. "I want you to keep it. You're going to need more luck. If what I hear you are planning is true. You're going to need it more than me."

"Thank you Keera." He stepped back from Keera adjusting the ring over his shirt.

"There's something I want to give you." Abel brandished the small, sparkling charm he found in his home in Gravope. "This was my mother's. She wore it, when…when she wanted to feel special. I hope it makes you feel like she did."

Keera looked at the jewelry glimmering in his hand. "It's lovely Abel. I never had a real necklace before. But I can't take that. I just can't. And you shouldn't ask me to."

"I'm not asking." Abel took Keera's hand and placed it over the pendant in his palm. He could feel her soft fingers slide over his hand as she took it. She placed it around her neck slowly, careful not to drop it. When she was done she looked up at Abel. "How do I look?"

"Like a queen." Abel put his hands around Keera and held her close to him. He intended to kiss her, but hesitated. What would it mean? How would it change their relationship? Maybe she would reject him. All the reasons why not to crossed his mind, then Keera leaned forward and kissed him softly. She held her lips over Abel's, teasing him. As she began to recoil Abel grabbed her tightly and kissed her again. He relaxed and Keera moved back to look at him. Who would have thought childhood friends from Gravope would find each other again in Bourdain and be brought together by a gangster? Before either one of them could express what they just shared they were interrupted by Isnor's unexpected entrance.

"You really had us worried Abel." He said wearily, oblivious to the sentimental moment the pair just shared. Abel turned around to see Isnor, Grise, Tommie and Forsum enter the room. While his attention was occupied, Keera used the opportunity to slip over to the doorway. Abel saw her leaving. "Hey…?"

Forsum responded thinking he was talking to him. "Hey, Abel."

Abel bared his teeth and waved off Forsum to let him know he was not talking to him.

"Let her go. We all need to talk." Isnor insisted.

"You'll have plenty of time for that later." Tommie smirked. He motioned his head toward Keera for emphasis. "Honestly this place is better than I remember. I don't know how Warden is recruiting these people, but he makes the stay worth your while, right?"

"He does." Forsum said mechanically.

Tommie answered the boy in his usual surly tone. "I wasn't talkin to…"

"Hey. Get your heads together." Isnor shot him a fierce look, more akin to a father figure than a disciplinarian. "We only have a few minutes before Warden comes calling. We need to discuss a plan."

"A plan." Abel said unclear where the merchant was

heading. "Didn't you hear? We're working with Warden now. He'll have some people under my command. With the data Tommie collected, Xonox doesn't stand a chance."

Isnor grimaced. Abel was no fool; maybe his mind was clouded from fatigue. "And you trust everything Warden said, 'cause I sure as heck don't. We've been here, more prisoners than guests. I've observed his people. They're fiercely loyal to him. I just can't see them following you so easily."

"You worry too much old man." Abel reasoned. "Warden needs us to take down Xonox. He can't do it alone."

The merchant knew the answer to his inner thoughts. "He's been operating on the fringe for this long, with his own personal army and now all of a sudden he needs strangers to take on Xonox? Doesn't sound right to me."

"I agree with him." Grise growled in a low tone. The group was gathered around in a half-circle around Abel, while Grise stood off in the corner adjacent to the doorway. Everyone paused, they turned slowly towards Grise. They looked at him as if he was a wild animal that suddenly decided to speak. Grise continued. "I don't trust him. Warden. He's nothing more than a glorified mercenary. And one thing I know about mercenaries, they only take action if it benefits them. You need to be careful Abel. We all do."

"Ok. This *is* serious." Tommie said in his animated manner pointing his rugged fingers at Grise. "Because that's the most I ever heard him say at one time."

"It is serious." Isnor's voice was unchanged. Abel looked back and forth from Grise to Isnor, he respected their opinions. They had seen more action combined than most people in the building. If their instincts said something was not quite right with Warden's proposition and acceptance into his camp, he had to take it seriously. Abel understood his role as the leader to this group, but he also knew he was only as strong as the support they gave him. There had to be a consensus among the group how they would proceed. In the end Grise was right. Warden had his inner-circle and followers loyal to him, Abel had to establish a similar buffer between himself and his new partner. "I believe you both." He said. "What are you suggesting Isnor?"

Isnor spelled out his strategy quickly. "I'm suggesting the

five of us stick together, watch one another's back and look out for Keera too."

"I can't speak for Tommie Gun, but I'm sure Forsum and Grise are in agreement." Abel said as the de facto leader of the bunch. Forsum and Grise nodded in affirmation. Abel looked at Tommie who had not spoken. "Well."

Tommie had gone silent. He looked at each man in the room, and then settled his eyes on Abel. "Hey, that business with Warden was just that, business. But if you're asking me to go against Warden...I don't know."

"That's not what I'm asking." Abel contested.

"Then what?"

"Look Tommie." Abel walked closer as he spoke to the hired gun. "I need guys that are with me, watching out for the other people with me. That includes everyone in this room and Keera."

"I like this whole five musketeer's vibe, but what am I getting out of it." His response was true to his reputation as a man who saw no value in a cause besides what it would gain him in the end.

"You have four other musketeers willing to stand with you. You think The Mountie is going to rest until you're dead?" Abel tried to use the safety in numbers approach. Even as he said it, he knew his psychology would look thin to a man he found traipsing through the Grazen Woods with no cares.

The rogue responded without taking a breath. "Yeah, but I've been dealing with guys like that my whole life."

"Then what do you want?" The group leader inquired.

"When I first met ya Abel, I wanted to kill you myself." Tommie's tone was not threatening, yet Grise began to walk toward the group.

"But now." He continued ignoring the large man's advance." I see you. I know you. I'll join up with your little team. But I want something."

"What is it?" Abel braced himself for a bizarre request.

"I don't know yet." Tommie admitted. "But I will when I see it."

The man from Gravope exhaled. "Fair enough."

"Good. It's settled." Isnor said taking the floor again. "There's six of us, so we need to try and stay in pairs as much as we can. I know Abel, Grise and Tommie are close up fighters. Keera and I are better with ranged weapons. Forsum I heard you were good with a rifle."

"One of the best in Gravope." Abel bragged, grinning at his friend.

The brashness of Abel's words gave Forsum confidence. "Just give me a clean gun, a clear lens and a soft wind and I can hit anything within two-hundred yards."

Isnor was comforted by the conviction in the young man's voice. "Ok. That skill will come in handy in the coming days. So be ready."

"I will." Forsum nodded.

"Make sure you get him a better rifle too. That piece of crap he has now may be good for hunting, but it won't be much in a firefight." Tommie warned.

Abel looked at the weapon slung over Forsum's back. "I'll talk to Warden."

"We all need better supplies." The merchant stated, looking at Abel.

A familiar voiced answered from the door entry. "And you'll get them." Luchi said obviously eavesdropping on their conversation. How much had he heard they wondered? "Warden sent me to find all of you. Relevant personnel are being summoned to go over the plans and formulate the attack strategy."

However long he had been listening, Abel was sure their internal meeting was now officially over. "We'll be there." He said as he walked near the referee. "Forsum and Tommie come with me. Grise, go with Isnor to find Keera and make your way to the meeting area from there."

CHAPTER 15
WAR ROOM

Abel entered the dark meeting room and took a seat next to Warden's tacticians. It was the room where he first met Warden and fought Goll. Now it was turned into a war room, with people packed in side-by-side waiting to hear Warden's analysis of the plans procured by Tommie Gun. Abel sat near the adjacent wall on the left side near the entry. In the middle on the wall opposite Warden was his inner-circle. He could see Luchi and seven others, whose names he had never learned, seated around the large table. On the far right he caught a familiar face staring at him. Goll sat in the middle front row, he proudly wore his vest with the red 'W' stitched over his chest. He nodded in a non-menacing manner, Abel returned the gesture. Neither man smiled, their differences put to the side temporarily to fight a common foe. Finally Keera, Grise and Isnor arrived. Forsum slid over so Keera could take the seat next to Abel.

"Did I miss anything?" Keera whispered.

"Not yet." Abel said as she sat down. "I think he's just getting started."

Warden stood at the front of the room, eyeballing each person that came in. He wanted them to know how serious this meeting was. He cracked open the water he was holding in his hand gulped it down and passed the empty bottle to one of his attendants. "Everyone. Please take your seat. We have much to discuss."

The room began to grow silent. Warden motioned to one of his inner-circle. "Dazshal. If you please."

Abel watched as the old projector sitting on the center table illuminated light in a large rectilinear shape against the wall. The large man seated in front of the projector took Tommie's drive off the table. It was about the size of a pen cap, but thin as a coin. He flipped it around and pushed one end into the side of the machine. The screen flickered and an image appeared next to Warden. It was a three-dimensional image of the eighty-nine story home of Xonox. Each area was color coded to designate servant quarters, entertainment, guest and Xonox's suite which took up the top five floors. A low murmur filled the room as people discussed what was shown. Forsum leaned over to Isnor. "We could put the whole city of Bourdain in that thing."

"Gravope too." Isnor reasoned.

"As you are all aware this is the home of Victor Xonox, the head of the House of Vancrew, the third house of the Collective, our enemy." Warden began. "You all know him as a dangerous man of unlimited means. This is the first time anyone outside the city has been allowed access to this information. I want to take this time to commend the man that made the viewing of this data possible." Tommie sat up in his chair as Warden continued. "Abel from Gravope. Without his bravery and courage, these plans may have been lost."

The room erupted in claps and cheers. Abel smiled. He stayed seated as he waved his hand to accept the applause. He looked behind him and he could see Tommie Gun fuming. His arms were crossed and he was biting his bottom lip. Abel leaned across the chairs and put his arm on his shoulder. "This is for you too."

"I didn't hear my name." Tommie snatched away from his hand. Abel looked at Warden and gestured towards Tommie. Warden reluctantly capitulated. He had to be careful giving out too much credit and he had more pressing matters. "And let us not forget Tommie Gun who risked his life for the plans as well."

Tommie stood up from his seat. "Mind if I say a few words there Warden?"

"I do." Warden shot him an icy stare. Tommie sat back down quickly as the clapping subsided. "Where was I? Yes,

Xonox's home. But before I proceed, I want to thank all the contacts to Gravope, Bourdain and Xonox's home city of XV1. Each one of these areas have committed thirty-men and women to this assault. I want to personally applaud everyone involved for their efforts. Also, we were able to secure more weapons through the Black Market. They came at a steep price, as everything does when dealing with rogues, but they were necessary for this mission. Taking the Water Facility will more than cover any losses. If you need more ammo, a newer weapon or something extra for your team, to complete your part of the mission, I need you to see Luchi. He will be in charge of the distribution. I want you all to be prepared. If we are prepared, we'll have no need for fear." The group nodded their heads in approval. "Up until now a lot of you thought we would be attacking the city, but that was never the case. An assault on Xonox would be virtual suicide at this point, but I know how we can greatly weaken him. Dazshal, go to the next image."

Dazshal clicked back and another three dimensional image popped up that everyone was familiar with, The Xonox Family Water Management Facility. The image spun around slowly on the screen. It was essentially broken down into three separate buildings forming a large 'U' shape. Water collection, purification and bottling occurred at the bottom of the 'U'. A large metal arm jutted from the back of the wall into the lake behind the facility. Water was being pulled in by the gallons. Along the lake, guards patrolled daily in front of the twenty foot high wall to insure no vandals had access to the resource. The building was long and rectilinear, the larger mass stepping down from the top to a smaller mass at the bottom, giving the look of an inverted stair. Shiny metal panels covered the building, as slivers of glass cut rhythmically around the structure. This detail failed to be expressed in the model, but all who visited the Facility were aware of the sculpture-like quality with which it was crafted. The remaining buildings were not as imposing, housing the guards living quarters on one side and the administrative services in the other. Each part ran smoothly towards the steel entry gate. Each side of the gate was controlled by a guard in the adjacent tower. The gates were closed and opened upon the Water Facility manager's command for heightened security. A twenty-foot high wall continued around the complex, with a guard tower positioned at each step in of the wall. Two towers were at the gate, two on each end of the long wall facing the entry gate. From either side the wall ran symmetrically, going along the side of the housing building, meeting a guard tower stepping in, then moving along the edge of the Water Facility until spreading out to encompass the body of water behind it. Warden moved in front of the pixalated scene and began to speak as the model adjusted over the entry and zoomed into the courtyard. "As you all know, Xonox sends and receives convoys carrying water on a daily basis. Tomorrow is the next water pickup and recycling exchange. They will be at the Facility in approximately ten hours, before they head back to the city in the morning. The convoy will pull into this area."

Warden circled the courtyard area in front of the main building as he continued to speak.

"The truck will be followed closely by a number of vehicles, with a well-armed battalion. Some of Xonox's best. The compound itself will be well guarded. With the convoy, I would say we can expect around six hundred Xonox loyalists."

The team assembled grumbled and shifted in their seats. With all the men and women under Warden, the cities of Bourdain, Gravope and XV1 were counted, they barely had an army of two hundred and fifty. "Believe me. Your concern is not without merit. We will have to use precision and the element of surprise to take the Facility. My plan is to break our army into three segments. The first part will be led by Dazshal and Luchi on the south side of the building. You will need to gather the best snipers to take out the guards in these towers." Warden pointed at the southeast entry tower and the southwest tower. Once that is done, your best marksmen will fire a ground to ground rocket into the side of the Administrative building. Hopefully the explosion will crumble part of the wall or at least severely damage it. That should be a big enough distraction to pull the majority of Distor's forces to the point of the explosion." Warden paused, looking around to make sure everyone was paying attention. "The second wave will be led by our new recruit Abel. Your team should be positioned on the opposite wall here." Warden pointed to the northwest wall near the main building. "I need you to set up with your best demolition man. When you hear the explosion at the Administrative building,

I need you to wait five minutes, and then blow a hole in the wall. Give their guards a chance to focus their attention on the first blast. You need to storm the courtyard and secure it as quickly as possible. Get someone up the entry towers and get the gates open. From there I'll lead the final frontal assault into the Facility. My team will form a blockade to prevent any survivors from fleeing. If we're smart we should have control of the Facility before Xonox can send reinforcements. The water will flow without ceasing that day."

The men cheered and the screen went blank. Warden stared around the room. "Seriously, we need to make every bullet count and treat the man next to you as a long lost friend. That is the only way we can hope to prevail over this tyranny. Since I was a boy I've strove to keep water around me, to keep it flowing. Like all of you I have seen the devastating effects of days without a drop. I never thought I would live to see a day where the people would come together and rise against our oppressors. A day where men of different ages, backgrounds and cities would come together to wreak terror on a House of the Collective. A day, where, if we are so destined by the Great Beyond, we can take control of one of the most productive Water Facilities ever built. If you would have told me, I would have not believed it. I would have said it was impossible. But here we stand shoulder to shoulder. Can the impossible become a reality? Only if you believe. Only if you fight for it with every fiber of your being. Only if you know the alternative will never be enough ever again. Stand with me and you will know victory my brothers and sisters! I say to you today, we will take the Water Facility, we will defeat Distor, and we will topple the House of Vancrew! XONOX WILL BE DEFEATED!!"

Everyone stood up from their seats, pumping their fists and screaming chants of victory. Warden gazed around the room knowing his people were ready for the arduous battle ahead. He extended his hands to quiet the people. "All of you get rested and get prepared, we leave before dawn."

The crowd dispersed, the people filing through the doors. A few hung around to talk to Warden and extend their gratitude for his leadership. Forsum was near Abel. "That speech. Warden is real inspiring. I see why you chose to align yourself with him Abel. He made me feel like we could win this thing."

Abel agreed. "Yeah. We need to bottle up that energy and release it on Xonox's guards tomorrow. You ready for this Forsum?"

"I…I think so." His friend said.

"You'll do fine. Just pretend like those guards are a deer or a bird in the forest and you need a hot meal." Abel patted Forsum on the back and they started toward their room. Suddenly, Abel felt someone grab his arm before he was able to take two steps. It was Keera pulling him back towards her. She had changed into a pair of faded jeans that were ripping at the edges and a tightly-fitted red short-sleeve shirt she had undoubtedly borrowed. Abel could not blame her, although the previous outfit was more alluring, it was not conducive to strategizing for war.

"Come with me." She beckoned.

Abel was focused on preparing for the task at hand. "I was heading to the room now."

Keera cocked her head to the side and stared at Abel as a smile spread across her face. So smart in some aspects, so slow in others, she thought. Forsum continued on, figuring Keera and Abel wanted time to talk.

"You know the whole gang will be in the room, Isnor and the rest." She said. He was missing Keera's subtle attempt at some time alone with him. He needed to make sure everything was organized, but after so many days away a few minutes alone with Keera could be just what he needed. "You're right. I don't think there's much privacy around here though."

"I know a place." Keera led him through the winding makeshift apartments into a larger space on the far end of Warden's home. As they walked through the door, Abel could see another door directly in front of them across the room about forty yards away. Only one thing impeded their progress as they made their way from one side of the room to the other. It was filled with children, young and old. Instantly upon opening the door there was a mix of playing, shouting, running and crying mixed in with the overall commotion of the children's activities. Some adults walked around supervising, officiating and separating them. After all, some of these young people were their own. As Keera and Abel made their way through the indoor playground, he could see the smaller children huddled in the corner with caregivers around them playing with wood, sticks and boxes building little structures. Kids ran back and forth at full speed, laughing and tagging the wall, engaged in their game oblivious to the intruders. One child perked up as she saw Keera, running over and grabbing her leg. "Keera! Play with me."

Keera rubbed the little girl on the head and wiped the dirt from her face as she responded.
"Sorry Peatra. Not now. Where is your mother?" Peatra did not answer, instead letting go of Keera's leg and running back across the room as fast as she could. Keera looked up at Abel and spoke as if reading his mind. "Naomi."

She pushed open the door to the outside and started towards the fence. The area was enclosed. Three men were talking around a diesel truck, they looked up, surveyed the pair and went back to their conversation. Keera stopped at the far gate, she placed her fingers through the square metal openings. She pressed her head close to the barrier and stared out into the darkness. It was pitch dark a few feet from her, the only light emanating from the moon, stars and the perimeter lights Warden's people had erected. She could hear the generator creaking and groaning as it ran in the distance. She tilted her head upward and breathed in deeply, absorbing her surroundings and all the reticent smells that came with it; old cars, greasy rags, smoke, smog, grizzled men, death, despair, renewal and hope. She put both hands on the fence and breathed out. Pushing all of the air out of herself and releasing the negative thoughts. Closing her eyes, Keera thought to herself, it's funny how the same structure could imprison you and the next moment it could be where you felt safest. It was all perspective.

Abel stood quietly behind her. It had been a long time since he stood silently outside and watched nothing in particular and thought of nothing in particular. He mimicked Keera's actions, staring off into the distance then looking up at the night sky. He sighed, contemplating the coming day. The attack on the Water Facility was just the beginning. If they could take it...When we take it, he thought, they still had to find a way to hold it. Would seizing the Facility be enough to disrupt Xonox? He was not sure. He did know there was no turning back now. He watched Keera as she hung off the screened wall, her combat boots giving her a little height, but not making her any more menacing. He had to keep an eye on her during all this. He had to keep an eye on them all; Isnor, Forsum, Grise and Tommie. They had trusted him with their lives and he could not let them down. They would find a way to prevail, he would make sure of that. Somehow he would make sure.

Keera began to speak without turning around. "Did I ever tell you about my father?"

Staring into the darkness he replied. "No. You never did."

She turned around to face Abel, her back flat against the fence. "You know he worked at the Water Facility. Xonox's Water Facility."

"I heard." Abel said quietly.

"That's why we left Gravope. I still remember the day he told me. It was just us two then." Keera paused. "Mother had died a few years before."

"I know. I'm sorry." Abel moved closer to Keera as she spoke.

"It's fine now." Keera's eyes met Abel's briefly, then she turned from him so he could only see one side of her face. Lost in her story, she continued. "He was so happy. It was such a privilege to be selected as a guard. I guess it still is. You know from that day forward, even though it may be rationed, you never have to worry about water or supplies again. We moved to the Facility a few days later and it was so different from Gravope. We had a small room, but it was clean and safe. The only odd thing was no children were allowed in the complex. So there were no girls or boys under sixteen years old. Children were sent to live with other family members or the family stayed in the adjacent city all together. Everyone at the Facility had to work in some capacity. I was in the collection and data production area. I was part of a team gathering production data and filtering the information to the head of the Facility. Everyone seemed so happy and healthy. You tended to forget about the outside world. Only when my father would go out on water delivery runs from the Facility to the city would he face the harsh reality. He would come back sometimes with stories of people struggling for just a few drops of water, the dehydrated laying in the streets. And here he was with a truck load of water and there was not one bottle to spare. He swore he would do something about it. I knew he could get in trouble, but it was hard telling my father otherwise when his mind was set. He began to take water from trucks, just a bottle at a time, then he started taking whole crates. At first he was trading to those in need, for anything they could spare. Then he was literally giving the water away. It took some time, but one of the higher ranking guards noticed. My father thought this meant certain death, so he told me to start packing my things and we could slip away in the night. But when the guard came to our room later that day, he assured my father he agreed with his generosity and together they could help more people. The next morning this man, my father and two other guards went out of the complex as part of a convoy. The plan was for them to lag behind and stop in some of the cities and give away free water…That was the last time I ever saw my father. Before they returned, one of my father's friends, Wilus came to my room in a panic. He had overheard the men's plans for my father and what they planned for me on their return. I was rushed to his room and hidden in the closet until the next day. The conspirators thought I had already escaped somehow. The next day Wilus was able to smuggle me to Bourdain. I lived there for the last couple years, struggling, trying not to die. Then I saw you."

Abel stared at Keera as she hung her head, exhausted from the tale. "I'm sorry about your father Keera. He was a good man."

Keera held her head up. "He was, Abel. And that's why I want to see Xonox pay as much as you do."

"He will. We'll find that guard too if he's alive. I swear." Abel turned back towards the darkness.

"I don't need to find him Abel, I already know where he is." Keera stated casually.

"You do?" Abel was confused. If Keera was in Bourdain this whole time, how could she know the guard's whereabouts?

"I do." She said.

Now Keera was being coy. Abel waited for her to tell him what she knew. It was evident she needed more prompting. "Well…?"

"He's still at the Water Facility." She said gripping the gate.

"Wait." Abel asked. "How do you know he's still there? Guards come and go."

"No. He's there. He's never left." Keera answered confidently.

"But how do you know?" He questioned.

"I know because after all these years I never forgot his name…His name was Connin Distor."

Abel's mouth dropped open. Then he closed it and gritted his teeth together, his brow furrowed, he clasped his hands together once. "Distor."

The name spat out of his mouth. How many families had he destroyed in his quest for power? Abel looked down at the ground and thought of what he would do to him. His eyes caught Keera's feet moving near him. He looked up at Keera and let the aggression slip from him, he would need that for the morning, he thought. Abel straightened himself, put his arm around Keera and they walked back towards the warehouse.

Off in the distance, past the fence, blending in with the shadows a familiar figure watched the whole scene play out. Even from one hundred yards, his goggles allowed him to zoom in and decipher the couple's words. He was sure this was the young man he saw in the Grazen Woods, but the woman was an unknown. The Mountie had surveyed the camp ever since he followed Tommie's trail from Gravope. While he watched the pair interact, he thought about assembling his rifle and killing them both. Escaping once was inexcusable, a second time was intolerable. Unfortunately, he was under strict orders from Xonox to observe and report. He had not glimpsed Tommie Gun yet, but based on the way Warden and his forces were mobilizing, he was sure they were planning their attack. The Mountie turned his back to the camp, jumped down behind a tree and pressed his wrist band once. "Xonox I'm here."

"And...?" His employer questioned.

"Everything is as you expected." The Mountie replied.

"Then you know what to do."

"Yes sir." The Mountie understood. The comm link went silent. The Mountie walked off into the darkness.

CHAPTER 16
THE WATER FACILITY

It was early morning, dark and still, the sun was yet to rise over the horizon. By the mask of night is how the three armies led by Dazshal, Abel and Warden were able to set up and take position around and near the building without drawing any attention from the inhabitants of the Water Facility. The topography around the complex sloped down into a depressed area on the east and north side, before flattening out to the west side of the building and south where the lake began. The steep change in the terrain allowed Dazshal's team, which consisted mainly of sharpshooters including Forum and Isnor, to set up on a nearby perch facing the north guard tower. Around thirty troops converged on this elevated area with a direct sight line to the towers. Grise, along with other hand-to-hand combatants, was along to watch the snipers' backs in case there was a close encounter with Distor's squad. The terrain sloped towards the east front gate and Dazshal watched the road intently waiting for a visual on Xonox's convoy. He was flat on his stomach, peering over the edge holding the oval shaped dull, gray metal binoculars up to his face. He sat motionless surveying the road from the Facility to the city. The marksmen were laid out in a line with their weapons readied, waiting on Dazshal to give the command. Just when the troops were beginning to get restless, and the tip of the sun began to peak over the landscape, Dazshal lifted his hand to make a fist, giving the 'get ready' symbol. First there was just dust, and then he could make out the outline of a truck, the sound of the vehicles soon followed, echoing off the land. The trucks ran in a straight line, with two hummers leading and two others behind. Dazshal could make out the double red 'XX's' on the front hoods. As the convoy approached the guards in the tower moved to open the gates. The large, steel doors began to slowly slide away from one another revealing the inner courtyard. The group of trucks hardly slowed down as they passed through the open gates. Guards leapt from the vehicles, securing the perimeter, as the gate closed behind them. They circled the water truck out of instinct more than necessity, the Facility was secure as far as they knew. As Dazshal watched and counted the number of the convoy, someone of impeccable dress and influence emerged from the Main Facility. His royal blue suit was crisp and clean from shoulder to ankle. The black dress shoes he wore shone from the glare of the sun. His visor covering his closely cropped blonde hair was that of a high ranking officer in the defunct military. Blue cloth lay above the black brim and double 'XX's' across the face of the headgear. Even his suit had metal bars of varying colors signifying some long forgotten military triumph. The only problem was he never served in a war. It was all a fabrication to project status. He was flanked by two armed guards and everyone stopped and straightened their backs as he approached. The way the men genuflected, Dazshal did not need to see his face to know who it was. As Distor shook the hand of the Captain in charge of the convoy and all the attention turned to the two men, Dazshal motioned for his team to start taking out the guards in the tower. There were two per tower and they needed to be hit almost simultaneously so no alarm was sounded.

Isnor and Forsum were trained on the southeast guard tower closest to the group. The two guards were standing on the opposite end of the tower both facing the courtyard. Forsum aimed his weapon and fired on the first guard; he doubled over and collapsed. Isnor's aim on the second guard was not as true. The foreground guard turned around as the bullet pierced his ear. He could see his fallen comrade on the floor. The guard's eyes widened as he lunged for the lever to sound the alarm. Forsum fired a second time and the guard fell to the floor in a heap. The guards in all four southern towers fell in the same manner. Now Forsum had to move quickly before the guard's suspicion was aroused. He put down the high powered rifle given to him by Luchi and opened a long crate laying on the ground. Lifting the heavy green rifle with an enlarged barrel, he checked the weight in his hands, and then he rested the gun between his legs, barrel up. He pulled out the single round of ammunition, a stick rocket. It was cone shaped with a rounded end, tipped with titanium. The front was six inches long with a four and a half inch diameter. Rectangular grooves were etched on four sides around the cone. A cylindrical, metal tail projected less than a foot from the bomb. Forsum grabbed the rocket by its metal stem and slid it into the barrel. He held the rifle up again with the bomb sticking awkwardly from the end. Balancing the weapon he came up to one knee, looked through the scope and adjusted slightly for the wind. He fixed the crosshairs on the side of the building, where four of the metal panels met. He breathed out slowly, flexed his finger. Suddenly he was interrupted by Dazshal.

"Take the shot kid. I can see the guards on the other side of the gate starting to look anxious."

Forsum was unresponsive as he zoned in on his target. He shifted the weapon so it would rest on his inside shoulder. He grabbed a clump of dirt and threw it up and away to check the wind again. He pulled the trigger. There was a loud noise as the rocket sped off towards the Facility. Forsum lurched with the kickback. The nose of the rocket rammed in between the metal panels and instantly small metallic arms sprouted from the cone and dug into the panel holding the bomb in place. Everyone crouched bracing for the impending explosion. But the bomb either was on a delay or it was defective. It was hard to tell when acquiring items from the Black Market, Forsum thought. Everything was silent, he stood up to get a better look. The bomb was in place and the arms were extended, it should have blown after the arms dug into the wall. Piece of crap, Forsum thought. Then he realized the seriousness of the situation. If the bomb did not blow, how would that affect Abel's assault? As Forsum was contemplating what to do next, fire shot through his right arm. He looked down to see blood coming from his bicep, the bullet had passed through cleanly. He knew the next bullet would be on the mark, but he was frozen in place. Isnor sensed Forsum was too stunned to react, running over he tackled Forsum to the ground as the second bullet whizzed past.

"Get down!"

The guards had repopulated the tower and were returning fire from the cover of the Facility walls. Dazshal's men were exposed and were having trouble getting a clean shot on the alerted guards. Forsum was not the only one injured. Several people were hit and not faring as well. Forsum laid on his back in pain as Isnor attempted to bandage his arm while not being shot.

"Get low and keep firing!" Dazshal instructed. "I need someone to fire on that bomb. Maybe that will set it off."

A young marksman from one of the cities volunteered for the task. "I think I can hit it."

She slid forward to get a better shot. The other sharpshooters tried to cover her as the bullets from the towers began to fall without ceasing. The young woman aimed her weapon and then her body went limp. She was sniped by one of the guards in the tower before she could show if she had the skills. The situation was beginning to turn dire.

"We can't hold much longer. This mission may be over." Isnor voiced the sentiment of the army around him.

Dazshal had no intention of standing down. "We have to hold and we have to detonate that bomb. If we need to we'll…"

A thunderous boom erupted as the stick bomb exploded causing a massive hole in the side of the facility and destroying part of the administrative wing. The guards fell backwards in the tower and Dazshal's forces pressed the attack.

Abel felt the explosion on the other side of the complex. He could hear the commotion as guards scrambled to fortify the southern position. With the cover of night he had led his team around the facility and set up near the northwest wall between the main facility and living quarters. Keera and Tommie Gun were near him with the other seventy men and women hugging and wrapping the wall like a snake. Abel motioned to Tommie and he slung the dingy backpack onto the ground. He pulled out the small square, red bomb, with three colored buttons positioned on the left. He gently placed the device on the building. His arm jerked as the magnet gripped to the wall. After pressing the three buttons in rapid sequence he stepped back holding the small palm detonator in his hand. Tommie had insisted on carrying the bomb even though Warden had assigned a bomb specialist to the group. Abel was unsure if Tommie could get the bomb from Warden's compound to the Water Facility without incident. It was up to Abel to make the decision on who carried the device, so he put his trust in Tommie. They had to start trusting one another if they planned to live through this assault. Abel signaled for everyone to move back. He needed to wait a few more minutes before he gave the order to Tommie. The group moved around the adjacent wall and crouched down in anticipation. The Facility was on high alert, gun fire and hurried commands rang out across the interior courtyard. The battle was clearly raging on the far side of the complex. Abel tapped his nose with his index finger to signify the all alert sign. The group gripped their weapons tighter as sweat dripped from their faces, a combination of anxiety and a fear of the unknown. Abel bent down with one knee on the ground, pointed to Tommie and braced himself. The wall blew open with a roar of air, shaking the foundation as smoke and debris erupted from the new entry. Abel stood up, shouted to his team and charged through the rubble. The guards were not expecting a rear flanking attack, as they rushed to regroup and redirect towards this new threat Abel was downing the guards at a rapid pace. He was not one to normally shoot his enemies in the back, but these were not normal circumstances. Tommie followed him with guns blazing, within minutes guards were laying around the courtyard. Keera was stuck to Abel's side, firing wildly at her targets as the mix of smoke, dust and gun fire swirled around them. Abel chalked her inaccuracy up to adrenaline; he knew Keera would calm down as they progressed through to the towers. The convoy was directly in front them in the middle of the courtyard. The guards were already starting to close ranks and adjust to Abel's team as more of the rebels poured through the opening. As Abel and Keera laid down cover, Tommie was literally cutting a path to the convoy, with his gun in one hand and a machete in the other.

Abel's plan was two-fold; Tommie and a faction of the team would keep the guards occupied, while his squad composed of Keera and a few others made their way to the guard tower controlling the gate. Once the gate was open and Warden could bring his forces to bear, the battle would swing in their favor. Time was the critical factor in the plan and Abel had little of it. He used the side of the buildings to shield his small team as he ordered a secondary group to back up Tommie and secure the courtyard as best they could. Any minute reinforcements would start streaming from the barracks. He had to cross in front of the living quarters to enter the stairwell that led to the tower. He started to signal for his five person team including Keera to move out, when he noticed one of the guards had made his way to a machine gun mounted on a hummer near the entry. Abel instinctively pressed himself against the building, pushing Keera hard against the wall in the process. Tommie and a few others were able to reach the water truck for cover before the heavy machine gun began to spray the area. Four of Abel's team were killed quickly as the others dove for cover. The guard tilted the gun up and rained bullets past Abel's position into the exploded wall opening. The hail of bullets and the curved metal shield protecting the gunman, made it difficult for Abel to get a good shot. More of Abel's group were being cut down, while half the force were still outside the wall. Abel knew they had to take out the gunman fast. He shouted to Tommie. "Got to bring that guy down! Now!"

"I got it boss!" Tommie responded sarcastically. He motioned to the rebels near him at the water truck. "Cover me." Before they could turn their weapons Tommie was off, rolling past the front of the truck and surprising the guards on the other side. They were scattered and weren't expecting anyone crazy enough to leave their cover and go on the offensive. That worked to Tommie's advantage. He thrust his knife into the neck of the first crouched guard and shot the second through his helmet. Using his momentum he crashed his right elbow into the head of the next guard as his next shot ripped through the chest of another. He raked his knife across the fallen guard to make sure he was dead while still making his way to the gunner. His team was close behind picking off stragglers and sending the remaining guards ducking for cover. Tommie drove his boot into the face of the last guard as he neared the hummer with the machine gun. The guard was so focused Tommie was upon before he realized. He tried to swing the gun around to shoot Tommie, but the rogue ducked under the turret and dug the knife deep under the guard's arms. Tommie was close enough to see his eyes through the dark visor and to hear his startled scream turn to a gasp as life left him. The group moved behind him trying to find cover as guards were firing from every direction in the courtyard. Tommie kicked the dead guard from the hummer and grabbed the machine gun. He began firing wildly into the corners of the courtyard. The guards were on the defensive. Abel's squad were coming through the wall again. This was Abel's time to move.

As the battle ensued the sun began to rise over the horizon revealing Warden's army southeast of the Facility gate. He was seated in the passenger seat of the semi-truck rig, observing his carefully laid plan as it fell into place. The first blast orchestrated by Dazshal's team had lit the sky, outlining the Water Facility with yellow and red streaks. He could see the smoke billowing from the second explosion. Tommie Gun's information was accurate and crucial to execute the attack. Still, he was not one to wait or guess and hope for the best. In the event that Abel had failed to bring back Tommie, he had a man on the inside of the Facility who would have been persuaded to provide plans of the layout.

He leaned over to the driver of the motionless rig. "Prepare everyone to move on my mark. The gates will be opening soon."

"Yes Warden." The man stepped from the truck and went vehicle to vehicle telling the drivers to be ready to move forward on Warden's command.

There were eleven all terrain trucks behind Warden's carrying four to eight armed militia. That left the majority of the army on foot. The driver approached a man standing silently in front of the ground army. He relayed the message and Goll turned around slowly and looked across the faces of the large strike force. The group was an assortment of Warden's army, grizzled and ready for action. Then there were the war veterans and hunters from the neighboring villages, they had an idea of the scale of the attack they were attempting. Lastly there were the inexperienced and weapon deficient men and women who despite their ragged appearance had a determination in their eyes. They were fed up with the way things were and knew they had to fight for the change they wanted, even if the battle cost them their lives. Among the bunch, women were few but capable. Of those handful of lady warriors one stood out above the rest. She had caught Goll's attention as they traveled to the Facility on foot. It was more of a run as they struggled to keep up with the trucks and jeeps and keep the convoy in their sights. Some of the poorly conditioned could not keep up and fell behind, but the woman known as Ayilise was not one of the stragglers. She was near the front of the brigade with Goll, her short, shoulder length hair bobbing as she kept pace. Her two guns were strapped to her waist and the scabbard on her back held her sword. The hilt was old and worn, the leather was serrated and was noticeable reworked, stretched and padded until the metal handle peaked through the gaps. The blade was inexplicably clean and sharp, showing little sign of wear. It shined as she pulled it out and quickly cut a tree branch for effect. As she stood with the group her brown long sleeve shirt covered her neck, lapping over her tight, black pants which fell over her boots. Goll was intrigued by her. Though he was more curious to see how she handled herself in a fight. Tree limbs never struck back, he thought. Goll took stock of the rest of the army. He had been promoted to a leader of Warden's ground assault. He knew it was an honor to be selected as well as a chance to show his ability outside of the arena. The two combatants who fought the final battle in the circle were now leading two separate forces. It was nothing more than a test for him and Abel, he thought. Goll wore his signature red vest over his bare chest with the 'W' insignia in bright red as if it was burned into the cloth. His shotgun hung over his right arm by a flat, black strap and a long knife dangled from his waist.

Goll growled as he spoke. "Gather your gear and weapons. We're moving toward the Facility. The gates will open soon or we'll tear them down ourselves when we reach them!"

Goll turned and began to march the troops towards the gates. Some of them had shouted, some had clapped, others were confused by his speech and why he was leading them. Goll did not have time to worry about their state of mind or if they were galvanized by his words. Any minute the gates would be open. And they would need to unite quickly to be ready for what they found inside.

The group neared the Water Facility approaching from the side where all the fighting occurred. Dazshal's snipers were firing back and forth with the tower guards. The solid metal gate was shut and lay still as if it would never open again. Abel's team may have reached the internal compound, but they had not reached the gate controls in the adjacent tower. Suddenly, a shot rang past

Goll's group. One of the men crumpled to the ground before Goll could react. They were taking fire from the guard tower. Goll ordered the team to seek cover behind the trees and rocks on the edge of the sand colored road. He should have been more careful, but he assumed the guards were preoccupied with the assault occurring around the complex. His team began returning fire, but many had short range weapons that would have little chance of hitting their targets. He ordered the useless firing to cease and only allowed a select few to return fire as he formulated a plan. Goll's first thought was to wait for Abel to take over the tower. As his squad was pended down he reasoned that he might be waiting for a while. Goll was behind a large tree at the edge of the dirt road leading to the Facility. He could hear the bullets zinging past him and the occasional scream when the bullet found an exposed target. As Goll assessed the situation, one of the suppliers who worked in the armory and often secured weapons from the Black Market slid beside him. Brot was akin to his name, a stout man who filled out his armor plated vest with ease. His weapon of choice was a short axe magnetically clipped to his leg and the sawn off shotgun holstered on the other side. He liked to get up close and personal in combat. Goll knew Warden valued him because of his keen knowledge of weapons and his ability to negotiate good trades.

Brot stood in front of Goll with a pair of gloves in his hands. "Goll."

The strike force leader responded. "Brot, make sure you're covered from the snipers. I need you around to execute with my plan."

"That's what I was coming to talk to you about." Brot said.

Goll did not wait for the arms dealer to finish his thoughts. "So you were thinking about using the riot shields we have to get closer to those towers."

"No, I...." Brot searched for the words to clarify what he was proposing.

"How many shields do we have?" Goll inquired, cutting off Brot before he could began.

"Roughly four or five in good condition I think." Brot answered quickly.

"That will do." The man from parts unknown said. "Get the strongest four people we have. We'll use them to form a barrier with the shields. I'll gather the best shooters among the group to bring up the rear."

"Got it." Brot slapped the gloves around in his hands and reluctantly moved towards the group. He needed to figure out where the shields were and who would carry them. Goll gathered the most accurate shooters and the two met up minutes later.

"Ok. I've got our shield carriers." Brot pointed to the small force separated from the group. "Two are from our compound, Jatke & Ueram. Two of the others are city people and they are strong with no fear in their eyes."

"Good." Goll said. "I've got the sharpshooters. I think we're ready. When I give the word we'll start firing at the tower in alternating waves to throw off the guards. It will also provide some cover so we can get into place and advance. Get ready."

Brot knew Goll wanted him to move, but he had an idea he needed to share. "Before we go…"

"Brot, we have to move now." Goll stated impatiently.

"This will be quick." The weapon specialist assured. "I know you are under pressure, but this may be of help."

Goll stared at Brot. He was more than perturbed, feeling that Brot was trying to usurp his authority. He wanted to make his thoughts plain. "If Warden relieves me of this duty, I won't forget it."

Brot answered wearily. "I know."

"Go ahead then." The ground leader intoned.

Brot pulled out the black, puffy gloves and flipped them over so Goll could see the palm and fingertips. Embedded in the cloth were small metal rectangles. At first Goll did not see the significance, then Goll put the gloves together and they stuck quickly. Brot had to force the fingers of the gloves apart. Brot answered Goll's question before he could ask. "These are rare neodymium magnets. You can see how strongly they attract to one another." He pulled a flap of cloth away from his vest to reveal the metal plate. As he swung the gloves towards the plate they instantly pulled to his vest and adhered with a clinking sound. "My breastplate is a magnet too. I think you can see what I'm getting at."

Goll looked confused. Brot began to explain as he pointed to the Water Facility. "The side of that tower is all metal. We have these magnet embedded gloves and vests. If I can get close enough I can scale the wall and personally take out those guards sniping from the tower."

Goll grabbed one of the gloves from his hands and felt the magnets. They were firmly affixed to the fabric. "Have you done anything like this before?"

"At our home, the warehouse, yes." Brot revealed. "But nothing on this scale."

"I'd hate for you to get up there and fall. And by yourself. Seems too risky." Goll looked towards the Facility and shook his head as he spoke.

"Actually I have another set of gloves and a vest. So if someone else is game..." Brot's voiced trailed off as his proposition to Goll hung in the air. Off to the side of the pair, Ayilise had been listening with interest. She hardly saw advanced technology, let alone was given the chance to experiment with such things. She piped up. "I'll try it."

The two men turned to Ayilise as she walked up. Brot grinned. "I knew I could get a volunteer."

Goll grimaced. "It's too dangerous."

Ayilise ignored Goll as she took the extra pair of gloves from Brot and fit them over her hands. They were bigger than she thought, but the gloves expanded, then tightened on her wrists. She stared at the gloves as she countered Goll's grim look with a matter of fact tone. "Die by the fall or die by a bullet. Same difference."

Brot put the vest over her. Goll was silent as he watched her being outfitted. He thought about ordering her not to go, but it was something about her aggressive demeanor that was all too familiar. As Ayilise stood looking at Goll and Brot with her hands at her side, she could feel the tug of her pistols attracting to the hand magnets.

She lifted her hands and stared at the magnets on her open palms. "Strong."

Goll acquiesced. "Then it's settled. Let's move out."

The group moved rapidly in a coordinated manner across the dirt road towards the Facility. Bullets pinged off the side and face of the riot shields. Brot and Ayilise fired off shots to try and keep the tower snipers at bay. When they were within twenty yards of the wall, the pair broke free from the moving shields and ran full speed to their destination. Within a foot of the metallic structure their vest pulled them tightly face first onto the structure. Brot braced his body meeting the impact with his head up. Ayilise was thrown off by the sudden pull and met the wall with the thump of her head.

She looked over at Brot. "Thanks for the warning."

"Sorry about that. The warehouse attraction isn't as strong." Brot said stoically.

Ayilise stared up at the seventy foot high tower. "You sure this is going to work?"

"I sure hope so." Brot did not look at Ayilise as he answered. He dug the tips of his fingers into the top of the metal panels lining the wall and pulled himself up. The magnet in his chest adhered comfortably to the structure. He was nearly a full story up before Ayilise began to follow. Now that she was at the base of the building the bravado she displayed early had gone from her. As she dug in the metal panel seam with the magnetic gloves she could only think, how did I get myself into this? She already knew the answer, she was constantly trying to prove herself, show her skills and show her lack of fear. It had helped her as she had grown to adulthood in these savage lands. Her grandmother had migrated here from China before the Collective came to power. She was a well-known sculptress among the artisans in the House of Vancrew. Ayilise, unlike her mother, exhibited none of her family's elegance with stone. She kept close to her father, a transplant from the Australian outback, who taught her how to shoot. Those lessons at their makeshift firing range came in handy at times like these. This was not the first time a desire to prove her worth had thrust her unnecessarily into a life and death situation. She pulled herself up feeling the weight shift to the front of her vest.

Brot was moving smoothly along the wall using the grooved panels to pull him along notching his boots into the panels below him. He looked down to his left side to see Ayilise a few feet below him. She was not making her way as smoothly, but climbing nonetheless. Brot was nearing the opening to the tower when a bullet pinged off the wall next to him. Another shot rang out bouncing off the back of his armored vest. He was under attack, but from where? He turned his head to the right and he could see the glint of the rifle scope from the tower on the other side of the gate. They apparently had spotted him. He slid to his left closer to Ayilise as he tried to give them a less visible target. The guards continued to fire making it hard for them to continue their ascent. Brot had his shotgun and axe, but both weapons were useless at this range. Even the small stick of dynamite he kept tucked in the side of his boot was of little use. He shouted at Ayilise trying to get her attention, but she was too focused on gripping the next panel. He decided his only way to get out of harm's way was to keep going up. Without warning the gunfire ceased on his position. He looked over again to see a man screaming as he fell from the tower, splattering against the ground below. His vision was obscured as he tried to look into the tower to see what occurred. Maybe the interior forces had reached the tower, he thought. Whatever had occurred, he and Ayilise needed to move quickly. Brot pulled himself along the wall with renewed vigor. He rested below the opening to the tower. He could see the rifle of the guards above him. The first guard would stick his rifle out and shoot until they exhausted their ammunition. Then the second guard would take his place firing upon Goll's position. Brot inched himself closer and tensed as he held himself in place with his right arm. The rifle fired its last round then retreated into the room. The next rifle peered over the wall. Before the rifle could fire a shot, Brot yanked the end of the barrel, sending the weapon and the gunman nose diving to the ground. The guard was too shocked to scream, impacting the ground with a thud. The second guard approached the window with the end of his gun facing down coming face to face with Brot. The man's eyes narrowed as he prepared for the kill, then they expanded and his eyes glazed over as Ayilise thrown dagger sunk into the side of his neck. He dropped the weapon instinctively grabbing at the handle of the knife. He gurgled blood and his eyes rolled to the back of his head as he fell to his death.

"Good shot." Brot yelled.

Ayilise repositioned herself. "Thanks."

Brot and Ayilise climbed through the opening unaware of the last soldier in the corner of the room. He charged Brot with his sword, flailing wildly at the mercenary. The blade missed wide and Brot slammed his fist into the man's face. As he stumbled back,

Brot pressed the attack putting his left arm behind the man's neck and right hand in front. As his right forearm pushed forward, he heard the bone crunch as the guard's neck snapped. His head rolled around his shoulders as his body went limp. They looked at each other and breathed a sigh of relief. Brot looked out of the tower opening. "I wouldn't want to do that again."

"Why not?" Ayilise asked as she searched the room in case there was another surprise. "I had a blast."

Brot was not sure if she was being sarcastic or not. "You're a real adrenaline junkie, huh?"

"You don't know the half." She said throwing Brot a sideways glance.

They surveyed the room to make sure there were no more surprises. Brot closed the cloth flap on his vest concealing the magnet. He pulled the comm device from his waist. "Goll. We're in the tower."

"I know I saw the whole thing from here. I guess those suits worked after all." Goll said dryly.

"Yeah. Who would have guessed?" Brot said trying to hide his excitement. "I think Lady Luck was on our side."

Goll could sense the triumph in Brot's voice, but was averse to giving him the satisfaction. "That's one way to put it."

"What do you want us to do now?" The arms dealer asked.

"Clear the area, figure out a way to get that gate open, then wait for my orders. Goll out."

Brot looked at Ayilise as he placed the comm back in his belt.

"He's a gem." She said with a smirk.

"You don't know the half." Brot said. They shared a laugh as they searched the room for some way to open the gate.

CHAPTER 17
ADVANCED TECHNOLOGY

While Tommie had the guards occupied, Abel decided this was his chance to make a break for the tower entry. He looked back at Keera and grabbed three others from the ranks behind them, while instructing the remaining fighters to provide cover. They needed to make their way past the guard barracks to the left side of them. There were two openings into the building, one near them and the other at the far end. As he passed the first entry, Abel shot blindly into the open space in hopes of dissuading Distor's armed guards from advancing on their position. He motioned for Keera and the team following him to do the same as they moved along the metal wall. On the opposite side of them Tommie was continuing to spray the courtyard forces with his new found weapon. Abel neared the other end of the barracks and he could see a guard emerging with his gun raised towards Tommie's position. Abel waited for the foe to lock in on Tommie before he fired sending the guard crumpling to the ground. The second adversary pushed forward swinging his machine gun in the direction of Abel letting off a few rounds. Abel ducked the ensuing barrage, but one of his team members reacted too slowly taking the hot lead squarely in the chest. Shooting from his crouched position, Abel cracked the helmet of the guard sending him falling backwards to the ground. Abel quickly rushed the opening pulling a small grenade from his vest. He stripped the pin and flung the grenade against the interior wall. It bounced into the room and exploded. The guards inside yelled out as the shrapnel shredded their bodies. Abel capitalized on the confusion by shooting into the room as he walked past. Keera and the others followed suit. They were past their first obstacle and facing the door leading upward to the tower. Abel laid his weight against the heavy door as he turned the knob slowly. The hinges of the door groaned as he pushed it open revealing a small hallway leading to a dark stairway that led straight up. The stairs were lined with small, square yellow lights inset in the wall. Abel crept quietly up the stairs with his gun intently focused on the darkness above. He was not sure what he would find at the landing, but he knew whatever it was his tiny band had to complete their task; clear the area, reach the guard tower and get the gate open. Nearing the top of the stairs, Abel could hear voices echoing from the hall above. Abel peered into the hallway where he could see three guards standing in front of a door.

The Captain was barking orders at the other two. "No one gets through these doors. We need to hold the gate until reinforcements arrive from the city. Is that clear?"

"Yes sir!" The man and woman answered in unison. The ranking officer turned and walked through the door into the guard tower. He could hear the guards inside the tower firing their weapons on Warden's forces beyond the wall. Abel leaned his head against the wall. He knew a direct assault would alert them to his presence and they would barricade access to the tower. They only had one shot at getting through. His thoughts were interrupted by the hushed whispers of one of the men with him. His name was Shashak and he had served with Warden for a few years now. "How many are there?"

"Two on the outside." Abel responded. "Maybe three to four more in the tower."

"What are we waiting on? We can take those guards easily." Shashak stated boldly.

Keera chimed into the conversation. "We kill those guards, they lock down the tower, mission over."

Shashak dismissed Keera's comments. He had never taken strategies of war from a woman and he was not about to start now. "We have another bomb. We can blow the door."

Abel and Keera looked at one another astounded by the ignorance of Shashak. Abel explained why his plan was flawed. "If we blow the door we risk damaging the controls. If we damage the controls how do you suggest we get that two ton gate to slide open?"

Shashak looked back as he tried to reason out his approach in his mind. It was obvious he had not thought his plan out thoroughly. Abel turned back to Keera. "We need to figure out a way to get down the hall quietly and get past the guards without alerting those within the tower."

"I've got an idea." Keera said.

Abel shrugged. "Good, because I'm all out."

Keera reached out her weapon to Rheem, the other man from Warden's compound that joined them. He took the weapon unsure what Keera was planning next. A puzzled look crossed Abel's face as Keera removed the belt from her waist with the gun holster and dagger hanging from it. She handed the items to Rheem and he placed them over his shoulder. "I'm going to walk up to guards unarmed, act like I am lost and was ushered into this area. With any luck the two of you can shoot the guards as they start to let me into the secure area."

Abel stared at Shashak then back at Keera. "That's the best plan we've got?"

"Not unless you have another idea?" Keera said as she ruffled her fingers through her hair trying to present a more haggard appearance. "But time is running out."

Abel had exhausted his ideas and she was right, they had to get in the tower soon. "Okay. Let's go with it."

Keera brushed both hands through her hair and breathed out slowly she began to step into the hallway when they heard the door to the tower come open and the guards inside clamoring about.

The Captain stepped forth. "You two get in here. We need more firepower. These filthy rebels are scaling the building somehow." His voice was tinged with anger, disgust and disbelief. The guards rushed into the room.

Keera grabbed the gun back from Rheem and strapped the belt around her waist. She was a few yards behind the exterior guards as they entered the tower. Two men were positioned inside shooting out towards the trees where Goll's forces were located. The Captain pointed to the rifles on the wall then out to the tower across the breadth of the gate. Keera could not make out what they said, but she could tell their movements were urgent. She knew they would not be occupied long. As she continued her cautious approach she could hear one of the guards as he grabbed the rifle and took aim across to the next tower. "I see him. I got him. Watch this."

Suddenly his head jerked forward as his helmet exploded from the gunshot. Keera's aim was true. The bodies of the remaining two guards went limp as the barrels of Abel and Rheem's guns spat fire. Shashak rushed past them pushing one of the gunmen out the tower. The Captain was stunned by the efficiency of the attack. All his men were dead before he had time to unsheathe his blade. He lunged at Shashak and the blade cut deep contacting the armor plate beneath his vest with a spark. Shashak fell back and regained his balance for the next attack. The Captain slashed downward violently hoping to end the fray quickly and turn his attention to the approaching foes. To the Captain's surprise Shashak sidestepped the blow as the sword scratched a deep groove into the face of the control panel. Shashak caught the wrist of the Captain's sword hand as he head-butted him in the face. The Captain's nose broke with a crunching sound. Shashak used his right arm to hook the Captain under the shoulder, and then drove the man's own blade into his chest.

The Captain met the mercenary's eyes with cold defiance. "You'll die like a dog under Xonox's boot."

"Not today." Shashak pushed the sword in deeper as the life slipped from the man. He pulled the sword out and his soulless body fell to the floor.

Abel reached Shashak as he dropped the blade on the ground. "Anyone alive?"

Shashak eyes scrolled around the room. "Not anymore."

"We should have kept one of them alive. Now how are we going to get this gate open?" Abel wondered, clearly perturbed by Shashak's tone.

"Warden said no prisoners." Shashak reminded Abel. "We're already outnumbered three to one. We can't take a chance leaving anyone breathing."

"Then I'll leave you the task of opening the gate." Abel said as he touched one of the dead guards searching for a pulse.

Before Shashak could retort, Keera stepped between the pair. "I scanned the controls and I think I know how it works."

"How?" Abel was surprised she had figured out the multitude of levers in such a short time.

Keera pointed to a lever protruding from the control panel. It was wide as her palm. Above the handle, etched into the panel was the word 'close'. She ran her finger downward to the point where the grooves stopped and could see the word 'open'.

"Well. It's a bit complex, but I think if we move this lever down the gate will open."

They all shared a chuckle at the simplicity of operating equipment in a technologically advanced building. Keera grabbed the lever and pulled down. The lever did not move. Maybe it was stuck, she thought. She pulled down harder, and then used both hands with all her might. Nothing. Shashak moved forward and gripped the handle with his large hand. He fared no better than Keera.

Abel grimaced. "So much for simplicity."

"Try this." Rheem was knelt over the fallen Captain. He held a small cylindrical, metal piece in his hand. It was notched and grooved.

"What is it?" Abel asked.

Keera turned to see the small, metal shape in Rheem's hand. "It looks like some kind of key."

"That's what I was thinking." Rheem walked over to Abel and handed him the key.

"Where does it go?" Abel questioned. The group looked at the control panel and around the room, looking for an opening that would receive the key. They had looked for a few minutes with no luck. "It's four of us in here. We need to spread out and figure this out."

They each took a wall working their eyes and fingers around the surface looking for a hidden door.

"I found it." Keera exclaimed.

She was standing over the lever again and reaching back for the key. Abel handed it to her. She bent down to get a closer look as she slid the key into the right side of the lever arm. The key locked in. She could feel the energy pulsing from the handle. She gripped the handle with her left hand using her thumb to push the key in further. The lever began to move down towards the 'open' sign. As soon as the lever stopped, the gate groaned and began to slide open.

Shashak took out a small comm device from his pants. "I'll contact Warden and let him know." He spoke gruffly into the microphone. "Warden, this is Shashak. We're in."

The words were scarcely from Shashak's lips before Warden's caravan of trucks were spotted speeding towards the entry to the Water Facility. The vehicles turned sideways to form a barricade in front of the gate. Warden's rig was off to the left side facing the steel complex. Goll's forces began to make their way from the brush no longer in danger of being fired upon by the snipers. Warden smiled to himself. Everything was going as planned.

In the courtyard, Tommie Gun had pushed the majority of Distor's forces back to the main building where the water was converted and packaged. The guards in the barracks were pinned down and now Goll's squad was starting to enter the courtyard to help secure the area. Without warning the water truck Tommie's team used for cover roared to life. All around the vehicle were surprised. Apparently there were guards in the truck and they had decided the odds were not in their favor. The engine revved and the truck rocked as it was thrown into reverse. Tommie only had seconds to jump from the Hummer before the water truck slammed into the vehicle sending it flipping over and sliding into the wall. The water truck continued, not concerned with the makeshift barricade Warden had created outside the gate. The rebels scrambled out of the way at the approach of the trailer. The driver angled the rig to split the two trucks blocking the escape route. The jerking of the wheel combined with speed of the impact lifted the right wheels of the trailer and cab off the ground. Turning the wheel to the right, the driver tried to compensate for the imbalance, but it was too late. The truck smashed into the dirt creating a deep impression as it careened to a stop at the edge of the woods almost killing some of Goll's army. A crackling flame emitted from the cab. The guards in the cab did not scramble from the internal fire; they were already dead from the impact. Warden's people cheered at the sight. They poured into the compound linking their forces. Distor's guards were being depleted at a rapid rate. They fell back to the main building attempting to regroup, protect the water generation and their leader.

Abel was in the tower looking at the wreckage of the truck and chaos that ensued in the courtyard. He reached out his hand for Shashak's comm device to contact Warden. "This is Abel."

"Great job Abel." Warden intoned. "We've got the outside secure and we still need to secure the interior. From what I understand there is still a good portion of their forces in the barracks and Distor is in the main building. I'm sending in Goll with half our army to help Tommie Gun hold their position. I need you to get to Distor before he can notify Xonox, if he hasn't already. I'll keep the remaining forces out here in case we have company."

"I'm on it Warden." Abel handed the comm back to Shashak as he spoke to the group. "We need to gather a small, formidable group and make our way to the main Facility. We need to find Distor. I know we can't go through the front door so we need to find another way in."

"From what I remember from the plans, there is another way in." Keera pointed across the courtyard to the main building. "We can make our way through one of the towers into a side entry. It should bring us to the floor where Distor has his office.

"Good." Abel said. "Let's move. We've got to get to him before Xonox gets to us."

CHAPTER 18
DISTOR

Distor cut the formalities with the Captain of Xonox's convoy and retreated to the main building as soon as he heard the first explosion. He always followed the Collective Water Distribution Protocol to the letter. This attention to detail had allowed for his rapid ascension. He recited Article 11 section 5 in his head; in the event of imminent threat against water generation, fall back to the place of distribution, fortify your position and immediately notify your superior to provide reinforcement. The next chain in the command led him to Xonox. He sent four to five snipers to each tower so they would have a good view of their attackers; he rounded up his personal guard and fell back to the main building with a small army. The soldiers in the barracks would start to push from their position, assess the situation and swarm the courtyard soon. His primary concern was water generation and getting word to Xonox.

From his office he had just ended communication with Xonox. The First of the House of Vancrew did not seem surprised the Facility was under siege. The casual nature of how Xonox responded to the full-scale attack had caught Distor off guard. Xonox told Distor to hold the area, keep the gate closed and assured him reinforcements were forthcoming. The fact that reinforcements were already on the way told Distor that Xonox had anticipated a rebel attack. Somehow he was always a step ahead of everyone else, Distor thought. But why was he not notified of the impending offensive? He would have been at the ready instead of getting ready. As another explosion shook the building, Distor turned to his monitor and he could see the courtyard being overrun with ruffians from the surrounding villages. One of the gates was already open. The water truck lay smashed and burning on the outside of the building. The situation was dire, but Distor was confident he could hold the Facility until Xonox's forces arrived. He had every entry and exit covered. His guards in the courtyard did not stand a chance against the rebel marauders, but he could not trouble himself with their lost lives.   There were more important things to consider. The water production had to be sustained for the Xonox family, for the House of Vancrew, if he had any hopes of advancing into the Xonox home. He had to hold, he thought.

Distor leaned over from his desk requesting a status report from his second in command, Lucrid Hergof, even though it was evident on the monitors around the room the rebels had taken a large part of the Facility. "Status, Hergof."

"Sir, we have currently lost approximately one-hundred and thirty two of our people in the courtyard and towers. The rebels are continuing to press their attack on the barracks. We have one hundred and seventy-three guards in the barracks, but they are pinned down and struggling to fight their way out. There are another one-hundred and twenty people in the administrative area. Some are armed, many are not." Hergof reported, pausing slightly for questions from the Facility commander. "We're communicating with officers in the wing and telling them to brace themselves for the impending battle. There are well over a hundred armed fighters in this Facility, including your personal guard, not counting the technicians keeping the water process flowing."

"And how is the water generation?" Distor asked, bored with his second's assessment of the guards.

"It's unfazed." Hergof stated. "We're still at one-hundred percent capacity. As long as we keep this building free of those vermin, the generation will continue. Unfortunately, as you see on the monitors, the water truck has been…incapacitated."

"Yes, I can see that." Distor said, the distaste dripping from his voice.

"Yes sir." Hergof responded as he awaited further orders.

"Alright, keep me informed on any changes. I want an

update ever five minutes. We have to stay on top of this situation or it can easily spiral out of my control."

"I'll station twenty of your personal guards outside this entry and down the adjacent corridors." Hergof promised.

Distor waved his hand dismissively. "Thank you. That will be all."

Hergof nodded his head and exited the room. No sooner did the door slide behind him, Distor heard the echo of gunfire in the halls. The rebels had breached the complex and were undoubtedly heading towards his office. He thought about what Xonox said on their call, suspecting that the well organized and coordinated attack was due to the rebels having a precise layout.

Distor pressed his comm link. "Hergof, status report. Hergof, status!"

The comm link crackled with silence. Distor closed communications and stood from his desk. He brushed the lint from the bill of his visor before placing it on his head. Sometimes you have to handle matters personally, he thought. He pressed a button on his desk and the side door slide open revealing the small pistol, still shining from the fresh morning polish. Snapping out the barrel, he placed the six armor piercing bullets into the revolver. He holstered the weapon on his right hip. He lifted the top of the drawer and pulled a semi-automatic handgun from a case and notched the holster onto his belt. Walking towards the wall, he ran his eyes over the handle of the cutlass sheathed in a scabbard hanging from a hook. He grabbed the metal handle padded with leather and protected by the soup ladle style shell guard. The polished brass basket hand protector was shined to mirror perfection. He admired the gold threads stitched through the leather handle as he fixed the sword to his hip. The reflective surface on the wall shot back a dashing figure. He squared his shoulders and passed through the door into the hall. As he turned the corner he could see the bodies of his guards and the rebels strewn about the area. Further down the corridor, he could see the factions of each force diving in and out of the door depression for cover as they advanced on his position. He raised the semi-automatic weapon in his left hand and fired two shots downing the two rebels he targeted. He started to move towards the enemy's position, firing shots and attempting to turn back the small band.

As he walked past one of the doorways, the door suddenly burst open and two of the rebels lunged at him. Distor pulled the cutlass from his side and slashed across the man's chest and face. The aggressor looked shocked as the crimson streak burned across his body. His eyes rolled to the back of his head and he fell to the ground. Distor had his weapon trained on the second rebel, but he hesitated to pull the trigger. He replaced the sword in his sheath. Keera dropped her weapon as she stared back at the Facility commander.

A look of delighted surprise crossed Distor's face. "I know you…Your father worked here once." As Distor spoke he began to unclip his revolver with his right hand.

"You have no right to talk about my father." Keera said in a surly tone, arms raised above her head.

"No right." Distor laughed at her insolence. "Do not fool yourself. What, do you think this raid is going to shift the balance of power? You think Xonox will stop being the head of the House of Vancrew? You think the other Houses will lose anything from this little attack? The Water Facility is still at full power. This has been nothing more than an annoyance. It has done nothing. It's changed nothing. In a few minutes Xonox's reinforcements will arrive and all your friends will be killed. And the ones that aren't killed initially will be questioned, tortured, and then killed. That's what happens when a rat attacks a bear. It's eaten." Distor spoke the last sentence through his clinched teeth with disdain.

Keera was not intimidated. "Not before the bear is bit in his ass." Her eyes looked menacingly at the commander.

Distor lowered his left hand as he brought the execution pistol up to Keera's face. "This will be a pleasure. I'm just glad you're standing. I would hate for you to die on your knees, begging and pleading like your father."

Keera stared at the man with defiance. She could not stop the tears from welling in her eyes. "No matter what you say, you'll never be the man he was."

"Thank the gods." Distor spat back. Flexing his finger to pull the trigger, Distor heard a voice behind him.

"Hey you." Distor turned in time to feel Abel's blow land on the side of his face. He collapsed back into the corner of the doorway. Keera stumbled past Distor as Abel grabbed her.

"Are you okay?" He said.

"I'm fine now." Keera said as she composed herself.

Abel slide Keera behind him as he held the gun in his hand looking down at Distor. The Facility leader's gun was lying next to him, but not close enough to do him any good. Distor took the palm of his hand and wiped the blood from the corner of his mouth as he gathered himself. He stood to his feet, his eyes fixed on Abel. "That's the best you've got. No wonder all you scum are all dying of dehydration."

"But somehow here I stand." Abel said pointing his gun at the commander.

"Well everyone has a lapsed moment. You can't blame me for that." Distor raised his hands.

Abel's eyes were cold as ice as he stared at Distor. "You don't remember me do you?"

"I don't remember the name of the man who shines my shoes on a daily basis." Distor responded. "So why would I remember the name of a vagrant."

"Well, I'll help jog your memory." Abel kept the weapon trained on Distor as he recounted his journey. "My name is Abel. You landed in Gravope weeks ago. You killed my father for violating the Water Protocol and left my mother for dead, all under Xonox's orders. My path to Xonox has led me to you. Isn't it strange how quickly things change?"

Distor was unmoved. "What's changed? I'm still the commander of this Facility. And you're still nothing. You and your girlfriend."

"You know." Abel began as his hand tightened on the handle of the gun. "I thought you were going to beg for mercy, but I'm glad you didn't."

"So what now? Are you going to shoot me? That's fine as long as you know you won't make it out of this place alive." Distor threatened.

Abel holstered his weapon. "No. I'm not going to shoot you. That would be too easy."

Keera was shocked. "Abel what are you doing. Just shoot him."

"No. He embarrassed and killed both of our fathers. I want to give him a taste of how it feels to be on the other end." Abel walked towards Distor. The commander began to lower his hands and his head cringed as if he were cowering before them. Abel thought he was submitting to try and soften the punishment. When Abel was in range, Distor whispered under his breath. "You really are ignorant."

Distor charged Abel and slammed him into the wall on the other side of the room. Abel was stunned by the man's speed and aggressiveness. He had not expected Distor to fight back at all. Pain shot up Abel's spine as the corner of the wall dug into his back. He was able to gain his composure and hook Distor under his arms, slinging him into the adjacent door. Distor regained his balance quicker than Abel expected. The commander punched him in the ribs. Abel groaned as another blow landed on the opposite side of his body. Distor stepped forward to land another shot. Abel blocked and slammed his fist into the side of the Facility leader's face. Distor fell back and Abel pressed the attack. He rushed in using his forearm under Distor's neck to bar him against the wall. The commander struggled free turning Abel to the wall and punching him in the kidney. The arena champion spun around and swung wide and slow, missing his mark. Distor did not, as the uppercut connected with Abel's chin sending him to the ground.

Keera shouted from behind. "No! Abel!"

Distor twisted and struck Keera in the face with the edge of his elbow. She flew across the room and slumped against the door. Blood dripped from her nose onto her shirt as she lay unconscious. Distor looked down at Abel watching his opponent struggle to regain his senses. He slid the cutlass slowly from his scabbard and held it at waist level.

"I know what you're thinking." Distor smiled as he spoke. "You underestimated me and you should not have. People have done it my whole life and I've used it to my advantage. It's one of the reasons I've risen through the ranks so rapidly. It's my discipline, it's my training. It's the reason the good of the Collective will always overcome the evil of you rabble-rousers."

Lifting the cutlass high above his head, Distor prepared to end this battle with one strike. Abel was clearly in no position to protest. Distor held the blade above his head. "Well. This is a first. You're not going to beg? Your kind normally does."

"Never." Abel declared.

Distor flexed his arm and gritted his teeth. His cutlass swung forward and simultaneously Abel kicked his right knee throwing him off balance. Distor fell into the doorway, as Abel rose to his feet. He wiped the sweat from his face with the back of his arm, watching the sword in his opponent's hand. The commander held the sword out with two hands, creating a barrier between him and Abel. Distor thought about reaching for his gun, but he knew there was no time. He would have to put the boy down with his sword. As he looked at the cold lenses of Abel's eyes shooting daggers at him, he thought it may be easier said than done. Distor steadied himself and lunged at Abel, swiping the sword across his body. The man from Gravope contorted his torso as he jumped back, the tip of the blade dangerously close to cutting him in half. Abel sprung forward catching Distor and smashing his head into the wall. The commander flailed almost injuring Abel with the blade. He wrestled the sword from Distor and punched him in the throat. The commander clutched his neck as his breathing became labored. Abel knew he had him now. He moved in for the kill when suddenly Distor pulled out the semi-automatic handgun and shot twice. Abel rolled away instinctively. He was sure the next shot would find him. Distor trained the gun on him, but he never pulled the trigger as his body lurched involuntarily and he dropped the weapon, it clanged against the floor. The man who's every action centered around ascension to the House of Vancrew, looked down at the red circle growing large on his chest. His arms slackened, confusion spread across his face. It was almost as if he was asking, how did this happen? His body stiffened like a wooden board and he fell back flat with a thud. Keera held the revolver in her hand. She had used the same pistol to end the executioner's life that he had used to extinguish the lives of countless others. Abel slowly stood up and made his way across the room holding the of his head. "Thanks. I owe you one."

Keera dabbed the fluids from her face with her forearm sleeve. "I think that makes us even now."

"Fair enough." Abel reached out his hand to help her up.

"I think...I think I'll stay here for a second." She said

"I understand." Abel could hear Warden's people clearing the corridor, so he knew they were safe for the moment. He took out the comm device and patched in to Warden. "Warden. Distor's dead. We're clearing some of the guards now. Send reinforcements when you can. We'll work from the top of the facility to the bottom. You do the reverse."

"I'm sending more of Goll's team now." Warden replied. "Tommie and Goll are still clearing the courtyard."

"Good. We're almost there…" Abel was cut off in the middle of his sentence.

"Not now…" Warden remarked. His voice trailed off.

"Warden? Warden what is it?"

Before Warden could respond, Abel could hear the muzzled roar of the motorcycle engines through the comm growing louder as they approached. Abel knew the sound all too well, bike gangs. And there was a large number if the sound was any indication. The last thing Abel heard was Warden shouting commands as the comm went silent.

CHAPTER 19
INNER CIRCLE

The Scorpions were closing fast, a huge cloud of dust rose behind them. It was a band of raiders, thieves and murderers converging on the Facility. They were spread out across the expanse of the dirt road numbering in the hundreds, with Warden's forces square in their sights. Warden barked orders to his stalwart group as he fell behind the barricade of the vehicles preparing for the impending barrage. On his right side, Goll's warriors were streaming from the woods, but now at a faster pace. One voiced boomed over the wail of the engines.

The leader of the gang rode in the center of the group and screamed one last order. "Kill everything that moves."

No sooner had Reaper spoke his murderous words the gang yelled their moniker in maniacal unison. "Scorpions!"

Reaper stopped short, almost one hundred yards off the Facility entry. He stayed back with twenty-five ruffians and a large, red truck behind him. The former ice cream truck was painted a deep red, with a black scorpion across each door. One claw of the scorpion was open, the other claw was closed. The rest of the bikers closed in and separated into two lines, each motorcycle wheel inches from the rider in front and behind them. The lead gang member fired his weapon on Warden's position, the bullets from the Uzi clanked off the side of the trucks in rapid succession. The bikes looped in an arching U-turn as the next biker fired on their position and so on down the line. Shooting indiscriminately from the choreographed two looping ovals, the gang was causing significant damage to Warden's opposing force.

Members of Goll's group were struck down as they attempted to reach the barrier between the gang and the building. Others dove for cover and poked their heads from behind their respective shields to get a good shot on the gang. As Warden's sharpshooters in the tower began to return fire on the miscreants, bikes began to slide out of formation and off into the forest as the rider lost control. The wheel of one of the metal horses was shot out and the bike crashed into the jeep on Warden's right flank. Twisted metal entangled the biker as the woman's mangled form draped over the front of the wheel. Still holding the handlebar in one hand, the gang member pulled the pin of a grenade with the other. The vehicle exploded, flipping back towards the Water Facility walls, killing the usurpers inside and around it. Some of the bikers began dismounting and charging the Facility with hands gripping their knives and hoisting their guns in the air, screaming like wild dogs, the scarves covering their faces only revealing the madness of their red eyes. The gangs attacked with a ferocity that quickly started to overcome the untrained townspeople in Warden's army. Warden's inner circle was holding strong, but the objective of the battle had turned. They had gone from flanking and securing the Facility to countering the outside attack, while suppressing the forces within. Goll was in the middle of the battle, using one end of his shotgun to end biker's lives and the other end to severely injure them. He also used his gloved leather hands to crush in the face of one biker and the throat of another. Luchi was also faring well, with his spiked mace in one hand and pistol in the other. He was a whirlwind of death, sweeping the leg of one Scorpion, crashing the mace across the chest of another and finishing the fallen biker with his pistol. Even with the skills of Warden's inner circle on display, the Scorpions were steadily advancing. Worse yet, Warden's forces were being overwhelmed and were falling all about him. He could see a few of the villagers, who swore to look fear in the eye this day, scrambling into the woods to escape the carnage. Warden finally pulled his gun shooting a Scorpion closing in on his position. He fired again sending another rogue to his grave. Warden smashed his fist into the side of another biker's face, and then took out his comm device. Taking a breath, as he surveyed the battle around him, Warden radioed to Dazshal to start advancing down from the ridge to give them more cover. The snipers were doing their best, but there were too many of the gang members to be effective. His platoon was being beaten back. He had to get to the Scorpions' leader and even the battle out. Warden stepped back and adjusted the belt around his waist. The brown thick leather strap ran to a buckle, and then branched up to a taut harness that ran across his body up to his left shoulder. In the middle of the strap was a rectangular, metallic fastener. Upon first glance there was nothing out of the ordinary about the clip. But upon further inspection, those with knowledge of war and weaponry knew exactly what Warden possessed and why he used it sparingly. He pressed on the circular impression in the center of the fastener, and then moved his hand away. He could feel the surge of energy and the crackle of blue sparks began to expand from the circle until they formed a curved barrier in front of him. As if on cue a bullet deflected off the energy field. Warden pulled out his sword with his other hand, jumped onto the front wheel of the truck in front of him and propelled himself over the vehicle into the fray. He landed in the middle of three bikers. The first attacker's bullet ricocheted off his shield. Warden wasted no time, shooting him between the eyes, thrusting his sword into the second and spinning around to slam his elbow into the third. He finished him off with a single shot. No sooner had the shot repeated when a hulking gang member yelled a war cry as he drove a sledgehammer down towards him. Warden blocked the attack with his sword and brought the gun up to the man's bare chest. As his skin exploded red, Warden ducked as a bat swung over his head. Rolling on his back he kicked his feet out to catch the biker in the chest. He landed on her and stabbed the sword down once, while firing on two more gang members in succession. He ran towards four more bikers, with no fear of their weapons. He plowed his knees into the men's faces hearing the bones crack on impact. Before he hit the ground he shot another biker and beheaded the other. Warden began to clear a path to the leader. Bullets and knives were being repelled by the shield. When the gang members realized there was an invisible force protecting Warden, they were gurgling blood from his blow. In a matter of minutes, Warden had used his speed, weapons, knees and elbows to send twenty bikers sprawling across the dirt. His gun had run out of ammunition and he had no time to reload. Using the butt of the gun, he slammed the weapon into the face of the stream of aggressors. He plunged the sword through another's body. The man held the blade taut, causing Warden to loosen his grip. He spun around, crashing the palm of his left hand into a biker's face, crushing the larynx of another with his right hand. He smashed his elbow against a biker's chest and punched another to the ground. One biker shouted his outrage in the calamity and rushed Warden barehanded hoping to grab him in a bear hug. Warden flipped backwards, landed on his feet and with blinding speed killed two more bikers. The large biker rushed again, but Warden was too quick, avoiding his grasp and still maiming gang members. Finally Warden tired of the game. The man rushed him again, but instead of retreating, he shot forward using the top of his head as a weapon. The biker fell back with his face a red cloud of gore. He was dead before he hit the ground. All of a sudden, as the tide of the battle was turning in the rebel's favor, two metallic disks landed near two of the remaining trucks forming the barricade. The vehicles erupted in flames killing the Warden's soldiers and the Scorpions alike. A man stepped from the brush with his long trench coat, metal plated breastplate and colored goggles. The Mountie began firing rounds at his targets and Warden's people were dying quicker than they were before. Warden shifted his body as he retrieved his sword to down another biker and began to make his way to the mercenary. Another of his followers fell near him as the bullets pierced the 'W' stitched onto his vest. Before Warden could clear the distance, yet another rebel met a similar fate. The Mountie was squeezing the trigger faster than rebel leader's legs would move.

From the ridge a figure charged The Mountie firing wildly at his blindside. The bullets pinged off the killer's solid armor. Dazshal bore down on his opponent, hoping to distract him long enough to allow Warden to get to the mercenary. The Mountie spun, dropped to one knee and shot Dazshal in the right leg and arm. Carried on by adrenaline, Dazshal continued his attack raising his knife high above his head to deal the finishing blow. The Mountie twisted, caught the man's wrist with his forearm, pulled a knife from his coat and sunk the blade under the armored chest of Dazshal. Surprise quickly flashed across Dazshal's face. He knew of the The Mountie's quickness and accuracy, but he never would have thought the man could block his fiercest blow.

Another of Warden's inner circle slumped to the ground as death gripped his cold body.

Warden finally cleared the group as he made his way toward the mercenary, bullets rapidly pinging off his shield. He was a few yards away from The Mountie when the disk dropped at his feet. He braced for the impact as he was thrown backwards into the crowd of fighters, sliding along the ground until his momentum was stopped by the side of the building. The shield crackled and fizzled away, damaged beyond repair, but not before it saved his life. Warden slowly gained his senses, he reloaded his gun and raised it in the direction of The Mountie. He scanned the area, but there was no sign of his attacker, he had disappeared as abruptly as he emerged. His brief involvement had urged the bikers on, as they fought with renewed vigor.

Luchi had continued on to Reaper. The gang leader stood broad-chested holding a short bat in his hand waiting on a worthy opponent. Luchi emerged from the fighting and kicked Reaper across the face. The Scorpion leader spat droplets of blood on the brown dirt. Luchi moved to hit Reaper with the butt of his gun, but was blocked by the leader's weapon with a speed and effortlessness he had not expected. Reaper spun and kneed Luchi in the ribs. Falling backwards, Luchi fired a shot and watched as the bullet careened off Reaper's body armor. Before he could gain his balance, Reaper's bat smashed the side of Luchi's face sending him spiraling unconsciously to the ground. The Scorpion leader stalked toward him looking cautiously for any signs of movement. When he was sure the man was without fight, Reaper let the bat fall one more time splattering the ground with the referee's blood.

Warden jumped to his feet. The fight with Reaper had unfolded quickly and seemed to favor Luchi from the outset. Now another of his inner-circle had fallen under the heels of the gang's onslaught. Warden holstered his pistol, pulled his sword and picked up another blade from a fallen biker. He ran into the melee, cutting a path to Reaper with a savagery that barely distinguished friend from foe. The bikers were falling all round him.

Reaper could see the rage in the eyes of his mortal enemy. He grinned and hit the hood of the truck behind him twice. The driver emerged from the vehicle and rushed to Reaper's side. The fear in his eyes turned to dread as the leader spoke through his blood-stained teeth.

"Release the Beast."

The lone biker walked to the back of the truck and faced the two large doors held closed with a thick, silver chain with a brass lock. As the gang member fumbled for the key, he could hear the low breathing coming from the cab turning into a growl. He fidgeted with the lock, removed it, and then slowly slid the chain past the iron handles trying not to raise the ire of the creature within. He opened the doors and quickly hurried back from the truck. Lurking in the darkness a figure lifted his head and stepped from the cabin of the truck stretching its body to the full nine foot height. His muscles flexed and glistened on his oily, yellow tinged body, a side effect of genetic mutation gone wrong. Scientists who hoped to create super soldiers in the past often ended up with grotesques like The Beast. The data for these experiments were long burned and forgotten, but the results were a lot harder to destroy. The Beast's head was bald and muscular with his green eyes sunken in beneath the scowl of his brow. His nose was two dots on the front of his face. Green, yellow and red jagged daggers of teeth crowded his mouth. He brought his forearms together and clanged the huge wrist gauntlets attached to his arm. It was a war cry that startled the forces behind him, friend and foe alike. He looked down at the pants he wore, stitched together in a patchwork of colors, down to the steel-toed custom boots on his feet. Growling as he breathed in the harsh, untainted air, free from captivity the monster looked at the gang member who released him. The keyholder pointed a feeble finger in the direction of The Beast's prey. The monster turned and reached back into the truck pulling out a long machine gun normally mounted on a truck due to its weight. He picked it up with ease, his muscles tensing as he lumbered around the truck that carried him. Once in position, he began to spray the fighting with bullets. Bikers screamed with the rebels as they were cut down by The Beast's gun. Anyone in The Beast's direct path or opposing him would be brought down. The bikers who remembered the last time The Beast was released knew to get out of the creature's way as he lumbered towards the rebels. The sound of the machine gun echoed louder than the cries of its fallen foes. The larger armor piercing bullets tore through Warden's ranks. Warden's followers were yelling and dying. Some tried to flee, but were cut down all the same. The brave ones that turned and attempted to face The Beast were greeted with a bloody death. Their shouts soundly silenced. When the ammunition was spent the hulk threw the gun at its nearest adversary, crushing the nearest rebel under the weight. He moved towards the fallen and crushed his head beneath his boot. The Beast reared back its leg and kicked another of Warden's comrades, collapsing the woman's body into a heap of shatters bones as her body flew across the dust. He grabbed another man by the head and squeezed until no sound came from him. Flinging the body like a weapon, he slammed the man into two more of the rebels. The Beast roared taking pleasure in the mayhem he created.

Goll ran from the crowd firing his shotgun at the Beast, at the last second the mutant lifted his large bracelets and the shells bounced off his wrists. As Goll stood in awe of the blocked attack, the Beast lifted his massive boot and kicked Goll shattering his ribcage and causing him to collapse to the ground. The Beast lumbered toward him, stopping to grab a rebel and throw him across the dirt. Goll grabbed a pistol near him and fired off shots in succession as the monster came closer. The bullets bounced off his body armor and steel bracelets as The Beast held his right forearm in front of his face. The bullets finding his exposed skin seemed to have as much effect as a mosquito bite. Goll was helpless and looked on in horror as The Beast dug his fingers into his shoulder. The man from parts unknown's muscles ripped as he was picked off the ground. Goll yelled in pain. A rebel tried to come to his rescue, but was slapped away with the creature's powerful arms snapping the man's neck.

The Beast looked into Goll's eyes. "I can see your fear."

Goll flailed as the pain shot through his body. He tried to reach for his axe, but his arm would not move. He could feel the hot breath of the monster as he bit into his neck. Goll's agony was silenced by the blood filling his lungs. As he dangled from The Beast's right hand, the monster severed Goll's head from his body. He threw the headless body down like a rag doll. Goll's head rolled into the dirt.

Warden made his way to The Beast, but it was too late as he saw his protégé ripped apart in front of him. He shot at The Beast's chest and the bullet pinged off the woven, chained armor.

The second shot was blocked by the bracelets. Warden maneuvered around the mutant looking for an opening. The Beast suddenly uncrossed his hands, surprising Warden with his quickness. He spun so as not to receive the full brunt of the blow and was slapped across the dirty plain, his body coming to rest with a thud. Warden quickly rose to his feet staring at the brute. The Beast bellowed another blood curling howl as he advanced, crushing rebels beneath his feet.

Abel made his way to the Water Facility gate, pausing to view the ensuing melee around him. The eruption of flames, death and dread filled his senses. The battle was not going in their favor. Tommie Gun was still fighting the remains of Distor's army inside the Facility. Now Warden was fighting a monstrosity. Abel had heard stories of mutants and their awesome power. He also knew they were rare. But here he stood, surveying the mayhem caused by the towering creature. Abel knew he had to eliminate this new threat if they had any hope of holding the Facility.

The Beast stalked toward Warden to finish him off. Warden grabbed a discarded mace as he rushed the monster and slapped the mutant across the side of the face with the sharp spikes. He rolled to the other side of The Beast, bashing the weapon into the back of his right leg. The hulking biker recovered quickly with a snarl, swatting Warden with a massive backhand that sent the rebel leader flying across the dirt and the mace from his hand. The Beast turned to Abel, upon seeing the rebel unarmed he stooped low, balled his hands into fists and let out a long, deep, bone-chilling growl. Abel fought down his fear as the behemoth approached for the killing blow. Warden used the distraction to slash across the back of The Beast, piercing his armor. The creature roared. Warden smiled. If you can hurt him, you can kill him, he thought. The Beast swung his arm around quickly and Warden rolled under it towards Abel. The battle raged all around them, but the trio had carved out an area for their personal fight. The Beast stretched out his hands and crouched low. He growled deep at the pair, daring them to challenge him. Pulling the 9mm from the small of his back, Abel fired the gun at the monstrosities head until the clip was empty. The Beast slow reaction deflected the first bullet off the iron bracelets, the hot lead cut into the creature's brow, causing a gash. Crimson fluid dripped into The Beast's right eye clouding his vision. Instinctively, the creature grabbed at his face to stop the bleeding. The sharp nails from The Beast's fingers dug into the gash making the cut worse. Warden ran towards the mutant and slashed his sword across his right leg. The Beast dropped to one knee. Abel spotted a sword laying a few feet in front of him. He leapt to his feet and grabbed the weapon without losing stride. With his momentum carrying him, he jumped high in the air and plunged the sword into the scaled chest of the creature with both hands. The mutant fell back howling in shock unable to fight off his assailant. Abel pushed down until the hilt of the blade rested on leathery, tanned skin. Some of the bikers began to fall back, the death of The Beast shaking the gang's morale and putting into doubt their confidence in an assured victory. Abel looked up and realized the mutant had fallen in front of the gang leader. Reaper smiled raising his weapon, undaunted by his best warrior lying dead in front of him. Abel stared back at him, his gun was spent, the sword was deep in his last opponent. Maybe he would not taste victory today, Abel thought. He rose slowly as Reaper trained the gun on him.

"So this is how it ends." Reaper said as he gripped the weapon.

"I guess so." Abel responded.

Reaper squeezed the trigger and Abel flinched. But no sound came from the gun. The trigger was stuck as Reaper tried to force it with his finger. He used his other hand to violently tap the top of the gun hoping to knock some of the grime from it. Abel reached down and gripped the hilt of the sword; with one solid thrust he freed the blade from his adversary's unmoving chest. As Reaper continued to hit the defective weapon, Abel slowly approached. Reaper dropped his weapon and pulled a knife from his waist. The knife had a thick handle, the blade separated into four serrated ends. A dangerous weapon, but no match for the sword Abel carried.

"How did you say it? This is how it ends." Abel mocked.

"Yeah. But not how you'd like." Reaper said confidently.

Abel felt a smirk come across his face. Reaper was smug to the end. Abel held the sword tightly in his left hand, expecting Reaper to run at him at any moment. Abel was unfamiliar with Reaper's custom knife, what the gang leader held in his hand was no ordinary blade. The leader was waiting for Abel to get a little closer, as he held the knife tip pointed straight at his opponent. Abel stepped closer, suddenly the tip of the knife exploded towards him. Abel's eyes widened as he braced for the impact, abruptly a figure lunged in front of him taking the ballistic knife in the chest. The man who saved Abel fell limp to the ground on his side. Abel dropped his sword as he caught Grise. In a flash, Warden came from Reaper's left side. He swung the sword once. The gang leader's head was on the ground before his body could react.

As Grise turned on his back with the knife protruding from his heart, he looked up at Abel and grinned, and then his eyes closed.

Abel grabbed the man's strong hand as red fluid formed in the corner of his mouth. "Grise, hold on. There's a medical bay here. What were you thinking?"

Grise opened his eyes and exhaled his last words. "I'm just an old soldier doing my duty…I swore to protect you…" His voice trailed off and his unblinking eyes were affixed on Abel. His hand slackened, falling from Abel's grip. Abel touched his hand to Grise's chests and thought words of honor to befit his fallen friend. He placed Grise on the ground carefully, then turned to see Isnor and Forsum staring at him. They shared a knowing nod and began walking back to the entry.

Reaper and The Beast dead, as well as many of the gang members, the Scorpions had begun their retreat. A small group of Warden's army followed until the gang was out of range. The rebels left alive had no rest. They were tasked with rounding up the last of Distor's guards and completely securing the Water Facility. Time was of the essence. There was no telling when Xonox would send the next wave.

As they neared the building, Warden finally spoke.

"In his life, he fought to stay out of the angel of death's shadow. In his death, we shall remember how he lived and sacrificed himself for the greater cause. Let our solemn words be the death song of the lost as they died as heroes going home. Their lives were not in vain Abel."

Abel looked at Warden, wondering if all the lives lost today were worth what they had gained. "He said he was a soldier. He will be honored as a friend."

"He will." Warden assured. "Well done Abel."

"Thanks. But it's not over yet." Abel said realizing they still needed to clear the Facility.

A familiar voice came from the side of the group. "Actually it is." Tommie explained.

"What? How?" Abel asked.

Keera answered instead. "Once the guards realized Distor was dead the smart ones started surrendering."

"Yeah, even have a few guards that want to join with you, help you run the Facility." The rogue suggested.

"You trust them?" Abel wondered aloud. "I mean, can we trust them?'

"I don't trust nobody." Tommie reminded him.

"I think we can." Keera said. "I know some of these families they were just looking for a better life."

"Do they know we're going to be under constant alert for attack and the battle is far from over?" Abel asked. "The Collective won't let us just take there greatest resource. They'll find some way to get it back."

Warden interjected. "That's why we have to stay on the offensive. I want to personally meet every woman and man that wants to stay at the Facility. I will assess their worth."

"You mean, we." Abel was not going to take a backseat to Warden. He had shown his mettle in battle.

Warden surveyed all the bodies on the ground. His inner-circle was in shambles. He could see Brot rounding up Distor's guards with a rugged woman by his his side. It was time to rebuild, he thought. "You're right Abel, we. You have proven yourself this day."

Abel nodded in agreement. He knew that Warden was in no position to resist his terms.

"Abel, let me talk to you." Tommie grabbed Abel's arm.

"Sure. What is it?" Abel was not sure what Tommie wanted. The man worked hard to be unpredictable.

Tommie pulled Abel to the side and eyed the gold plated pistol holstered around his waist. "Let me see that pistol."

"This?" Abel pulled the gun from his holster and handed it to Tommie with the barrel facing out.

"Man. This here is a fine weapon." Tommie whistled.

"Where'd you get it?"

"Took it off Distor's cold body." Abel spat the man's name.

"Oh, right." Tommie looked at Abel knowing the significance of the weapon.

"Let me see that holster too." Abel unbuckled the holster and held it out to Tommie. It took Abel a minute to figure out where Tommie was heading, but now he was sure. Abel stood silently.

"Remember what we discussed at Warden's compound?" Tommie said as he wrapped the holster around his waist.

"We discussed a lot of things." Abel feigned ignorance.

"The most important thing." The rogue said, putting the gun in the holster.

The silence between them lingered for a moment. Abel thought to say something, try to tell Tommie the importance of the weapon used to kill his father. Maybe Tommie would bargain for something else. But he knew better.

"I remember."

"This will do. Going to fetch a nice price on the Black Market." Tommie pulled the weapon out and fondled it again. He turned and began walking towards the trees. Abel was still stunned by the transaction, but managed to call out to Tommie as he neared the edge of the foliage.

"Tommie, where you going?" Abel said.

"Into the woods to do a little scouting. I'll be back. Don't wait up though." Tommie replied.

With that last sentence Tommie disappeared into the woods. Just then Keera walked up and grabbed Abel's hand, holding it tightly. "Hey, don't look so sad. I'm still here."

"I know, it's just...we have a lot of work to do to secure this Facility." Abel stated.

Keera knew the real issue, but focused on the task at hand. "With you and Warden, I know we'll find others and we'll protect it."

"I know you're right. It'll all work out." Abel was not so concerned about keeping the prize they had gained, as he was about pressing the attack against Xonox. They turned to look on the wreckage around them. There was a lot to be done in the next few days. They needed to salvage supplies from the slain and the vehicles, close the gates, repair the wall and prepare for another raid. They would be on the defensive this time. If they were lucky they could stand against another assault. Then they would go on the offensive. Abel narrowed his eyes as the cold thoughts of revenge sent chills through his body.

EPILOGUE

Weeks had passed since the rebels took control of the Water Facility. The uprising was said to be organized by three people; a warlord mercenary; a rogue who once worked as Xonox personal guard; and a third person who remained a mystery but was said to have remarkable skills in battle. It had to be true as they had infiltrated a compound with well over four-hundred armed guards, destroyed a water convoy protected by one of his best Captains, killed the Scorpion gang leader and Distor was believed to be dead. The Mountie had reported all that transpired. He had wanted to join the battle, but Xonox had stopped the mercenary. He had lost too much in one day to lose his most loyal and fierce executioner. Upon Xonox's orders The Mountie had withdrawn with much coercion, but not before being promised another battle to satiate his appetite. Xonox sat up in the chair in his study watching the monitor and madness ensuing in the city streets. Friend against friend, brothers fighting sisters, guards killing one another in cold blood over water. Xonox found it fascinating to watch the breakdown of society into its most base animalistic nature. The city had literally run dry in a matter of days with no new deliveries from the Water Facility. Xonox attempted to secure the water distribution again, but the rebels were too well prepared, destroying the bulk of his two-hundred militia. It was seen as a rare miscalculation on Xonox's part. With the water supply dwindling he should have helped the guards to secure the city. That was the whispers coming from the lower ranking officials within the House of Vancrew. Suddenly, there was an eruption. Even on the seventieth level, Xonox could feel the building rumbling. His door opened with a start.

Dante spoke frantically. "Sir, there you are."

"What is the meaning of this intrusion Dante?" Xonox voiced his displeasure. "I specifically asked to be left to my thoughts today. Are you becoming deaf or am I becoming too nice in my old age as my orders are not heeded?"

Dante continued unfazed by Xonox's threats. "Sir, the rebels are in the building and they are advancing on this floor."

"What? Impossible!" The First of the House stated with impunity.

"It must have been some coordinated attack." Dante explained. "I'm sure they are being helped by some of the House guards."

Xonox was surprised by the bold assault. "They would dare turn against the First of Vancrew? I'll see their bodies lashed and dragged through the streets."

"I don't doubt it sir." Dante said, his voice providing no reassurance to his master's proclamation. "But for now we need to move. Your helicopter is prepared and waiting on the roof heli-pad. Your personal guards will escort us."

"Now?" Xonox looked down at his silk robe. "Like this?"

Dante looked at the monitor as it showed rebels advancing on the fiftieth floor. Xonox followed his eyes and was visibly startled at how quickly the rebels were taking each floor. Maybe Dante was right, but Xonox refused to show any fear or a need to rush his escape. "I see your point Dante."

Xonox began to move across the room with more intent than normal. Dante ushered him through the doorway, down the hall and to his private elevator. Dante briefed Xonox on the way to the helicopter pad. "You have everything you need in the helicopter. You can change on the way. I've already sent a convoy ahead with your most personal belongings."

"Very well, Dante." Xonox smiled. "You are always aware of what I need. I trust you have Pheona's belongings as well?"

Dante was silent. Xonox repeated the question as the elevator opened up. The guards stepped from the elevator connecting with the guards already waiting. They created a procession across the bridge to the helicopter with its wings already spinning.

Dante stammered through his words. "Sir…Sir there was no time. Pheona…she was on the lower levels. We could not reach her."

Xonox grabbed Dante by the shoulders of his suit and threw him against the outside of the elevator. "Is she dead?"

"No sir. But…the rebels probably have her." Dante answered fearfully.

"Then we need to go back for her." Xonox turned to his Captain of the guards. "I want you to take as many as you can to Pheona's last location and bring her to me."

Before the Captain could answer shots rang out from the stairwell sixty-feet from the elevator. Dante moved to shield Xonox catching a bullet in the back. The Captain stepped forward and was shot, his orders turned into gibberish. One of the guards moved forward pushing Xonox low to the ground and firing back at the rebels, many of whom wore the same uniforms, double 'XX's' across their breast. Xonox was hurried to the waiting helicopter as his elite guards fought valiantly to hold back the rebel charge. From the height of the chopper, Xonox could see the last of his personal guards being overrun as the rebels lifted their weapons cheering. He turned away from the window and for the first time in many years had an emotional thought of someone other than himself. What had they done with Pheona? He clinched his fist and swore he would get his daughter back or kill those rebel dogs in the process.

The helicopter was in the air for a few minutes before Xonox realized they were not headed to Croman's home. The collapse of a House protocol under the Collective regulations stated the head of the House would seek refuge with the House above him, lest his pursuers find him at a weaker House and topple it. Xonox laughed to himself. When he, Mordal and Croman had written those rules, it was with the lesser families in mind. He never dreamed he would be a victim of a fallen House. Xonox leaned towards the pilot. "Where are we heading?"

"Northeast sir." The pilot said mechanically.

"What's our final destination?" Xonox asked again a little perturbed.

The pilot seemed puzzled but answered anyway. "The

House of Saran, the First of Firsts is expecting you sir."

Xonox reclined in his seat. It was not what he expected, but maybe this was the best move for him. With Mordal's protection and resources he could get Pheona back, more importantly he would get back what he lost.

The helicopter landed on one of the many landing pads and was greeted by armed guards. They were in all red suits with black boots and helmets, the black "YM" on their chests. The symbol always reminded Xonox of a martini glass in the middle of an inverted table. Mordal's guards gripped their weapons as if they were ready for an enemy, not the acceptance of the third of the Collective. Xonox waited for the propeller to die down, and then he stepped from the helicopter with seven of his militia in tow, not including the pilot. All his escorts were unarmed. If a problem did present itself, Xonox was in no position to fight so he opted for his guards to leave their weapons behind. Xonox stopped at the edge of the bridge connecting the landing pad to the receiving area. He noticed Mordal's sentries tensing as he continued his approach. Appearing from a dark hallway he saw two men step forward in unison. No doubt Mordal's sons. They bowed to Xonox and he returned the gesture. They stepped to either side of the path, taking their place in front of the guards, but not telling anyone to lower or holster their weapons. The minutes dragged on as Xonox stood facing the dark opening, waiting with as much patience as he could muster. Finally a figure appeared from the shadow of the opening, his long silk red robe dragging on the ground. The lining was trimmed with gold, as were his cloth shoes. Two dignitaries were on either side of him, dressed in impeccable suits. They were followed by fourteen guards, with no helmets, a handgun and a sword hung from either side of their waists. These were Mordal's elite guards. As he approached, all of Mordal's guards near Xonox fell to one knee. They spoke in unison as their eyes stayed affixed on the ground.

"The First of Firsts."

When Mordal had walked far enough, stopping a few yards in front of Xonox, his aides and personal guards, as well as his sons, fell to one knee. Mordal looked at Xonox with a cold stare. The former king of the House of Vancrew knew what was expected. As he knelt to one knee with his hand over his chest, he thought of all he had lost and how he would regain it. The men behind Xonox mimicked their master.

"Hail Mordal, The First of Firsts."

- End-

ABOUT THE AUTHOR

Kenan Hillard grew up on X-Men comic books, Mad Max movies and Final Fantasy video games. It's no wonder his love of a good story led him to try his hand at writing. In his roaming 20's his creative mind led him to pursue design degrees in Architecture from Washington University and The Georgia Institute of Technology. In between designing he continued to read X-Men comic books, watch Mad Max movies, play Fallout games (had to replace Final Fantasy) and most importantly write. Follow him on twitter @collectivekh.